Common Decency

www.penguin.co.uk

Also by Susannah Dickey

TENNIS LESSONS

Common Decency

SUSANNAH DICKEY

doubleday

TRANSWORLD PUBLISHERS
Penguin Random House, One Embassy Gardens,
8 Viaduct Gardens, London SW11 7BW
www.penguin.co.uk

Transworld is part of the Penguin Random House group of companies
whose addresses can be found at global.penguinrandomhouse.com

Penguin
Random House
UK

First published in Great Britain in 2022 by Doubleday
an imprint of Transworld Publishers

A CIP catalogue record for this book is available from the British Library.

ISBNs 9780857526885 (cased)
9780857529015 (tpb)

Typeset in 12/15.5 pt Bembo Std by Jouve (UK), Milton Keynes
Printed and bound in Great Britain by Clays Ltd, Elcograf S.p.A.

The authorized representative in the EEA is Penguin Random House Ireland,
Morrison Chambers, 32 Nassau Street, Dublin D02 YH68.

Penguin Random House is committed to a sustainable
future for our business, our readers and our planet. This book
is made from Forest Stewardship Council® certified paper.

For S.D.

'Life becomes actual only when it is identified with ourselves.'

– William Carlos Williams

'As if what we did next were given with the mere act of naming. As if there were only one thing called "talking about a thing". Whereas in fact we do the most various things with our sentences.'

– Ludwig Wittgenstein

'And taking a look at the long-range forecast, continued snow, darkness, and extreme cold.'

– *Dinosaurs* (American sitcom, 1991–4)

LILY

She leaves her flat at 3.30 p.m. and idles to the supermarket around the corner. The day is giving off its last vestiges of bright and the Belfast sky is like Peach Melba. A person in a floral dress passes her on the footpath, taking wide, load-bearing steps to accommodate an enormous box of Heineken. In the supermarket she buys a packet of rectangular caramel shortbread. Each comes in a pink paper casing – they look like artisanal sex toys. She takes them home and eats them in bed. She feels the sun go down.

SIOBHÁN

She tries for a prurient whisper, conjuring mental images of Scandinavian women from crime dramas for inspiration. She imagines herself as elusive and leggy; she has poreless skin, possibly a motorcycle.

'Fuck me,' she says, huskily. He takes a breath.

'I will,' he says, then pauses. 'In a minute.' His expression is tortured. She rolls on to her back and stares at the ceiling.

LILY

She was born with unusually long fingernails. 'You were this soft ball of a thing, with these sudden sharp surprises – like finding bits of eggshell in your omelette,' her mother said once. A nurse offered to trim them, but she declined. 'I liked that you were born capable of inflicting damage,' she said. 'In my post-labour fugue state it made me less anxious, less worried about my own competency.'

She presses one thumbnail into the skin behind the other until red appears under the nail's crescent, like a slow geyser of tomato juice. She peels the nails off, one by one, then arranges them in a spherical cluster on the bedsheet in front of her. They look like an astrolabe. When she's finished she deposits them into a mug. The empty plastic box from the shortbreads sits on the counter, the shed pink skins susurrating against one another as she flips the pages of a calendar. It is the first Saturday in February, and her mother has been dead for seven months.

Earlier, on her way in from the supermarket, she encountered Siobhán in the foyer of their building. Siobhán was standing by the noticeboard, which looks like a steamrollered tennis ball. She was staring fixedly at her phone, ignoring the flyer for the dehumidifier for sale, the notice of roadworks scheduled for March and the handwritten, cloying request for people to stop overfilling the bins. She had a shopping bag on the floor next to her, bottles of red wine visible inside. Her feet were positioned in a stance of indecipherable intent, as though in the next moment she was as likely to sit down as she was to perform an emergency tracheotomy.

Lily pulled the front door closed behind her and strode past, steeling herself for a relaxed interaction. She'd been preparing for this moment. At the entrance to the stairwell she turned.

'Are you coming this way?' she asked. She hadn't spoken to anyone that day, and her voice crackled like timber, expanding in the heat. Siobhán looked up, frowning, and Lily blushed from bungling her delivery.

'Sorry?' Siobhán said.

Lily tried to avoid sounding impatient. Siobhán ought not to be held accountable for her malfunctions.

'Upstairs,' she said, more clearly this time. 'Are you coming upstairs?' She jiggled the door a little, to emphasize the relative time-sensitivity of the question. Siobhán looked at the door as though it was her first time seeing a door.

'Oh,' she said. 'Yeah, sorry, in a sec. You go ahead.'

'I can wait,' Lily said.

'Oh,' Siobhán said again. She put her phone in her pocket and picked up the shopping. The carrier bag clinked. 'Thanks,' she said, as she reached out to assume the weight of the door.

'That's all right,' Lily said. She smiled widely. Siobhán smiled back. A pause as they showed their teeth to each other.

'Do you live in the building?' Siobhán said.

The building is officially listed as Benson Tower, but the first E and the second O from the signage have been missing for as long as Lily has lived there. The remaining letters are stuck, tarnished and worn, above the doorway, sandwiching the faint echoes of their former colleagues and listing slightly, as though with survivor's guilt. They spell out Bnson Twer. Her mother would have liked this – she liked playing with the phonetics of acronyms, typos, numerals. MRSA was 'Morrissey'; the IV full of chemicals was her 'four'.

The foyer is tiled with black and white and the occasional aberrant triangle of matte grey where they've chipped to reveal the grout. There are burgundy-coloured mailboxes with patinas around their keyholes and two thick-trunked artificial ficus plants in orange-brown planters. The colour scheme is like standing in a Tupperware lunchbox that once, however briefly, housed leftover Bolognese.

The day before she moved in, when she was still sleeping in a sleeping bag on the undressed mattress of her mother's erstwhile bed, she brought two final suitcases' worth of saucepans and towels and Pyrex dishes and long-handled rubber spoons to Bnson Twer. She slid two postcards into her postbox and tried to forget having done so. The next day, after trotting upstairs, opening the windows and boiling the kettle, she returned to the postbox with her newly acquired key. There were two postcards waiting for her, one a print of Brian Ballard's *Flower and Skull*, the other a print of John Luke's *The Three Dancers*. In one, thick brushstrokes in gloomy blues and greys capture light landing on bone and porcelain. Six angular blooms in coral and umber sit in a vase alongside, perforating the dusk. In the other, three people balance on their toes and cock their arms in a sloping, layered valley. The precarious balancing of the triumvirate seems to imply something about their dependences upon one another. She stared at the A6

Luke print and felt herself transposed into its language; she was flat and rampant on the matte background of her new existence.

On the back of the Ballard postcard it said, 'Congratulations on your new job,' and on the back of the Luke, 'Welcome to your new home.' Both messages were written in her handwriting. She took them upstairs and secured them to the fridge with a magnet. She made a cup of tea and suppressed the reflex to call out, 'You want tea?'

She had actually met Siobhán three times already. The first time, she had approached her from behind. Siobhán was standing in the doorway of the building, looking out. Lily had at that point already lurked for too long in the stairwell, having watched Siobhán's head bob down and around each landing, not wanting to risk the awkwardness of Siobhán turning around, spotting Lily looming above her like a buzzard over some carrion, of them having to exchange small talk from different vantage points. In the foyer, there was nowhere to go but forward, so she proceeded quietly, and then they were side by side, watching the December rain and the cars and the sporadic people, stationary and mobile. Siobhán's head came up to Lily's chin, and Lily tried to draw her arms into her torso to seem smaller.

'It's raining,' Lily said, and Siobhán said, 'Not even the rain has such small hands.' She laughed brusquely, then drew her scarf over her head – it was thin, silky, maroon – and walked out. Her tan-coloured ankle boots had wide openings and no zips, and Lily wondered if they would fill with water, like novelty flowerpots.

The second time they met was unavoidably in the stairwell.

6

Lily was descending, Siobhán ascending. Before Siobhán looked up Lily watched the top of her head growing steadily in her field of vision, her centre parting and thick hair that fell in waves, its thickness such that it sat up from her scalp in a plume. Lily wondered if she ever worried about losing it, if she considered her beauty a fragile thing to be clung to as it risked erosion by time. She wondered if Siobhán worried about the precariousness of good things, and she felt an impulse to tell Siobhán about the time she had sinusitis for five days; how she sipped Sprite through a straw and whimpered at intervals like a lame sheep; how when it finally dissipated she vowed to never take a painless face for granted. She retreated into the banister and allowed Siobhán to pass. Her scarf this time had an art deco print, geometric zigzags overlaid with gold-beige deltas that matched the coppery strands of hair around her face. Without looking up, eyes fixed on her phone, Siobhán intoned, 'Thanks,' to Lily's feet. Lily glanced into the canvas tote bag suspended by one strap from Siobhán's shoulder – it was filled with small, pale blue exercise books. Lily said, 'No problem,' and once past Siobhán said, 'They could do with fixing that, couldn't they?' and gestured vaguely with her free hand at the flickering tube of electrical light protruding from the wall. Lily nodded, but Siobhán wasn't looking. 'Maybe I'll email the estate agents,' she muttered, then walked on. The bulb is still flickering, Morse-coding something indecipherable.

The third time they met was last week. Siobhán was trying to forcibly inject her key into the crusty lock of her postbox. Lily wanted to tell her that sometimes it helps to jerk it once in an anticlockwise direction, then once in a clockwise, like starting a car. She said nothing. One of the ficus plants had a Santa hat perched on top – a lingering side effect of

7

December. 'The Venn diagram of days before Christmas and days after Christmas is a circle,' her mother said once.

Siobhán rattled the key, swearing under her breath, then gave up. She began searching in her bag, and without looking up propelled herself forward. Her shoulder collided with Lily's chest and Lily made an *oooft* noise. 'Oh God, sorry,' Siobhán said. Lily said, 'That's all right,' and Siobhán, still fixated on her bag, muttered, 'One of those days,' then performed an apologetic shrug with her shoulders. She disappeared into the stairwell and Lily stood, watching the spaces she no longer occupied.

It was in this moment that an idea began to assemble itself in the fraying distortion of her mind – the idea that Siobhán could help her. Siobhán's concurrence with her surroundings, the ease with which even her transgressions and apologies seemed to occur, the way their innocuous interactions had almost managed, for a few, fleeting instances, to concretize Lily. Although still an ersatz person, for a moment she felt realer. Her blood, which had become mulchy and frozen, seemed capable of thawing. She went to Siobhán's postbox that wouldn't open and forcibly extricated the envelope that was half in, half out of the slot. She opened it. It was from the Student Loan Company, and Lily decided that this was the first thing she could do for Siobhán: remove this gloomy portent of debt. She took the letter upstairs and hid it in her wardrobe. She spent the rest of the week feeling like this was a beginning, as if the vapour of grief could maybe be compressed, made to share her mind with something else.

'Do you live in the building?' Siobhán said as they exchanged the stairwell door. For a moment Lily said nothing. Clearly,

Siobhán thought they were meeting for the first time. Lily's cheeks went hot. To ascribe undue weight to an interaction is so much more shameful than to have forgotten the interaction, she realized. Forgetfulness is the luxury of a rich existence. She wanted to redress the balance. She wanted to say, 'We've actually met multiple times,' and for Siobhán to say, 'I'm so sorry it's just—', which Lily could interrupt with, 'Personal occupation doesn't absolve you of poor manners.' She wanted Siobhán to blush, then apologize profusely, till her apologies reached the ceiling of their intensity, wilted under their own mass.

She said nothing, though, and nodded, and Siobhán said, 'Me too. See you about.' She commenced climbing the stairs, and Lily once again hung back, watching the muscles in Siobhán's legs tauten and slacken in her tights as she ascended. Back in her flat, she took the caramel shortbreads from her bag and ate them without tasting.

'Common decency' was a phrase her mother had used often. She had been a Biology teacher at one of Derry's more pernicious secondary schools, and after an especially challenging day she was prone to say that common decency ought to be taught to teenagers, rather than cellular meiosis. Lily wasn't sure what impact this model would have had upon her job – if all disciplines would get subsumed into a more generalized intent to bestow good manners, or if it was just Biology. She forgot to ask.

One night, years ago, when Lily was a teenager, her mother sat on the blue, sausagey sofa in the living room, eating yoghurt-covered raisins. Lily had been in the park, pulling blackberries off bushes in anticipation of jam. Each removal involved the same stretching out of the floricane, then its pinging back as the fruit came loose. As the incorrigible evening oozed in she sat on a swing and ate some. There were three boys lolling on the climbing frame, and the low-slungness of their jeans made them look like walruses. Lily heard one say, 'Watch this,' and a moment later a pebble bit her on the shin. She looked up and they averted their eyes, laughing. A moment later another pebble landed next to her feet and she heard the first boy say, 'Nice shot, spastic,' and another respond, 'Fuck off.' A third stone hit her on the hand and she dropped the box of blackberries. They bounced on to the spongy black terrain – that material ubiquitous in children's play parks. The boys laughed again, and when she looked up they held her gaze, their expressions goading. She bent over and salvaged a few of the berries, sad and pearlescent on the ground. She got up and left, the skin on her leg stinging.

She spent the drive home imagining progressively more violent methods of retaliation. Her mother was on the sofa when she got in, dressed in her greying T-shirt that had a drawing of breasts on it in an anatomically incorrect place. She had a stack of exams on her lap and a red biro in her hand, the raisins next to her. Lily relayed some of her revenge fantasies: knotted electrical wire and garrotes and barrels of water. Her mother placed a hand on her knee and rubbed, saying nothing for a moment. Finally she said, 'Revenge is like cleaning your bathroom to impress a ghost.'

Lily sighed and put her fingers to her temple. 'What does that even mean?' she said. This was a common inversion of their prescribed dynamic – Lily as exasperated guardian, her mother boisterous theorist.

'Ghosts don't care if there's hair in the drain,' her mother said. Lily frowned at her, then took a raisin, chewed, contemplative.

'Wait,' she said. 'Wait, no. Wait – what?'

'Damn,' her mother said. 'I thought maybe I'd got away with it.'

'No,' Lily said. 'Explain.'

'Sorry,' she said. 'I'm feeling my way through the thought.' There was a companionable silence, then: 'Maybe people perceive revenge differently from cruelty, because it's in retaliation to a wrong, but actually both are teleological. Perhaps cruelty isn't altered by its motivating factor. Perhaps revenge is just cruelty with a hat on.'

'Oh.'

'You get it?'

'Yeah, but—'

'What?'

'I think you just reinvented, through gross overcomplication, the very familiar concept of "Two wrongs don't make a right."'

Her mother laughed.

'Plus,' Lily said.

'What?'

'Maybe it's easy to frame revenge that way if you have the luxury of neutrality. Maybe revenge and cruelty only seem synonymous—'

'Good word.'

'Shut up. I'm just saying,' Lily said, 'seems like this perspective might be enabled by a position of lofty detachment.'

Her mother laughed again.

'And also,' Lily said, 'what does any of this have to do with ghosts?'

'I feel silly postulating, now you've put me so firmly in my place.'

'No, please. Postulate away.'

'Well,' her mother said, 'maybe if the bathroom needs cleaning, you'll clean it. The ghosts are neither here nor there.'

'I think that's the generally accepted position on ghosts,' Lily said.

'You know what I mean.'

That year Lily wrote 'Ghosts are neither here nor there' inside a birthday card. When her mother opened it she laughed the sort of laugh elicited by an old joke, forgotten in the interim. The kind of joke that wouldn't survive the duration of its own explanation, a joke contingent on the closeness of two people.

When Lily was clearing out the house she found the card inside a copy of *Wuthering Heights*. All the cards she'd ever given her mother were secreted inside books.

After finishing the caramel shortbreads, Lily washed her hands till they smelt of chemical lavender. The sky was the black treacle of late winter.

She thought of how the cruelties that had exacted themselves upon her mother, though numerous, were largely faceless – you can't enact revenge upon a wet road, a precipitous coastal shelf, a slow-acting disease, a fast-acting disease. Maybe the intangible, spectral nature of her enemies was what provoked her mother's benevolence. Kindness as an alternative to impotent rage. In the muggy, poorly ventilated air of her flat, Lily edged her way up the bed and adhered her thoughts to the ceiling, Siobhán's floor.

Sometimes, when she's quiet, she can hear the music from Siobhán's laptop, or the sound of her laughing on the phone. She has a microwave that squeals like a pig when the food's cooked.

★

Lily's father died when her mother was six months pregnant, on the wet road traversing the border and tethering Culmore to Donegal. A man in a red Toyota saw through the rain's onslaught the motorbike careen to one side, yearn to right itself, then capitulate, capsizing. It slid across the road's uneven surface and into the path of an approaching black Honda. He saw the figure in the helmet bounce heavily at the kerb and the Honda's driver burst through the windshield to splay among broken glass. He called an ambulance, and both men were dead upon arrival at Altnagelvin. Lily was born three months later, a week later than her due date.

'Maybe I was reluctant to be told the bad news,' Lily said.

'What?' her mother said. 'That you'd be stuck with just me?'

'Exactly,' Lily said.

After taking the student-loan letter from Siobhán's postbox several weeks ago, Lily climbed one flight of stairs too many to inspect Siobhán's doorway. The tiled floor of the stairwell seemed to increase in stickiness as she rose, each footstep emitting a wetter Velcro sound, as though trying to hold her in place. The light from the wall sconces in the small hallway flickered on with her arrival, and she saw six pairs of shoes outside Siobhán's door, on a silver, expandable shoe rack. There were two pairs of the same style of ankle boot, one black and one brown, a pair of pink-and-purple running shoes, a pair of black trainers and two pairs of black high heels. They were all a size five. This, as well as their being displayed so casually outside her door, seemed to yield the promise of something. The blithe naivety required to abandon her shoes outside her home, potentially prey to the interference of others; the quiet assuredness of her own dominion over this space. It was this manner of living that Lily wanted for herself, wanted Siobhán to teach her. It's this manner of living that she now decides to target.

She spends the next day formulating the tentative beginnings of a plan. After that, she contemplates the boxes in the corner of her room. They've been there for six months. She goes to the uppermost box and lifts a flap covered in strips of formerly adhesive packaging tape, then glances into its depths. Her mother's books sit inside, clammy. She moves the box from the stack on to the floor, then sits cross-legged before it. She removes a book, turns it over in her hands, replaces it, conceals the contents with the flaps. At 6 p.m. she gets into bed, and the premature darkness allows her to sleep through the evening and into the night, her thoughts nonsensical and swaddled in auburn hair.

SIOBHÁN

The points of contact between them – their thighs, their upper arms – have cultured a warm, sticky moistness. To move would require peeling herself off him. She listens to his breathing, her eyes pointed upwards. A long-legged spider turns slowly in the corner.

When they spend longer than two days together he invariably turns guilty. She can sense it, the moment he wakes up – the space between them on the mattress will have widened since they fell asleep, will feel curated with plausible deniability in mind. Her motions and movements will be newly dictated by his anticipated reception of them, and this will make her reticent and apologetic. Once, on day three of a weekend in Galway, she tried to hold his hand. He squeezed hers for half a second, then put both hands in his pockets and glanced around, fearful. She said nothing, but felt like a child, chastened by a disappointed parent.

Sometimes, she wakes to discover that he's put on pyjamas in the night, and they might as well be a chastity belt. If she tries to snake a hand surreptitiously towards his crotch he'll catch her wrist with his fingers, will sigh and say, 'Sweetheart,' in a tone more pleading than warning but that she knows means, 'Back off. Please.' Sometimes he'll roll away from her, as though magnetically repelled, muttering, 'I should take a shower,' before departing with his phone to the bathroom. She's left forsaken on the bed, tragic in her great nakedness: her breasts wilting across her chest and torso, her nipples hard from the air-conditioning. This was back when they still stayed at hotels. As the shower faucet hissed she would sometimes rise and take a thumb-sized bottle of vodka from the mini fridge. She'd say aloud, 'What, is there a global shortage?' and imagine a studio audience laughing. The whole thing seems less pathetic if she pretends somebody is getting a kick out of it.

She wonders which of them will cave first. It's invariably her, but today, like always, she contemplates assuming the risk of alienating him. She sighs an aggrieved sigh and folds her arms across her abdomen. 'Just this once,' she thinks in his direction. 'Just this once, you be the one to restabilize things.' In her peripheral vision she can see him rubbing his face like an anguished otter. 'No,' she thinks to herself. 'No. Stay strong – don't always be the one to capitulate.'

Moments later she turns towards him.

'You okay?' she says. He rolls into her side and buries his face in her neck.

'You're fantastic,' he murmurs.

'You're beautiful,' she whispers back.

She can't stand herself.

When she breaks the silence and offers accord she doesn't consider it a gesture of compromise, of subjugating her own needs for his happiness. She used to think that, at the beginning. 'Love makes you selfless,' she thought, grandiose, after he'd cancelled their five-months-in-the-making plans, or forgot her birthday, and she still neglected her own work to talk him through an ontological crisis. Now, she thinks it's more that she can't bear the thought of having someone un-love her. She lacks the courage to risk existing undesired, and the longer a relationship is permitted to go on, the more daunting the prospect of extrication. She's weak, she supposes, but that's not love's fault. She's always been weak.

They met three summers ago, when she was about to start her PGCE. She was two years graduated from her BA and was renting a room in a cold, tall house off the Lisburn Road, with high ceilings and wet walls. She had four cohabitants she strove to avoid – two smug medical students, a barista and a bearded man who was known to sit in the park every day but pretended to be an accountant if you ever asked. She was working in a small hotel off Botanic, not far from where she lives now – she did bar work and occasionally reception, sometimes shepherding lower-budget bridal parties.

She met him in early June. He was being put up in the hotel for a university conference, and she noticed him immediately. Necklaces on men normally made her think of interrailers or interchangeable uncles at wakes, but his was a barely conspicuous gold crucifix on a thin chain, and the intermittent gleam of it beyond his shirt placket and among his just visible chest hair made something inside her tighten with lust. When the day's talks were over the attendees returned to the hotel and congregated in the bar, standing in clusters or squashing on stools around small tables. He kept appearing in front of her to order drinks, and each time she made a little more eye contact, made herself a little more gregarious. On his fourth expedition he hovered his hands over the bar, and when she smiled he set them down on the just-wiped counter and leaned forward. He was painfully polite, what she has always thought of as 'Presbyterian polite': half eager, half restrained. It seemed like he'd been aching to have a very specific conversation for years, and now that he was he was frightened of ruining it. That's something she still finds addictive about him: he has the power to make her feel apotropaic and precious.

'The usual?' she said, on that fourth visit to the bar.

'I've always wanted to have a usual somewhere,' he said, and although this response would have aggravated her from someone else – she had a no-chat, maximum-efficiency approach to customer service – she was thrilled that he wanted to prolong the transaction.

'Me too,' she said. 'I'm sometimes tempted to choose somewhere at random, go in and say, "The usual!" just to see what happens.'

He laughed, and she felt bolstered.

'"The usual, please, Greg," I'd say,' she continued. 'And the barman would say, "Who the hell is Greg?" and I'd say, "Oh, Greg, how I've missed your irreverent and off-piste humour."'

He laughed again, for longer than the joke deserved, and she took this as further encouragement. She felt overstimulated and giddy.

'"Oh, Greggy boy, Gregosaurus. It's been a rough ol' week, Greg,"' she said. She could feel Clodagh, another server, eyeing her steadily. '"Wait till you hear what the wife's been putting me through this week, Greg!"' she concluded, blushing slightly.

With hindsight, she's surprised this final line wasn't sufficient to subdue him, as any passing reference to wives usually does. Instead, he just smiled at her. Something she has realized about him since is that he rarely engages with the joke – he's too serious, or too nervous around her to be fully uninhibited – but he always laughs, and his general reticence to reciprocate makes it feel all the more special when she can occasionally coax silliness from him.

He watched her pour his pint, never having confirmed that it was what he wanted. She beamed at him, then swore when, distracted, the beer rose over the rim of the glass and over her fingers.

'So, what would your usual be?' he said, and she wanted to atone for her clumsiness by being memorable.

'Sausage in a glass,' she said, then immediately, 'God, sorry – I don't know why I said that,' but he was already laughing again, and it occurred to her, even then, that he was the kind of person who gave you the permission you needed to forgive yourself.

Looking back on it now, the nebulousness of it makes it seem all the more like it was unavoidable. The combination of variables that led him to her, that isolated him from the others in the bar to grant her the chance to perceive him as an individual. The precise arrangement of his characteristics, gestural and physical; characteristics that she couldn't do justice to if describing them to someone else but that made him, to her, the most beautiful thing. What was unjustifiable about her attraction is what made it real, and that is why she knows that, regardless of what happens, regardless of the extent to which she will compartmentalize her needs to keep him, she will always want him.

She loitered after her shift was over, trying not to think. She sat in the blue-lit lobby with a book she found on a shelf behind reception, though it might as well have been a stuffed ferret for how much attention she paid. At 7 p.m. the students and lecturers and consortium staff began to drip-feed out of the bar. She kept her eyes down, not so much on the page but near the page. She heard someone say, 'You coming for a bite to eat, Andrew?' and she heard him reply, 'No, thanks, I'm going to turn in. I'll see you in the morning.'

When she was sixteen she and her best friend, Tara, would attend every performance of the French debate club, sometimes even getting the bus to Lisburn or Downpatrick after school, just so they could listen to a boy in the year above named Hugo Diamond. They'd never spoken to him in person, and in another context they'd probably have been cruel about him, but behind a lectern, flanked by his team, they were entranced. They called his voice 'velvet chocolate', and that night, when she heard Andrew say, 'No, thanks, I'm going to turn in,' she felt the same thing she used to feel listening to Hugo Diamond argue against recreational drug use: as if all she needed in the world was to have that voice say her name.

With every muscle in her body she willed him towards her, and when she saw his feet next to her chair she felt telekinetic, as though her lust was sanctioned by unseen forces. He said, 'How is it?' and she said, 'I don't know – I can't read,' and he laughed. She turned the book over and was surprised to see that it was *Daisy Miller*. He said, 'I really love *The Portrait of a Lady*,' and she, grasping in the chambers of her memory for any information, said, 'It's good, but my favourite is "The Turning of the Shrew".' He laughed again. He has an easy laugh, which she theorizes comes partly from his innate need to please people, but also from a genuine pleasure he takes in living, given the chance. He said, 'Would you like to have a drink with me?' and she said, 'Yes,' and they decamped to another archipelago of chairs in an empty lounge. They spent the next two and a half hours cross-legged on a sofa, facing one another. He seemed young to her, but not in the way she now knows her students to seem young – brash, so as not to betray their ignorance. He seemed young like conversation wasn't about using the other person's contributions as stepping stones to his own, young like it didn't matter to him whether he spoke at all.

She stayed behind after work three days in a row, spent all her tips on pints and chips of varying undercooked- and over-cookedness. She was defensive about letting him spend money on her – she worried it would gesture to an imbalance already possibly denoted by their age difference. Clodagh and Nathan behind the bar were incorrigible – her winking; him pretending to fellate the cola hose. 'Fuck *off*,' Siobhán hissed each time she ordered more drinks, before turning on her heels and becoming winsome again. At 9 p.m. each night she would begin her campaign to convince him to stay downstairs for longer, but at nine thirty he'd rub his thighs as if he were trying to get a fire going, put his palm on her bare forearm for a moment, then retreat to his room. She'd trudge home in the waning colours of the etiolated summer sky, then masturbate under her duvet.

He told her about his wife and daughter on the first night, and later she was irritated with herself for being shocked, given his wedding ring, given the disproportionate gratitude he showed her, which could only have come from a man who hadn't felt wanted in a long time. They held hands for three uninterrupted minutes on the second night, while he told her that he'd never leave his family; that he couldn't. They kissed on the third – close-mouthed and chaste, his mouth seasoned with chip vinegar. When he checked out on the final morning he left a note for her at reception, with his email address rather than his phone number, as though that might absolve them. They exchanged emails every day for a month. A fortnight in, she wrote that she loved him. A fortnight later, he wrote it back. A month later, he asked if they could meet.

The day before they saw one another, she spent the afternoon on Royal Avenue, trying on skirts and sheer blouses. That morning she curled her hair and put on layers and layers of mascara, till her lashes were huge and rigid. When she saw him walk through the station doors, from the platform on to the concourse, she felt pangs of regret at all the ways she could have looked better. He took four equine bounds towards her and then her face was pressed to his neck. Afterwards he would reminisce about how it felt to hold her and hear her breath catch in her throat. A lot of their moments together are like this – they feel scripted in their enormity.

He'd booked them a room in a hotel off Donegall Square, with a great pavlova of a bed. When they entered the room she was coy in her attempts to conceal her feelings of coyness. He closed the door behind them, set his overnight bag on the floor, and said, 'Come here.' Although he was born in Donegal, his accent has been neutralized, hybridized, made unplaceable; the result of moving to Coventry when he was five, then back to Donegal at sixteen, then to Dublin for a decade of elite tertiary education. When he said, 'Come here,' a traitorous, bucolic growl emerged, and he looked at her in a way that felt feral. She went to him, and he wrapped his hands in her hair and kissed her. This time, she felt her breath catch, and she wanted to roll her eyes at herself. He whispered, 'This is pretty,' as he lifted her new top over her head, and when he unhooked her bra and took her bare breast in his hand he groaned and said, 'Oh my God.' When he put his hand to the damp gusset of her knickers she was briefly ashamed at how tangible his effect on her was, but when she saw the effect his effect on her had on him she was grateful for her body's lack of reactive subtlety. By some statistical anomaly she'd never been with someone uncircumcised before, and she was delighted by the sensitivity of him, how it made her feel powerful. When she slid his foreskin down and pressed her tongue to the amaranth-coloured dome of his penis his whole body shook in her grip. Afterwards they lay with him on top of her, her hands on the damp skin of his back, him whispering, 'I love you, I love you,' into her ear and her whispering it back, but also worrying that his sweat was turning her hair frizzy.

They spent the evening in the Cathedral Quarter, eating market-price fish (her seabass, him crab) and getting progressively drunk on New Zealand Sauvignon. He was used to Dublin prices, and his delight at the comparative cheapness of Belfast led to an extreme and excitable profligacy. They had desserts, dessert wine, coffee, shots of sambuca. They went back to the hotel bar, where a lissome woman was singing Bonnie Raitt's 'I Can't Make You Love Me', his favourite song. Re-installed in their room, she cried, then he cried, and then they slept for three-hour intervals between bouts of sex that felt both animalistic and transcendent. She resented their sleeping at all, because their time together was so limited, but in the morning he was impossible to rouse, so she watched the strengthening light percolate through the curtains, begging the cosmos to officiate their union. She watched how the rising sun illuminated the escarpments of his biceps, draped heavily across her torso.

A fan of hotel breakfasts, he insisted they availed themselves of theirs, so they trotted downstairs and ate shrunken pastries and ham omelettes, exchanging meaningful looks over orange juice. He likes smaller versions of regular things, which are never in greater abundance than at a hotel buffet. Siobhán wondered about this later – if the comedy of seeing something's proportions changed briefly distracted from some latent fear regarding the smallness of the self, of its susceptibility to forces beyond its control. This seemed apt, she thought, for someone who'd found himself in an inescapable, unhappy marriage, with a child he was biologically compelled to prioritize. Alternatively, maybe a small pain au chocolat is funny on its own terms – a sad scarab beetle mewing, 'I'm so small.'

He'd struggled to achieve orgasm with a condom on – 'They make them so restrictive,' he'd said, plaintively contemplating his strictured penis – so after she'd accompanied him to the station she went to the walk-in clinic and acquired three months' worth of combined contraceptive pill. When the doctor asked if she wanted some free prophylactics she replied, 'No, thank you,' with the smugness of someone who has captured monogamy.

Something about him made her different, recalibrated her emotional vocabulary. She was suddenly tender and saccharine, prone to lengthy pontificating about her feelings. If he devoted a paragraph to telling her how meeting her had changed his life, she devoted two. It became an emotional one-upmanship: who could feel *more* and express it *better*, which led to an agonizing sense of exposure when she was the more superlative.

Soon, it stopped being a conscious decision and she was the person she'd been emulating: she had become his emotional protégée. After a couple of days spent together she'd return to her dark, sticky room, the atmosphere like sorbet and the surfaces piled with dishevelled coursework, and weep. She'd weep for the injustice thrust upon her, for the pain of wanting him, of being denied him.

They still talk often about how they met. They discuss it at length: the immediate attraction; the initial resistance to the immediate attraction; the ultimate futility of such resistance. He talks about how beautiful she looked, even in her hotel uniform with her hair pulled back. She says, 'No, there's no way,' because she knows her small-featured, egg-shaped face is one that benefits from some hair around it. 'Yes,' he insists, and then he says that it wasn't just how she looked, that from the first conversation he felt understood in a way that he never had, that she delighted him, that she was inimitable and clever and witty, that she made him feel young, that she made him feel wanted. She reciprocates. She tells him that he's the most handsome man she's ever seen, that she's never wanted anyone the way she wanted him. Through repeated framings of their history they solidify their love as mythic, canonical, almost pre-ordained. This belies the more sordid elements of their pairing and casts them as beyond logic, beyond pedestrian questions of morality. She thinks they both mean it when they say that they are the loves of each other's lives. Or at least, they think they mean it, which she supposes is the same thing.

A couple of months in she came to understand the negatives of being the extraneous attachment to an intact couple. She was on her first placement, in a school that elicited the same unsavoury response from everyone it was mentioned to. A response fuelled by some composite of cultural tribalism, stereotyping of location and sufficient anecdotal material to affirm those stereotypes. That said, the school did lack resources, and things were difficult. One Friday afternoon, during a film screening, one child had a seizure. Siobhán quickly learned that ten- and eleven-year-olds are an unsettling mix of cynical and deranged. They know enough about the world to feign an authority, thereby making it apparent how little they know about the world. She arrived home with greasy skin, a throbbing shoulder and a faint smell of urine on her clothes. When she messaged Andrew to ask if she could call him, the response came an hour and a half later: *Sweetheart, you know we can't talk on the phone when I'm at home.*

The following day they messaged for several hours about his daughter's tantrums and newly acquired fear of zips, and then he had to disappear to cook spaghetti hoops and replace the fastenings on her fleece with Velcro. Tara called to ask how the placement was going, but somehow Tara's comfort felt less worthwhile than his would have been. She answered Tara's sensitive, probing questions with non-committal mumblings, said she was too tired to talk. This was something else her relationship with Andrew had done – invalidated the attention of the other people in her life. She needed his attention, only his.

At 12 p.m. the alarm on his phone goes off. They've been lying, naked and silent, for forty-five minutes – him dozing, her marbled with frustration.

He turns the alarm off and repels himself from the bed.

'Sorry, sweetheart,' he says. He sits up and commences dressing. She props herself on one elbow and watches him. She's always loved to look at him, particularly in the moments after sex, when he is soft but unselfconscious and she can take in his totality without the distraction of his erection. These moments, if she can suppress their context, are when she can most convince herself that theirs is a real relationship, with all the intimacy and vulnerability that a slack and pendulous cock implies. He's got good legs, she's always thought – long and lean with a forward-slash severity of definition on each thigh. He has broad shoulders and pronounced collarbones, biceps that have been visibly strengthened through weighty living, rather than vanity. He's got the most tentative beginnings of a belly, and the convex of it is far more attractive than a flat abdomen would be. His foreskin is ruched and sleeve-y, concealing the head. He's avoiding looking at her, as though attention might inspire her to say something he doesn't want to deal with.

'So,' she says, and she doesn't think it's her imagination that he flinches, 'can we see each other soon?'

'I hope so, sweetheart.'

'When?'

'I'll check my calendar and we'll get something figured out.'

He used to not like staying at her flat. She thinks that its oppressive dankness depresses him – it's a visual metaphor for infidelity. Something that's important to him is their logos: the idea that what they are is unique. They're star-crossed, held apart by the vagaries of fate, but their connection is too formidable to overcome. They're not like other extramarital pairings, clichéd and lewd. She once drew parallels between their situation and that of Constance Chatterley and Oliver Mellors. 'I, too, think men would be less pecuniary-minded and more content were they to simply wear red trousers,' she said. He didn't laugh. Her flat, with the passata stain from a former resident and the blinking fridge light and the discoloured showerhead, serves to negate the idea that what they are is beautiful. Idealism aside, though: his daughter is getting older, is persistently outgrowing her shoes, and his wife is angling for a house she can extend the kitchen on. He's had to cut back on spending, and though she will never say it, Siobhán resents being a victim of this asceticism, given that she will reap none of the benefits of his parsimony. Still, no more hotel rooms.

He finally turns to look at her. She's arranged her hair over one shoulder so only one breast is on display – she hopes she looks like a toppled, well-formed caryatid. He groans.

'God, you look amazing,' he says, and she takes that as an invitation to clamber on to her knees and wrap her arms around him. He bends over and kisses her on the forehead. He says, 'I love you.'

'I love you.'

'Speak soon, sweetheart.'

The front door clicks behind him. She rolls on to her front and groans into the pillow.

The afternoon meanders. At four she goes to the supermarket, devotes what seems an acceptable amount of time to contemplating the fresh produce – the apples with their bruises turned to face the wall, a butternut squash the size of a lamp – before buying two bottles of wine. She lurks in the foyer and watches the clock – when it reaches five she will deem it appropriate to start drinking. She glances at the fake eucalyptus plants, then at her phone, willing him to message. She goes to her postbox but doesn't bother attempting to open it – she's given up rubbing her palm raw on the key's edge. She notices that the student-loan letter she's been pointedly ignoring for weeks has disappeared from the slot, and she shrugs to the empty room. She looks at her phone. Two messages from her mother: a link to a tweet with a video of fox cubs, and also: *Have you started making student loan repayments yet?* 'My mum is a clairvoyant of wretched bureaucracy,' Siobhán said to Tara once. She ignores both messages, glares at the unyielding 4:45 of the clock. The odd woman from downstairs walks in and makes a pantomime of holding open the stairwell door. Siobhán tries to make conversation but is met with empty-eyed hostility. She interprets this as a deus ex machina. She goes upstairs.

She sometimes thinks about dying. Not in a way that would give anyone just cause for concern, but in a way that brings her comfort – knowing that she has the means and the autonomy to bow out, were it to become necessary or preferable. A girl she went to school with ate a snail as part of a drinking game, the summer after their A levels. It was carrying a toxic parasite, and the girl now lives in the hospital. Alive, but only in the strictest sense.

Some days she feels so inescapably joyless that living seems an unnecessary expenditure of energy. She doesn't know if these feelings are legitimate, or merely petulant, superlative responses to not having exactly what she wants. She feels partially ashamed at contemplating death simply because her boyfriend won't leave his wife, and partially comforted by what seems to her the very sage nihilism of viewing death as a contingency plan, something to assume dominion over, rather than something to be daunted by.

★

She knocks on Caz's door with the fist that's wrapped around the neck of the bottle of red wine, and when she hears the multisyllabled, lilting 'Yes?' from inside she clinks the glasses in her other hand against the bottle's flank. Caz calls, 'Coming!'

She met Caz a few weeks after moving into Benson Tower. She'd been to town to buy clothes for her new job: long skirts and high-necked tops and heeled boots in black and brown permutations. Caz was on her knees, peering into the fat terracotta pot in the foyer, her wide posterior swaying arhythmically in front of the eucalyptus. Siobhán had no intention of speaking to her, but as she headed to the stairwell she heard Caz announce, 'This plant is plastic.'

Siobhán paused by the door. 'What's that?'

'I've been watering it.'

Siobhán set her bags down and approached. She bent over – in the pot there was a thick cube of synthetic foam, holding the synthetic trunk in place. The foam was submerged in three inches of water.

'How long have you been doing this?' she said.

Caz's tone was calm but slightly bewildered. 'Two months,' she said.

Siobhán's voice cracked a little. 'Two months,' she repeated.

'Two months,' Caz said.

It was then that Siobhán laughed. A few seconds later, Caz joined in, and Siobhán was grateful, for Caz's sake, to have been there; a humiliating thing always neutralized by a co-conspirator. Caz invited her to the flat for wine, and after several glasses she put on her hotel uniform and concierged Siobhán's shopping bags around the open-plan living room-cum-kitchen.

During those first few months Siobhán became a frequent

visitor at Caz's. She had never thought of herself as someone who would be friends with her neighbours – she thought ingratiating herself with the residents of Benson Tower would be like placing an unripe banana in a bowl of ripe bananas – but that night, as she struggled to breathe over the force of her laughter, watching Caz barrel around the room, it briefly didn't matter that Andrew hadn't messaged her back, and it didn't matter that she was a nascent teacher with a new, baleful flat. It didn't matter that her life seemed suddenly to have sidled just beyond what she could handle.

Caz opens the door. 'Hello, angel,' she says, then bows. Her hair is tumbling around her shoulders in ringlets and she's wearing her satin dressing gown: ivory, with a cherry-blossom pattern. She got it in a charity shop and she told Siobhán that she found a used tissue in the pocket. When Siobhán grimaced, Caz said, 'Don't disrespect the sundries of the dead,' and when Siobhán asked what she'd done with the tissue she said, 'Buried it, of course.' Siobhán sometimes wonders if Caz has cultivated various eccentricities to distract from her not being clever.

Siobhán attempts a half-curtsey, then feels immediately conscious of having done so. Caz arranges herself on the sofa then pats the cushion next to her folded legs. 'Come,' she says. 'Tell me about your week. Tell me about the children.'
    'Well,' Siobhán says, 'we had a quiz yesterday, so that's always an epistemological maelstrom. One kid answered "How did the Romans transport water?" with "Jugs".'
    Caz laughs.
    'And another kid cried for two hours because he answered

the question "What type of triangle has three equal angles?" with "A normal one".'

Caz closes her eyes in performed rapture. 'Ah, were we not all so deep-feeling?' she says.

'For sure,' Siobhán says. 'He's a real Jonathan Swift.' If Andrew were here, he would laugh, but all Caz does is the polite, closed-mouth smile of encouragement, without understanding.

Sometimes Siobhán is grateful that she and Andrew conduct so much of their relationship via messaging. It allows her easy access to Google, so she can feign the bibliophilia necessary to understand everything he says. He studied Literature for all three of his degrees, while she did History at undergrad and stumbled through Donne and Sheridan and Rhys at A level. That he never condescends to what she's more likely to know is flattering, and it makes it seem all the more momentous when she can make a joke within his frame of reference. It makes the conversations that aren't centred around their mutual adoration feel like a challenge, and often, subsequently, she'll repeat the jokes when she's talking to other people, and when they don't understand she feels once more convinced of her and Andrew's ineffable well-suitedness.

Caz takes the wine from Siobhán and rises, strides to the counter. Siobhán isn't sure how Caz has managed it, but her flat is beautiful. There's a vase of fluffy faux catkins and pine cones in one corner, apothecary jars with tea lights in them scattered upon surfaces. The sofa is draped in sumptuous Merlot-coloured blankets and there's an antique coffee table with a fist-sized statue of a woman in a red swimsuit sitting on a stack of magazines. Caz has conjured intimacy and gentle kitsch in a building that feels held together by the scar tissue of water damage and dead skin. Caz takes an industrial bronze corkscrew from a drawer and gets to work on unleashing the wine. Siobhán doesn't own a corkscrew, has relied on screw caps her entire adult life, and watching Caz use hers, which looks weighty and dangerous, makes Siobhán's life feel more romantic.

'Here you go, angel,' Caz says.

'Thanks, Caz. Oh, before I forget' – Siobhán reaches into her bag – 'I brought that spare key,' she says. She places it in Caz's hand, and Caz deposits it in a drawer. She produces her own, and Siobhán puts it in her wallet. She glances at her phone – the screen remains blank. She sighs.

Caz repositions herself at the far end of the sofa – her dressing gown falls open slightly to reveal the chickeny skin on her chest. Siobhán has no idea of Caz's true age, but the anachronism of her full lips and smooth forehead with the craquelure on the backs of her hands makes Siobhán suspect she's younger than parts of her look, just sun-damaged. Caz exhales like a contented cat.

'All good, Caz?'

Her eyes are closed. 'Mmm,' she says, conducting an invisible orchestra with the long-stemmed glass. 'Dorothy died,' she says, so under-breathily Siobhán just hears it.

'Oh?'

'The glamorous old woman who lived in the hotel.'

'Oh no.'

'I never knew a woman to spend so much time in a jacuzzi bath.' Caz gazes at the wall. 'I used to wonder if she wasn't old at all,' she says. 'I wondered if she was just pruned from the bath water.'

'Hmm. Presumably the glaucoma medication somewhat dispelled that, though.'

Caz laughs.

'You doing okay?'

'Yeah. She was a nice woman.'

Siobhán waits. Caz continues. 'She used to say that her final adversary would be death.'

'Good grief.'

'Which struck me as very wise.'

'But isn't everyone's final adversary death?'

Caz frowns slightly. 'I suppose,' she says.

'Provided they've had earlier adversaries.'

The frown deepens. 'Also true.'

'And provided you view death as an adversary.'

'Huh,' Caz says. 'You are absolutely right, and much too clever for me.' She leans over and clinks her glass against Siobhán's.

'I guess,' Siobhán continues, enjoying following a thought that is Andrew-distinct while remaining still Andrew-trace-backable-to, 'the two options are to view death as an unassailable tyrant, or death as a comrade.'

'Which do you view it as?'

'Depends on the day, really.'

After meeting Andrew, Siobhán forced herself to read rapaciously, to become *au courant* with his interests, to become comfortable using *au courant* in a sentence. Over the first year of their relationship they spent a lot of nights texting until midnight. After they'd said goodnight, or while she was dutifully waiting to hear from him at all, she'd read the books he'd mentioned in passing, or she'd try to predict what he might one day wish to discuss. She read Lawrence and Saunders and Turgenev. Unaware, prior to knowing him, that poetry as an art form was not only still existent but thriving, she started reading the poets he was teaching on his Contemporary Literature modules and even revisited the ones she'd waded through dolorously at school: Hughes and Heaney. She came to like how poetry made her feel, although she was reluctant to interrogate the feeling too deeply, in case it wasn't so much the poems as it was poetry's cachet, and perhaps this is why she preferred reading it in public.

She was also reluctant to question too vociferously just what it was she was feeling, in case it was simply relief at being able to share a common interest with the man she loved, or hubris at being able to speak casually about an art form of which her immediate circle knew nothing. If her new-found joy in poetry was simply a means of making herself desirable to Andrew, then that implied the possibility that they weren't meant for each other, that he had an idealized vision of her that she would spend a lifetime striving to preserve. In this sense, to not broach literature with her friends seemed like a tacit betrayal of him, because she wanted to always be the version of herself that he wanted. And yet she was aware that when she announced, 'Not even the rain has such small hands,' while huddling under a smoking-area awning with Clodagh and Nathan, she was presenting herself as newly affected, and pretentious, and gauche. She'd carved out a new ontological space for herself, one founded upon simultaneous self-alienation and carefully contrived assimilation. She was losing her grip on any notion she'd ever had of her core personality, but it was worth it, she thought, to feel like somebody he could love.

★

On the third evening she ever spent at Caz's, Caz fell asleep to the Shiraz. Siobhán eased the not-quite-empty glass from her hand and set it on the table and disembarked the sofa. She padded around the kitchen, opening drawers at random. She went into the diamond-shaped vestibule at the flat's entrance, peeked into the bathroom, which was mint green and spotless. Then she tried door number three – the bedroom, which she'd never seen. Damp touched her face as soon as she opened it. In the dark she could make out the open window, the curtains threadbare. The bed was undressed and the mattress was an atlas of stains. In the corner of the room was a pile, half the height of Siobhán, of crumpled clothing and boxes and detritus. The room looked forgotten about. It smelt of neglect and stagnant water and filth. Siobhán closed the door, retreated back into the living room, resumed her place on the sofa. She never mentioned it, and hasn't gone in since.

She rolls her eyes demonstrably at Caz's jokes, as though she might need evidence later that her indulgence of Caz is not the same as their sharing a sensibility. Caz burrows deeper into her mound of pillows.

'What do you think your final adversary will be?' she says.

'Incontinence, I suspect,' Siobhán replies.

Caz laughs. 'You're too young and too beautiful to be so cynical.'

'I feel neither beautiful nor young.'

'The precious children should keep you young.'

'The precious children will probably be the death of me – a real H. G. Wells situation.'

'You love them, though.'

'Unfortunately.'

'And they love you.'

'Debatable.'

"Course they do. What's not to love?' Caz leans forward for another touching of glasses.

Siobhán wishes Andrew were here to hear someone else paying her compliments. She often tries to orchestrate scenarios in which he might witness someone else acknowledging her merits, in case it raises her market value in his perception (when they go out she ensures that they queue next to any elderly men sitting by the bar, in case they decide to call her 'lovely'). She thinks of her phone, in her bag by her feet. She feels the impulse to check it, but instead pours half the contents of her glass into her mouth. 'So,' she says, to interrupt her thoughts, 'if not death, what will your final adversary be, Caz?'

Caz leans back and bites her lip. Her teeth are like an Iron Age settlement. 'Hmm,' she murmurs. 'Maybe ageing.'

Siobhán looks at Caz's chest, says nothing.

'Or' – Caz abandons her lip, nibbles at one of her long thumbnails – 'maybe a lengthy legal dispute with a scorned stepchild.'

Siobhán inspects her own nails, which are anaemic and split. 'That's a good one,' she says.

'Yeah,' Caz says. 'I can see myself, all wizened in big sunglasses, giving cheek to some greedy little heiress in a courtroom.'

'What's she an heiress to?'

Caz gesticulates flippantly. 'Whatever empire my dead husband built from the ground up. Dog food, maybe. Salmon paste. More wine?'

'Absolutely.'

Caz sashays to the kitchen, her broad calves meeting and parting with each step. Siobhán wonders when Caz thinks this benefactor husband will show up to rescue her from a lonely and commonplace middle age. She thinks again of her phone. The thought of being like Caz in ten, or however many years, appals her.

It wasn't until she'd known Andrew for two months that she told him she was going to become a teacher. She usually avoided telling people until it became unavoidable, mostly to spite her mother. Before she started her PGCE she told people she worked in a hotel. Her mother hated that. If they were together when Siobhán said it her mother would interrupt and say, 'Oh, but she's starting a PGCE in the autumn,' as though anyone cared, as though the responses garnered through small talk survived the small talk's duration. Even after she'd commenced the PGCE she didn't tell people – she let people believe that she still *just* worked in a hotel, as her mother would put it. 'You don't *just* work in a hotel, Siobhán.' The satisfaction Siobhán got from doing this makes her worry that it's just an alternative symptom of the same classicism – if she didn't subconsciously view hotel work as inferior to teaching, would she think it a worthwhile deception? It's another thing she tries not to think about. Her mother is that peculiar, self-hating sort; didn't go to university but derides those who don't. When she hears about someone having gone, only to graduate and return to a job in the service industry, she gets a pained look in her eyes.

When Siobhán was seventeen her mother won some money on a scratch card. Not enough to warrant media interest, but enough to pay off her mortgage and reduce her hours in the kitchen showroom, devote herself to full-time neuroticism and trying to obviate thoughts of her humble beginnings.

Siobhán suspects her mother thinks being working class is just a side effect of chronic laziness.

When Siobhán finally did tell Andrew, he said, 'Sweetheart, that's superb! You'll be a wonderful teacher!' and though he had no basis for saying this, it still mattered that he thought so. On the day of her graduation a bouquet of lilies and assorted flora arrived at the tall, wet house. Her housemate, the bearded pretend-accountant, left it outside her bedroom door, where it immediately commenced staining the carpet with stamen dust. Siobhán went to graduation alone – she told her mother she wasn't attending at all, and Tara had just moved to Bangladesh to dig wells. Afterwards, as her coursemates attempted to shepherd their flustered, innumerable relatives towards restaurants, or the line for photographs, Siobhán went to the pub, ordered a double vodka and lemonade, and thought, 'Fuck, yes, I've done it.'

LILY

On Monday morning her body uncoils from sleep and she eats an orange, digging her thumbs into the porous skin. She stands at the counter, inert, listening for Siobhán's footsteps overhead. She hears the gaseous shriek of a kettle and then a *thunk* as Siobhán drops something.

It's a nice day – the sludge of dawn has been cut through and the air is now cold and clear, air like a breath mint. She crosses Botanic, goes up University Street, crosses University Road, cuts down Elmwood Avenue, heads towards the yellow box of the hospital. On the corner up ahead she can see the strange woman who wears the pink rara skirt and the balding fur coat and the yellow flip-flops. The constancy of this woman's dress and positioning within a small, fixed set of coordinates always comforts her, in the way the graffiti in the bus stop near the home she grew up in once seemed to vindicate the constancy of her own mind. She keeps her head down and veers across the road so they don't cross paths. She buys a muffin in the hospital café and eats it in the toilets by reception. 'Love your cunt. I wish I was dead,' is written in green pen on the wall of her cubicle, and she reads it as an affirmative mantra. When she's finished, she goes to the gift shop to start her shift. She sells an 'It's a boy!' card and a teddy bear to a woman who smells quite strongly of garlic, then some chocolate to a doctor with teeth of such enormous uniformity she suspects they're fake.

40

At 1 p.m. she uses the change she purloined from the doctor to buy herself a cheese sandwich. She eats it on a bench by the hospital's entrance, watches a man rapaciously smoke two cigarettes in succession then grind them into the pavement with his heel before crossing the threshold on to the hospital grounds. At 2 p.m. she goes back inside, heads for the small, unassuming bungalow beyond the main building.

She volunteers at a charity called the Hope Cancer Foundation. Instead of an 'o' in 'Hope' there's a small, curved-edge butterfly. The name strikes her as tautological: what cancer isn't hope cancer?

She doesn't view her functions in the office as 'charity work', because there's little to distinguish it from normal work. In the office she answers the phone and alphabetizes files and collects and processes and sends out post and counts the money in the collection cans and enters various people's details into various spreadsheets. Most of the files she alphabetizes contain the details of patients who have died from cancer, which she supposes is one way in which her work is distinguishable. The files of the still-alive patients live in a separate filing cabinet, although to qualify for one of these files it's insufficient just to be alive; you need to be a specific type of living where your continued living is at least somewhat in jeopardy. Lily wonders where the files come from, if the erroneous creation of a file for a healthy person might act as a carcinogen.

One advantage of her radical self-sequestering following her mother's death is that she doesn't have to navigate the assumptions someone might make regarding her volunteering for a cancer charity, people inferring a correlation – that personal tragedy has spurred her to work for a collective good. In reality, she started volunteering because she needed something to do between the hours of two and four on Mondays, Wednesdays, Fridays, at a location convenient to her job in the gift shop. She would just as happily volunteer at a meat-production plant or a tech start-up, although she can't speak for whether either would also require alphabetizing the files of the recently deceased.

When she walks into the office Marian is hunched over the desk closest to the door. Marian has puffy hair and false eyelashes and a prosthetic breast. She has a soft voice and intonation that turns everything into a question. She looks up from a form and says, 'Hello, love?'

Marian's life circumstances are such that they also have the potential to invite assumptions of correlation, although in Marian's case the assumptions are correct. Her teenage son died of Hodgkin lymphoma while Marian was undergoing chemotherapy for breast cancer. Lily found this out from Hannah, who told her in an anguished tone, as though she were providing the information unsolicited. Hannah has a clipped, fulsome English accent that can reach piccolo-redolent heights in pitch. She relays everything as though being coerced, which makes Lily wonder if her romantic partners feel like they're blackmailing her. She eats butter on white bread for lunch every day and overuses the word 'discourse'.

'Hi, Marian,' Lily says.

'All quiet?' Marian replies, her default greeting. Lily likes that, from Marian's perspective, quietude is akin to contentment.

'Yes, thanks.'

Lily wonders if Marian's perpetual question-asking is an

unconscious deference to the uncertainty of existence, given that her own has been punctuated so remorselessly with unexpected tragedy. Perhaps, for most people, the bawdy inevitability of death means you can occasionally put it from your mind. To have had it brush up against you, though, then retreat; how could you ever function not under its influence? Lily tries to avoid the reciprocation of idle enquiry with Marian, in case they get trapped in a loop.

'All quiet?'

'Yes, Marian, all quiet. And you – all quiet?'

'All quiet?'

'All quiet. All quiet?'

'All quiet?'

Marian dresses her gently lopsided torso in slim-fit, cotton-Lycra V-necks in navy or burgundy, sometimes with stripes. Today she's wearing a navy with white stripes, and small gold earrings shaped like shells. Lily wonders if she knows that the shape of shells amplifies all ambient noise; that it's not the sea you hear inside a shell but nondescript air in a cavity.

'I like your earrings,' she says instead.

'Thanks, love?' Marian says. Lily nods, takes a seat at the back of the office. The door opens again.

'Hello, party people.'

Hannah takes off her leather jacket. She's wearing a T-shirt that says 'Eat the rich.' Last week there was one that said 'No milky toasts' and another that said 'Smash the patriarchy.' Lily finds it difficult to believe that Hannah is chancing upon T-shirts that align so precisely with her political beliefs. It seems more likely that she's either adapted her beliefs to suit the T-shirts or she's going to great lengths to source them. Lily wants to ask Hannah if she's worried that her slogan T-shirts, particularly those espousing anti-capitalist ideals, might be innately counterintuitive.

'Hi,' she says instead.

'Hello, love?' Marian never comments on Hannah's T-shirts. Lily suspects she would like to.

'Hi, Marian,' Hannah says. She lifts her arms and sniffs both armpits, frowns slightly, then shrugs.

'All quiet?' Marian says.

Hannah looks pained. 'I *wish*, Marian,' she laments. 'What I wouldn't *give* for it to be all quiet.' She swoons into a chair by the door, typically reserved for visitors. Lily shares the back desk with the other volunteer, Anna, a teenager who works Tuesdays and Thursdays and typically leaves the internet browser open at sites for various Cambridge colleges. From here she can only see the back of Marian's head – its cotton-wool, butter-coloured halo tilts to one side. 'Oh dear?' Marian says.

Hannah wrings her hands. 'Oh, it's a whole thing, if you *must* know,' she says. 'I was out last night with a few of the ones from uni. It was meant to be just a quiet night in the pub, but things got out of hand really quickly. Eimear thought Noel was pissed off because Eimear told him she was bi, so Emma started an argument with him, but it turned out he hadn't even heard what Eimear had said, so then Eimear was upset that she'd started a drama, and then Colm got kicked out for trying to buy a round of drinks with a Subway loyalty card.'

Marian turns in her seat to include Lily, squinting her eyes.

'But anyway,' Hannah continues, 'so, most people left when Colm did, and then it was just Laura, Chris and me. Chris is Laura's – you know my friend Laura? Human rights paralegal? Loves MDMA and *Antiques Roadshow*? – well, *her* boyfriend.

And I know him, but not, like, *that* well, and while Laura was out for a smoke – get this! – he tried to get off with me! Can you believe that? And *then*, when Laura went home, he tried it again! At that point I was like, "No mate," and left. And I was going to keep it to myself, you know? Because why rock the boat, you know? Why cause trouble?'

Marian murmurs. Hannah seems to take it as tacit agreement.

'But just now,' she continues, 'I get a call from Laura, and turns out he's gone and told her, and not only that, he's made it sound like *I* instigated it! Can you believe that?'

'Oh dear?'

'Yeah! He's told her, "Oh, Hannah tried to kiss me, and then when you left she was all over me and tried it again!"' Hannah sighs a beleaguered sigh. 'It's not true,' she says, defeated. 'But because everyone else had gone home there's nobody to back me up.'

Lily suspects Marian would like a cup of tea and twenty minutes of uninterrupted silence. 'Oh dear?' she says.

'Anyway.' Hannah sighs another sigh. 'Yeah, it's a whole drama. It's just horrible to have to deal with.'

Marian tilts her head sympathetically. 'I'm sorry, love?'

Hannah grimaces dolefully. 'Thanks, Marian,' she says. 'Anyway. Has the new rep been in yet?'

'What's that, love?'

'The one with the weird hair – I'm supposed to go through some of the fundraising stuff with her.'

'Not yet, love?'

'Grand.' Hannah pulls a purple 'Hope Cancer Foundation' T-shirt from her bag and tugs it on over 'Eat the rich'. She goes to her desk and opens a priapic bottle of Lucozade. She glances at Lily, says, 'You doing all right, mate?' and Lily contemplates asking her if she's familiar with false memory syndrome; that, if she had the time or inclination, she could use recovered memory therapy to condition Chris into confabulating her version of events. She nods instead. 'Good stuff,' Hannah says.

Industry settles in the office: Marian resumes hunching over the stack of forms, Hannah has a lengthy conversation with a civil servant about procuring permits for a sponsored walk, Lily wheels herself to the filing cabinet. She glances at her hands. One holds a file, the other keeps the cabinet drawer steady. They are balded and raw-looking, the nail beds flayed and tender.

Her mother described certain scenarios as being like 'buns to elephants'. She was adamant it was a real expression, though she could never explain in any satisfactory way what it meant, and she used it in a wide variety of contexts. When Djokovic won Wimbledon in straight sets it was like buns to elephants. When she spent an hour convincing a student he was capable of handing his coursework in on time and going to university, only to catch him pissing in a bin that afternoon, words were wasted on him, like buns to elephants. She treated language like a pet ferret she could dress in different outfits, her idiosyncrasies translating into a hyperactive logorrhea. Her students thought her eccentric and odd, but they also revered her. They went to her with their unplanned pregnancies and their broken homes and their naked photos being promulgated around the school. They bought her inappropriate end-of-year gifts: socks with expletives and cheap Greek-style statuettes; their small, off-white penises somehow ruder for their smallness. They bore her assignments with a degree of magnanimity, and every year the departing batch of students would mention her in the flimsy, shoddily assembled yearbook, which was more a pamphlet of misdeeds – memories of stomach pumpings and salacious dalliances.

Lily went to the smaller, more sanitized school just outside the city. It shared its grounds with a former mental-health inpatient unit, and on the bus ride she would watch the small brown rabbits frolicking on the lawns outside; the horses in the field, pointing in the same direction. A phone-mast obelisk sat covertly among the trees, painted to look like a tree.

After her mother had ceased working her students would come to the house occasionally. If she was asleep Lily would stand in the doorway with her arms folded. She'd appraise their doleful eyes and limp bouquets of carnations, rustling in lurid cellophane. One girl, called Shannon, who had a septum piercing and a pink fringe and who refused to get to grips with osmosis versus diffusion, sniffed in the doorway. She informed Lily in a sonorous oration that everything happens for a reason. Lily allowed the disdain of her silence to snowball between them. After a while she said, 'You know, most people brought nicer flowers,' and closed the door. When her mother woke later Lily informed her of the exchange.

'You shouldn't be nasty to the tiny children.'

'They're not *that* much younger than me.'

'That's true, I suppose, although you amass a lot of wisdom in your twenties, all of which is proven to be spurious in your thirties.'

'What fun.'

'Plus, *your* wisdom belies your youth.'

'But they're more highly educated than me, too.'

'Like wisdom ever had anything to do with education.'

'Do you intentionally undermine your own profession? Or does it happen organically?'

'Little point worrying about it now, I suppose.'

'Apparently everything happens for a reason,' Lily said.

'Well, yeah – I have some very informative printouts about carcinogens and causality and cell mutation that would say the same.'

'I think she meant in more of a cosmic, higher-purpose sense.'

'Like buns to elephants.'

'Precisely.'

Lily wonders what Siobhán's students think of her – if they would wear black, child-sized pencil skirts and ill-fitting polyester jackets to her funeral, if they'd write 'Best Teacher Ever!' on stationery-shop condolence cards, if, for many of them, her death would be their first confrontation with what had been an abstract concept, a word tethered only to some vague notion of conclusion.

At 4 p.m. she stands, locks the drawers of the filing cabinet, returns the key to her desk. She half puts on her coat. Hannah removes her earphones.

'That you off?'

'Yeah.'

'Would you say it's an acceptable time for me to take a break?'

'I don't know – that's not really my prerogative.'

'Do you not realize you occupy a role of immense responsibility in my life?'

'Do I?'

'Your leaving marks my having been here long enough to have a snack.'

'Okay.'

'It's not that I *want* you to leave, it's more your leaving means good things are about to happen.'

Lily says nothing, and Hannah laughs. 'I'm kidding,' she says. 'I'd probably eat regardless.'

Lily resumes putting on her coat. 'Right,' she says.

'You're not a big talker, are you, Lily?'

Lily shrugs, wobbling the flaccid trunk of her empty coat sleeve.

'If I come down to the shop one day,' Hannah says, 'will you give me free sweets?'

'Probably not.'

'Not even one?'

'Doubtful.'

'Dammit,' Hannah says. She twists in her seat and liberates the tinfoil envelope of butter bread from her bag. She gestures it at Lily like it's a champagne flute. 'Here's to you!' she says. Lily gets to work on her zip.

'What?' Hannah says. 'You didn't appreciate my toast?'

'That's not toast,' Lily says. 'That's bread, idiot.' Hannah does a bray of a laugh. Lily picks up her bag.

'Bye,' she says to the room.

'Bye, love?' Marian mutters, trying to extricate her reading glasses from her hair.

Her first four months there she rarely spoke at all. At induction she handed Marian her AccessNI certificate in exchange for a welcome pack and a computer login and a T-shirt. 'We're so grateful to all our volunteers, love?' Marian said. 'There's a Facebook group, if you'd like to speak to any of them?' Lily ignored this. During her first week Marian asked her if she would like to sometimes work out-of-office, volunteering at events, but after several inauspicious coffee mornings where she stood, laconic and labouring over the opening mechanism on a pot of decaf, it was decided she was better suited to office work. At Hope, she found that just being in the vicinity of people supplanted the urge she was feeling for familiar conversations, relieved her of the need to speak. She wondered if this was how it was for chicken embryos grown under hot lamps in labs rather than under the warm underside of a broody hen. She googled this process one day and found a headline: 'French Artist Trying to Hatch Eggs Will Likely Kill Them All.'

In the office she sat with empty headphones in, to the muffled sounds of those around her and her own inner machinations. She worked to a rhythm that begat mindlessness. Outside, the wind and time functioned in tandem to move her days forward, and she found that the more aggressively industrious she was, the more easily she could sleep once she was home.

Once, on a drive home from the airport, her mother turned the car radio on.

'I love this song,' she said. 'Do you know this song?'

'We've been through this,' Lily said. 'I don't know any songs.'

'Of course you know songs.'

'I know three songs.'

'What are they?'

'"Happy Birthday", "Happy Birthday" in French, and that one about luft balloons.'

'Alice! Alice! Who the fuck is Alice?' her mother shouted suddenly. Lily jumped within the constraints of her seatbelt.

'What's happening?' she said.

'We used to dance to this at the Ballymena discos when I

was a teenager,' her mother said. 'Nineteen seventy ... five, maybe? Smokie.'

'Shall I open a window?' Lily said.

Her mother laughed.

'On the chorus that's what you shouted: Alice! Alice! Who the fuck is Alice?'

'Why?'

'Why does anyone do anything?'

'Narrative cogency?'

'How dull,' her mother said. 'Give it a go,' she said, and so Lily did, and with each repetition of the chorus she shouted, 'Alice! Alice! Who the fuck is Alice?'

'That's one more song you know,' her mother said afterwards. The sun was melting on to the shelf of the Glenshane Pass.

'That's not how it works, I'm afraid,' Lily said. 'I have finite memory space. I've just had to forget "Happy Birthday" in French.'

'Oh no,' her mother said.

'It's okay.' Lily shrugged. 'Luckily, I don't know any French people.'

'*Quel dommage.*'

'Oh no.'

On her way home Lily stops at the perpetually empty sushi place on the corner. Botanic is a mixture of dynamism and poverty: soft-haired students and Deliveroo drivers congregate under the porticos of new, freshly painted takeaways; homeless people sit ignored by the bins and by the automatic doors of the train station. The street is a blend of potential and deterioration. The pavement is pocked with old gum and there's a puddle of vomit by the kerb. In the sushi place she selects a neat, pre-packed tray. The tray comes with a tiny bottle of dark sauce and a set of chopsticks. The man behind the counter is handsome. He wishes her a nice evening. She stops at the supermarket and buys a packet of Wispas and a Diet Coke.

The sky is pitch black, but jubilant birdsong emerges from dense patches of nothing. There's a poster for a film on at the university cinema – a documentary about the world of competitive tickling. The poster is an image of an enormous feather, and Lily attributes the disembodied birdsong sputtering into the night to whatever enormous, artificial bird shed this feather. What's tickling, if not an exercise in falsehood? She cradles her sushi and Wispas and Diet Coke to her chest.

'Your dad and I used to dance to this song,' her mother said. Lily watched the first tentative raindrops get jettisoned off the windscreen by the wipers. They passed the old quarry, which over the course of Lily's life had become increasingly dismantled and increasingly obscured behind construction-company signage.

'Were you Sally or Alice in that scenario?' Lily said.

'I was Smokie,' her mother said. 'And your father was the driveway – the lesser-acknowledged fourth protagonist.'

'Was he a good dancer?'

'As good as your average driveway, probably,' her mother said.

Lily groaned. 'Do you have an off button?' she said.

'I'm sure I will do, at some stage.'

'Can't wait.'

Caz is in the foyer, pinning a flyer requesting that people don't put food waste in the recycling bins to the noticeboard. Her hotel uniform is a thick, stiff blazer and a pencil skirt. It accentuates every part of her. She glances behind her at the sound of the door, and when she sees Lily she removes a drawing pin from her mouth. Lily wonders how many people in the building have similarly transferred that pin from hand to mouth to board to hand to mouth. 'Dot died,' she says.

Caz has large, horseshoe dental arches and teeth like an amethyst cluster. She lives on the floor above Lily, next door to Siobhán. Talking to her is like being in a deep-space simulator.

'Oh,' Lily says.

'You know, the elderly woman who lived in the suite with the jacuzzi?'

'Right.'

'Nice lady.'

'Shame.'

'You doing okay?'

'Yeah.' Lily redistributes her items against her chest.

'You know,' Caz says, wistful, 'Dot used to say that her final adversary would be death.'

'Oh?'

'Which sounds wise,' Caz says, 'but I suppose everyone's final adversary is death.'

'Yeah.'

'Provided they've had earlier adversaries,' Caz says.

'A wet road, a mutinous motorcycle, a protracted illness,' Lily thinks. 'I suppose so,' she says instead. She glances impatiently at the translucent plastic of the sushi tray's lid. The tubes of sushi are salmon wrapped around green-flecked rice – they look like small, rolled-up sleeping bags. She's never had sushi, but she's hoping it might aid her cognitive maintenance.

Sometimes she remembers her mother's voice at a different pitch, or she has apocryphal eyebrows. Once these falsities introduce themselves, they're hard to expunge. The problem with fighting to retain the truth of your memories is that truth never had much to do with it.

'I've been meaning to say to you,' Caz says, and Lily looks up again, 'the girl next to me and I swapped spare keys yesterday, just in case there's ever a problem when one of us is out. You and I could do it too, if you wanted.'

'You and the girl next door have swapped keys?' Lily asks.

'You know, in case you ever leave a candle lit, or if you get locked out. Neighbourly-mindedness, you know?' She winks. 'Like in *Rear Window*.' Lily forgets to laugh. After a long pause she says, 'Yeah.'

'Obviously, if you're worried about me pilfering, there's no pressure,' Caz says.

Another pause. Lily offers another 'Yeah', and when Caz laughs in a hurt tone Lily realizes there was a correct response. They look at each other.

'What's that you've got there?' Caz says eventually. She nods at Lily's chest.

'Sushi,' Lily says, then, 'Bye, Caz.' She heads for the stairs.

'See you later, moonbeam,' Caz says, then returns the drawing pin to her mouth.

Lily first met Caz two months after moving in. Caz was reading a flyer and had a shopping bag full of wholegrain bread and packets of pre-sliced cheese and cherry tomatoes and full-fat milk. When she saw Lily she said, 'There's a party happening upstairs tonight, and apparently we're all invited. Isn't that weird and wonderful?' Lily glanced over her shoulder, and Caz said, 'I'm talking to you. You've just moved in, haven't you?' Lily nodded. 'Fancy it?' Caz said.

Lily's first impulse was to say no, but she decided to entertain the memory of her former receptivity. Caz said she would stop by her flat at seven and they could go up together, but that evening Lily couldn't get dressed. She knew instinctively that to leave the flat, to place herself at the scrutiny of others, would invite revulsion. She'd mutated somehow, was now like a child's drawing of a person. Her body seemed newly multifarious, shoddily assembled of components that she no longer fully understood as hers. She wasn't convinced people would be able to move successfully around her, that she wouldn't obstruct the motions of others like some great bezoar, like a lump of festering hair in a drain. She didn't want to be looked at, or listened to; she wanted to forget that she had a body.

When the knock came on the door Lily was on her bedroom floor with clothes in heaps around her, some ripped in frustration. One leg was halfway into a pair of grey trousers and the mirror in the corner was turned to face the wall. The knock happened again and she became still, trying not to breathe audibly. Caz's voice called through the door: 'Moonbeam? You there?' Lily hoped she couldn't see the light under the door. Eventually the knocks stopped and Caz left, and Lily stayed on the floor for another hour, muttering to the crepuscular gloom.

Two days later they bumped into one another again. Caz said, 'What happened to you the other night? You okay?' and Lily said that a friend's mother had died unexpectedly. Caz said, 'I'm so sorry,' and Lily stole the sentiment, intended for this imaginary friend. She reached out an arm to stroke the noticeboard and, after a moment, Caz said, 'You know, when I go to a party, I tell myself that I'm the best-looking person in the room.'

Lily tried to hide her scepticism.

'It gives me confidence,' Caz said.

'But what if you're not the best-looking person in the room?' Lily said.

'Why would that have anything to do with anything?' Caz replied, and this response, so reminiscent of something her mother might say – so joyfully unencumbered by any objective reality – made Lily feel an ache so pronounced she flinched. She said nothing.

'I'm sorry about your friend,' Caz said. 'You know, my mum—'

'How was the party?' Lily interrupted her.

'Fun,' Caz said. 'But there'll be others.' She headed for the stairwell.

'And were you?' Lily said quietly, half expecting not to be heard.

Caz turned. 'Was I what?'

'The best-looking person in the room.'

Caz laughed cheerfully. 'Like I said, why would that have anything to do with it?'

Lily has since wondered if, conversely to how she needs not to be seen, Caz needs to be seen, but as something different from what she is.

She entertains feeling bad for not speaking to Caz longer in the foyer, but she can't make it stick. She unpacks the small box of sushi – setting the finger-sized bottle of soy sauce to one side, unsheathing the chopsticks. The salmon is tinted to the artificial pink of aspiring salmon, the colour it once was, before farming prevented young fish from eating the red spheres of the river-bed, before they were processed to a flat platinum colour. She choreographs the chopsticks between her fingers, thinks about how it must be to become visually divorced from the colour you created, to have your defining characteristic live on beyond you through mimicry, after it has been lost to you for ever. The salmon is clammy, like a forehead. She puts a roll in her mouth and bites down, regrets it. There's too much and too little resistance – her teeth slide through soft coldness to encounter a snagging vein of thread. The rice below fills her mouth with cardamom and stagnancy, and though the soy sauce improves it, when she swallows, the roll fights its way back up her throat. She spits tapioca into the sink, then puts the remaining sushi in the bin. She eats the first Wispa. She pours Diet Coke on top.

An hour later, out in search of replacement dinner, she sees Siobhán outside the supermarket, collapsing her umbrella. She goes inside, and Lily pursues cautiously, at a distance.

Under the merciless lighting Lily keeps her hood up and lurks by the magazines, watching Siobhán inspect the produce. There's a hole in her tights, but she's coloured the skin underneath black, so when she moves non-intuitive slivers of white appear at intervals. Lily watches her debate the expiry dates on chicken breasts, before barrelling into the frozen section and tossing a pizza into her basket. She negotiates the supermarket like she negotiates having a hole in her tights, like how Lily suspects she negotiates everything: with guileless nonchalance. Outside, she doesn't bother to erect her umbrella, and from several metres behind Lily watches her shake her hair in the falling rain.

★

In bed, she lies still and lets the anarchy of dead fish settle in her stomach. She realizes she forgot to pay for the packet of Super Noodles she brought home from the shop. She listens to the heavy-footed ambling in the room above, and she thinks of the spare key in Caz's flat. She falls into the kind of sleep that has become common: dense and lengthy, filled with intangible dreams that she can't remember on waking but that imply a separate life, lived over the course of nine hours, then forgotten. She's estranged from herself a bit more each morning.

The funeral took place partly in a funeral home, partly in a nearby hotel.

'I don't want you to be saddled with a lot of entertaining and cleaning up,' her mother had said, as they planned it. 'This way you can leave when the mood strikes.'

'Is it bad if I leave your funeral early?' Lily said.

'Of course not,' her mother had said. 'I'm not planning on going at all.'

SIOBHÁN

By Sunday evening the treacherous vibrations of her phone, always heralding the wrong person, become unbearable. She scrolls through her messages looking for companions, deeming every possibility, in turn, an inferior alternative to no one. She goes for a drink by herself. While she waits to be served she watches the dynamics of a nearby table. A couple composed of a blonde woman and a shorn-headed man hold hands, across from another woman wearing a T-shirt that says 'Full Marx'. Siobhán wonders where you even get a T-shirt that says that, wonders if the woman had it made especially. They all seem drunk – there's a plethora of empty shot glasses on the table and they're shouting over one another. When the blonde woman leaves for a smoke the girl in the T-shirt reaches over and strokes the man's bristly head. Her hand lingers, then slides down his face, her thumb moving across his lower lip. She leans across the table and he looks stricken, then she puts her lips to his chastely. He pulls away and glances over his shoulder and she gives him a triumphant smirk. Siobhán looks to the front door, where the blonde woman is just visible through the glass, hunched over her lighter. The barman says, 'All right, love?' and Siobhán turns away from whatever it is that's happening.

An hour later, having read the last nine months of Whats-App correspondence between her and Andrew, she decides to go home. On her way out she sees the girl in the communist T-shirt, now sitting on the same side of the table as the shorn-headed man. She puts her lips to his ear lobe. The blonde woman is nowhere to be seen.

In the times between seeing each other she sometimes wonders if she exists, properly. In her memory of the last few years the times with Andrew remain vivid: abundant and sensory. She can see the pores on his nose and hear him listing with a confident clarity dishes in a restaurant, characteristically ordering too much. The time between feels indistinct in comparison, like being just able to hear someone else's music on a bus. Her work contributes to this hazy propulsion of time, which is good, in theory, because its simultaneous chaos and monotony accelerate the parts of life spent waiting to see him, which is most of her life. She seems to live truly only when he's with her: the rest of the time she feels nebulous and two-dimensional. It makes her sad that she has come to think of her job, the culmination of everything she's wanted and worked for, as a means to an end, and that end is the expenditure of time. She also worries about what will happen when she discovers she's accidentally leap-frogged into middle age. When she was in her early twenties she did what she referred to as the sleep diet – she'd overdose on antihistamines and sleep through her hunger. She woke up one day and realized she'd misplaced three weeks – she was seven pounds lighter and a month older.

On Monday morning the sky is a dark, saturated duvet, close and oppressive as she clops through the empty Holyland streets and across Ormeau Bridge. She gets to school at half seven, heads straight to the toilets nearest the P1 classrooms, takes a shit. The toilets are smaller than regular toilets, and she feels enormous. The heating doesn't come on until after eight, so she wraps herself in the blue polyester blanket she keeps in her desk drawer and thumbs through *Charlotte's Web*, highlighting sentences and making notes about possible class exercises: sentence construction; identifying nouns, verbs, adjectives; describing a place through senses; writing different points of view; writing from an animal's perspective; the grammar of dialogue. She turns a page in her notebook and writes, 'Frost v Nixon style interview – Mr Arable v Charlotte? Bit much?' Her phone vibrates on the desk. She picks it up and looks at the message preview on the lock screen.

Hi sweetheart.

She waits to see if there's more coming, then sets the phone down. It vibrates again. She picks it up.

You okay?

Eventually the old radiator yawns into consciousness, and she slaps her cheeks a couple of times. Her phone vibrates.

I'm sorry I've been so quiet.

She leaves the messages unopened. She takes A3 sheets of pale pink and blue paper from the cupboard and starts pulling the desks out of their rowed formations and pushing them into continent-shaped lumps. She places a sheet at the centre of each desk mass and scatters felt-tips around, testing every fourth or fifth to make sure it has ink. Her phone vibrates three more times. She puts it on mute and throws it into the top drawer.

At eight fifteen she goes to the canteen. The staff have hauled open the shutters, and Jean is emptying beans from an industrial vat into a cauldron.

'Hi, Jean.'

'All right, love?'

The kids that come in for breakfast filter in, rheumy and cold-looking. At lunchtime the canteen is psychotropic, the combination of noise and brightly painted murals on the walls making it jubilant and festive. In the morning, though, it all seems forced, like a feather boa on a dementia sufferer. The kids line up at the hatch, tiny convicts, and collect their beans on toast or cereal or porridge. Sophie appears at Siobhán's side – she gestures at a painting meant to resemble a dragon.

'I hate that fucking cat,' she says.

Siobhán laughs, too loud, and several kids look over. Sophie gives her a closed-mouth, satisfied smile, then wanders away. Siobhán gets a cup of tea and sits at the end of one table.

'You okay, Paul?'

Paul is tiny and thin and dirty – there are stains down his jumper. He nods, sullen. The steam sweeps off the top of Siobhán's paper cup and Paul pokes a small finger through the vapour. 'I need to go to the toilet,' he says, abruptly.

'Okay – want me to take you?'

He doesn't look at her. He nods.

In her first few weeks at the school she would sometimes peek around the doorframe of the boys' toilet, fascinated by the frailty and ineptitude of the boys' tiny penises. While Paul is inside she goes to a storeroom and gets him a better-looking jumper from a Lost and Found box, and when she returns with it he allows her to wipe around his mouth with damp toilet paper.

In the five minutes before the first bell rings she goes back to her classroom and checks her phone. Six messages.

Hi sweetheart.
You okay?
I'm sorry I've been so quiet.
I love you.
Message me whenever you get a chance.
xxx

She messages back: *Hey – sorry. Sorting out the kids. You don't need to be sorry. I love you xxx.*

He replies immediately. *Sweetheart.*

Her class trickles in – first Kimberly, who is precocious and has had her period already, qualifying her for alpha status. Then, some of her disciples: Kate, who's cleverer than Kimberly but chubbier and less assertive; Ayesha, Amy, Rebecca. They assemble around one of the table islands.

'Hey,' Siobhán says. 'Don't all lump together – let's try and get some variety in the groups. Kim, why don't you come here with Rebecca? Kate and Ayesha and Amy, you three go there.'

'Why, miss?' Kimberly has her hand on her hip, and Siobhán has the thought that Kimberly will be the thirteen-year-old who is convinced by a guy five years older than her to give him a blow job.

'Because, if I let you lot sit together, it might all get a bit Jeffrey Eugenides.'

Kimberly screws up her face. 'What, miss?'

'Because I say so,' Siobhán says. 'Now' – she claps her hands – 'disperse!'

It's strange knowing that they think of themselves as real people, which isn't to say that they aren't, but when Siobhán looks back on being ten years old it's a bit like having been a puppy with a cone on its head – only seeing a third of what's actually there, prohibited from chewing on your genitals. When all twenty-one of her students are distributed around the room she hands out the marked assignments from Friday.

Kimberly says, 'How was your weekend, miss?' and Amy parrots, 'Yeah, miss, how was your weekend?'

Siobhán thinks about saying, 'Well, my married boyfriend said, "In a minute," when I asked him to fuck me, so it was all a bit of a fucking farce, kids.'

'All the better for having had your marvellous assignments to captivate me,' she says instead.

'But what did you do, miss?' Ayesha says.

'I saw my friends and I read a little and I watched some TV.'

'Your hair looks nice, miss.'

'Thanks, Kimberly – I grew it myself,' she says. This always gets a laugh.

Siobhán wonders at what point a confidence like Kimberly's dims. She's tall now, but child-tall rarely translates to adult-tall, and her tits will cease to be novelties once she gets to secondary school. Siobhán doesn't think she dislikes her, but she also wonders if any fondness is dependent on the assumption that her life is about to get more difficult. Siobhán sets Kimberly's homework in front of her.

'Why'd I only get a seven, miss?' Her tone ferments. Others in the class look up from their work, eager.

Siobhán shrugs. 'You made some pretty basic errors, Kim – stuff we've been going over for weeks. It seemed like you didn't really try. I know you know this stuff.'

'Okay,' Kimberly says, then smirks, '*Siobhán*.'

Siobhán feels twenty pairs of spectators' eyes. Although she doesn't mean to, she lets her head roll back in irritation. 'Fuck you, you little ass-hat,' she thinks. 'Don't,' she says.

Kimberly feigns innocence. 'Don't what?'

'You know what. Out.'

Kimberly blinks. 'Actually?'

'Yes. Outside for five minutes. You know I'm not into that sort of carry-on.'

Kimberly closes the door in a way that suggests a slam was warranted. Siobhán raises her eyebrows. 'Anyone else feel like being a jerk?' she says. The forty eyes look at her. 'Good,' she says. 'Because I've got some fun stuff planned.'

During morning break Sophie ambles in, using a tube of Hobnobs as a lint roller. Siobhán is texting.

What are you wearing? he says.

Siobhán picks a hair off the front of her shapeless corduroy shirt. *Tight skirt, low-cut jumper, those boots you like*, she says.

Mmmm.

'Hey, thrill-seeker.' Sophie sits on the corner of Siobhán's desk. Siobhán locks her phone. It vibrates. It vibrates again. Siobhán looks at Sophie, who is dressed in an expensive-looking trench coat.

'Aren't you cold?' she says.

'I think what you mean to say is "Nice coat, Sophie."'

'Sorry,' Siobhán says. 'It's great.'

'It would need to be. It cost a bomb. Hence why I'll be wearing it for the foreseeable, and also why I won't be eating for the foreseeable.' The phone vibrates again. 'Someone likes you,' Sophie says. She passes Siobhán the biscuits – Siobhán takes two.

'Can't imagine why,' she says.

'I know – you're intolerable.'

'Right?'

'I saw Courtney Love standing outside earlier.'

Siobhán lowers her voice. 'Pain in the arse, that girl.'

'What'd she do?'

'Called me Siobhán.'

Sophie laughs behind her hand. 'Christ,' she says.

'I know.'

'Ever think we should be sterilizing some of these kids as a favour to humanity?'

'Sterilizing? Try euthanizing.' Siobhán takes another biscuit.

'Spot on.'

'You know, eugenics gets a bad rep, but . . .' Siobhán trails off, and Sophie laughs. 'Want to sort out the papier-mâché stuff later?' Siobhán says.

'You bet,' Sophie says. Siobhán's phone vibrates again. 'Whoever he is,' Sophie says, 'he's clearly obsessed with you.'

Things were easier before she had a full-time job. What she hadn't anticipated was how much the success of a relationship with a married man is predicated on having large gullies of availability through the day. When she was working at the hotel, and then when she was a student, she could text him in his breaks between lectures, during his office hours, on his train journeys to Galway or Cork for conferences or PhD. vivas. Even after she'd graduated, when she was relying on substitute work, she could still just about manage to carve out great swathes of time for him. Now, though, their free time is too often non-concentric. Sometimes she likes the sense of power she feels in being less accessible to him than she once was. Then she gets home and the power is quickly displaced by loneliness. The innumerable evenings of no touch, no talking, unreliable correspondence.

Kimberly is meeker for the rest of the day, until Siobhán catches her muttering behind her hand to Kate and gesturing at Siobhán's legs. Kate sees Siobhán looking and has the decency to blush. Siobhán doesn't begrudge Kate's acquiescence to Kimberly – she needs to be inconspicuous, until either her excellence becomes valued by her peers or she becomes pretty. Siobhán hates herself for doing it, but she glances down at her legs. There's a ladder in her tights. She looks up at Kimberly, who smiles, blithely. 'Little shit,' Siobhán thinks. She turns on her heels. 'Anyone have a black felt-tip?' she announces to the class.

No one says anything. She adopts a rousing, jovial tone.

'C'mon – no takers? Black felt-tip – I definitely scattered a few on some of the tables earlier.'

Jake, who has amblyopia and a corrective eye patch, raises his hand. 'I do, miss,' he says.

She takes it from him. 'Thanks, Jake – you're a lifesaver.' She returns to the front of the room. 'Was worried one of you might notice this,' she says, and she makes a show of colouring in the exposed rectangle of skin. The kids in the reassembled front row of desks start laughing, and the ones further back crane in their seats to see. 'There,' Siobhán says. 'Much better, and much less embarrassing.' She returns the pen to Jake, who smiles at her. She glances at his sheet, and the questions that trip most kids up at first he's answered correctly, immediately. She's filled with an absolute euphoria, so palpable she wants to applaud. She posits loudly, 'How about we play a game once everyone's done?' and the mood in the room turns lambent.

Siobhán beams at Kimberly. She's never had this kind of enmity with a student before. 'One-upping a ten-year-old,' she thinks to herself as she sits down. 'Aren't you a big fucking deal?' She wonders if this is the sort of thing people go to CBT for.

Twenty minutes later she's chaperoning a maniacal game of Heads Down, Thumbs Up. Nobody squeezes Kimberly's thumb, and Siobhán tries not to feel pleased.

At the end of the day she sheepdogs the kids into a pile for pick-up. Robbie and Christopher start shoving each other – Robbie shoves too hard and Christopher collides with Rebecca and Rebecca falls over, starts bawling.

'Guys, could you try to be a bit less terrible?' Siobhán says as she bends over and picks Rebecca up. 'It's okay, pal – don't worry, you're fine.' There's snot beckoning at the edge of Rebecca's nostril. She takes Rebecca's small hands in hers. 'Not even the rain has such small hands,' she thinks. She blows on the skin and gingerly removes the stones stuck to the palms.

'That really hurt,' Rebecca says.

'I know, I know, but it's okay. You're a trouper. You're okay.'

Siobhán looks up and sees Rebecca's mother by the gates – anxious, probably anorexic. Siobhán receives three or four emails from her a week.

'Your mum's here, see? You can go get a big hug from her and feel better.'

'I don't think I can walk,' Rebecca says, with quivering nobility. Siobhán suppresses a laugh.

Sometimes it's hard not to resent the lucky children their backgrounds – the ones with parents who care. She thinks of Paul, with his filthy jumper and sporadic father, who showed up two hours late one day to collect him. It's not Rebecca's fault she's accustomed to feeling like someone's priority. Siobhán strokes her back.

'Of course you can,' she says. 'You're a brave girl. C'mon.' She coaxes her towards the steps. The limp swaps sides at intervals.

'Off you go, Lazarus,' Siobhán says.

'Bye, miss.'

Rebecca's mother envelops her with thin arms.

After every child has been retrieved Sophie and Siobhán spend an hour tearing newspaper into strips and painting the former Action Men turned robots they papier-mâchéd the week before. A well-thumbed copy of *The Iron Man* sits on the desk.

'Do you think it's ethically questionable of us to have big Hughes on our curriculum?' Siobhán says, painting one foot.

'Why?' Sophie says, inspecting the seam down a leg. Her charm bracelet dangles – the high-heeled shoe, the dog and the cherub all niggle at the plastic paint palette. After three attempts to push the bracelet up her arm she takes it off, swearing under her breath.

'Well,' Siobhán says, when the bracelet is at the far end of the table, 'because of the infidelity, and possible battery.'

Sophie adopts a pained expression. 'Shiv,' she says, 'I really don't think *now* is the time to raise these concerns. This book was *your* idea and, besides, we got this approved months ago.'

'I know,' she says. 'Never mind. Plus, I guess the canon would take a pretty big dent if we started using a tiny thing like misogyny as an exclusionary criterion.'

Sophie dunks her paintbrush in water and laughs. 'Christ,' she says, 'you're cynical.'

'Plus' – Siobhán rotates the newspaper her model is standing on – 'the kids love the book, et cetera, et cetera.'

'That's the spirit.'

'Maybe it's all fine. Maybe Peter Handke getting the Nobel was just a necessary evil.'

'Okay, now you've lost me.'

'He's a Slobodan Milošević apologist.'

'Okay, yeah – that clears things right up.' Sophie rolls her eyes, shakes her head. They paint in silence for a moment.

'Plus,' Siobhán says. 'You know, where does it end? Next thing we won't do Roald Dahl with them either.'

'Why?' Sophie says. 'What's his deal?'

'Antisemite.'

'Seriously?'

'Yep.'

'God, can't trust anyone.'

'And it's a shame really – you know that story of his about the leg of lamb?'

'Sure.'

'I saw a really big butternut squash at the weekend – would have made an unbelievable murder weapon.'

Sophie laughs. When she laughs she looks like a bad drawing of herself. The radiator behind them commences its Gregorian chant.

'So,' Siobhán says, leaning back in her chair to survey her work. 'Reckon when we show this to the kids we should précis the whole Plath death followed by Plath-death-lite thing?'

'What's Plath-death-lite?'

'Hughes' partner after Plath killed herself in the same way Plath did.'

'No fucking way.'

'Way.'

'Christ.'

'I know.'

'Still though, Shiv,' Sophie says, '"Plath-death-*lite*"? Bit glib, even for you.'

'Sorry, it's been a day.'

They start adding a second coat to the backs of the legs. Siobhán's phone vibrates four times in succession in her bag.

'That the Hughes to your Plath then?' Sophie nods in the direction of the sound.

'For him to be my Hughes might necessitate more regular visitations.'

'God, you're exhaustingly cryptic.' Sophie reaches down to her bag. 'Here,' she says, setting a room-temperature can of non-alcoholic Carlsberg on the table. 'Shut up and have a drink.'

'Smuggling Carlsberg, eh? Didn't realize we were seventeen-year-old party boys at a barbecue.'

'Sorry, Your Highness – they were all out of Babycham.'

They laugh. The table wobbles and the robots sway. They take long drinks of not-cold beer.

'Here, want to know something faintly distressing I found out the other day?' Sophie says.

'Always.'

'I was up seeing my mum, and she decided to tell me a little origin story.'

'Right.'

'So, apparently,' Sophie says, 'when I was about three weeks old, she decided to take me to visit my great-grandparents on my dad's side, because they were old and it wasn't looking likely that they'd be around for much longer.'

'Okay.'

'So. Mum lands at the farm in Ahoghill, with me in a baby

carrier, and they already have a visitor – some bloke my mum thinks she recognizes but can't quite place. Well, it becomes apparent from the chat that this guy, whoever he is, is on day release from prison and decided to use part of his day of freedom to call in with my great-grandparents.'

'Oh my God.'

'So' – Sophie leans back – 'Mum's *really* wracking her brains now to figure out who he is, but it's not until the drive home that she works it out.'

'Who was it?'

'Shiv, it was a member of the fucking Glenanne Gang.'

'You're kidding.'

'Nope. Swear to God.'

'Fucking hell.'

'So, one of the first people to hold me as an infant, hold my soft and impressionable baby head, was a fucking convicted paramilitary.'

'That's a bit insane.'

'Right?'

'Still,' says Siobhán, 'I guess most people here have a story like that, don't they? Perks of the place.' She wonders at the veracity of this statement as it leaves her mouth, wonders what she's inadvertently suggesting about herself by saying it.

'Oh, yeah, I know,' Sophie says hurriedly. 'And obviously, like, I didn't have it bad or anything. It's just, I wish I'd known before, you know? It explains so much, maybe. Did I ever tell you how weird and horrible the vibe was when I was growing up and we'd go visit my grandparents?'

'Mm? No,' Siobhán says. She takes a mouthful of beer and thinks about her own father, who might have been able to provide her with some context, if he were alive, who might have been able to help her justify herself. She thinks Andrew fetishizes her being from here, and sometimes she thinks he would like her to have a more traumatic personal history – an uncle who was in the Crum or something. If she has one, any information died with her grandmother, her mother staying resolutely tight-lipped about his side of the family. She knows that a cousin stood as a nationalist candidate in Castlereagh in the early noughties, but he only got three hundred votes, so it doesn't seem worth mentioning.

'God,' Sophie says. 'My family, mate. Terminally uncommunicative.' She shakes her head in dismay, and Siobhán realizes she missed most of the story. She rubs Sophie's thigh. Sophie gives a rueful smile.

'So,' Siobhán says, trying to reorientate herself within the conversation, 'are you worried that, like, you're a loyalist sleeper agent? That maybe Mr Glenanne pressed down on your fontanelle and implanted ideas in you?' Siobhán sets down her can and raises her palms in surrender. 'Are you going to kill me the next time I cross myself?'

Sophie laughs, and the mood lightens. She reaches over and pokes Siobhán in the ribs. 'Shut up,' she says. 'And when do you *ever* cross yourself?'

'First time for everything.'

They walk home some of the way together, then part. 'See you tomorrow, Captain Ulster,' Siobhán says.

'Piss off,' Sophie says.

When Siobhán first started, Sophie used to invite her out a lot. They were the only two members of staff under thirty-five, without families, and they fell into step immediately. A few times Siobhán agreed – they'd go for drinks, or to the cinema, but Siobhán would always feel antsy. When it got to 9 p.m., or 10 p.m., Andrew would usually text, and she'd want to leave – to get home so they could talk properly, so that her attention could be entirely on him. A night spent not talking to him has never felt innocuous – it feels like every night has the potential to be the last. After a while, the risk seemed not worth it, so she stopped going, and after a while, Sophie stopped asking.

When Sophie walks off, Siobhán takes her phone out of her bag. Ten messages. She opens them.

I wish we were together right now.

I'd pull your tights down with one hand then put the other hand up your skirt.

I'd stroke your clit with one finger and bite your ear.

Then I'd turn you around and bend you over the table.

I'd fuck you from behind until you came.

You're so sexy.

How's your day going, sweetheart?

I hope the kids are being okay.

I'm going to pick Ellie up from school.

Message me later if you're free xxx

The rain starts, becomes torrential. Siobhán drops her phone into her bag and finds her umbrella. She puts it up and it inverts, becomes half satellite dish, half Labrador, pulling her along. She glances down at her legs and with each step the material of her tights moves slightly, revealing the white skin around the splodge of coloured-in black. She feels ashamed; ashamed at her triumph in doing it, in trying to best a child in psychological warfare; ashamed at anyone who might see it now, now that she's removed from the protective and logic-relativistic chamber of a children's environment. Embarrassment never neatly occupies the same temporal space as its source, and she already knows the thought of her felt-tipped skin will recur in her mind in the weeks to come. She makes her steps smaller, tries to make the hole less conspicuous.

In the supermarket she puts noodles, vegetables, sweet-and-sour sauce, chicken breasts into her basket, before muttering, 'Fuck it,' and adding a Hawaiian pizza and a packet of brownies. Turning the corner on to her street, she senses someone behind her and she wraps her keys up in her fist and accelerates. She realizes upon getting home that she forgot to buy toilet paper, so she dries between her legs with the scratchy, paperless roll. Standing over the toilet, with her pants and tights still around her ankles, she looks at her phone. Another message.

Let me know if you're okay x

She replies: *Shit, sorry. Busy day, then stayed late to do lesson stuff with Sophie. Just got home. How are you? xxx*

For the rest of the evening she checks her phone at intervals, allowing herself to look at when he was last online after every four worksheets she marks. The phone stays obstinately silent. She goes on to his profile page on the university website and looks at his picture. She flicks through the limited number of photos that are public on his social media, because they're not allowed to be friends online. She changes her profile picture to one of five-years-younger-her, topless in a hot tub with strategically placed pina coladas, just in case he decides to look. She recognizes the futility of this gesture as she does it, because her profile has the maximum privacy settings and a Gaelicized version of her surname, to prevent her students or students' parents finding her. Still, it feels preferable to doing nothing. She puts a brownie in the microwave, and when the timer *dings* she opens the door to find wet chocolate offal dripping from the microwave ceiling and walls. She slams the door, opens it, slams it, opens, slams, opens, slams.

'Fuck fuck fuck fucking *fuck*.'

She abandons the mire of the microwave and eats another brownie, cold. At eleven fifteen, her phone *voot-voots* on the pillow next to her, and she rolls over to check it.

Have you done anything about driving lessons yet?? Her mother.

She ignores it. She turns off the light. She lies in the dark, more awake than she's felt all day – overfed and unbearably melancholic.

Her father died when she was three, but her parents had already separated. He fell off a hotel balcony, trying to pour beer into a bucket his friend was holding on the balcony below. It was a stag do. As far as Siobhán knows, the wedding went ahead.

When her mother is most irritated at Siobhán she says she is just like her father, which, to her mother, is the greatest slight that can be levelled at a person. Siobhán was named after her paternal great-grandmother, a decision her mother now calls misty-headed and foolishly sentimental. 'It makes no sense for *me* to have a daughter called Siobhán,' she says. Her mother is ostensibly Methodist, although Siobhán can't remember the last time she set foot in a church; her mother's Sundays are for dusting the skirting boards and bidding unsuccessfully on ceramic tat online. When Siobhán was little her father's mother would take her to Mass, and each February she would line up to receive the ashy blob on her forehead. Her grandmother was a neat woman with a grey bob and progressive trousers who used obsessive community work to stave off ageing and who was opposed, in a briskly affectionate way, to reminiscence. When she died – pneumonia, following a hip fracture – she took with her not just the only positive opinions ever expressed to Siobhán about her father but also any enthusiasm Siobhán had for organized religion.

Siobhán has no particular allegiance to the ghost of her father, but she can't imagine he was the sole villain in her parents' marriage. She's seen photos, and he looked a little like Keith Harris.

Once, when she was twelve, she brought her violin home from school with a broken string. She'd been playing with it on the bus, letting her friends pluck at it with their nasty, acrylic nails and pass it about like a conch. Her mother asked her if she was going to practise the violin that evening, and she said she would, then didn't. Her mother insisted she bring it to the kitchen and practise in front of her. When she saw the broken string she went quiet, said, 'Did you already know the string was broken?' Siobhán said, 'No,' and her mother said, 'You're lying.' Siobhán said, 'No I'm not.' Her mother paced the floor, repeating, 'Don't lie to me.' Siobhán said, 'I'm not.' Her mother's face slowly reddened. She opened the fridge and brought out a packet of individually wrapped triangles of cream cheese, did a kind of strangled scream, said, 'Liar,' and started throwing them. One hit the wall next to Siobhán's head, one hit the kettle, and one hit the big saucepan hanging from a hook. Siobhán left the room. The next day she found some cheese in her school bag, which had been sitting, open, by the kitchen table.

LILY

She looks at the curtains. It's too early for light, and she muses on how much of the day her curtains spend purposeless – the hour or so they devote to actually prohibiting light versus the many hours they spend either framing their enemy or shielding against its absence. She can hear the rain hissing behind them.

She rips her fingernails, picking at one thumbnail's edge with her other thumbnail until there's a split. She pulls, like removing the adhesive strip from an envelope. She drops it into the mug which sits on the counter, next to the urn full of her mother.

The mug is white and has a picture of Chris Hemsworth on one side, a still from the film *Thor*. It's the scene where Thor is in the coffee shop. He takes a mouthful of coffee and says, 'This drink, I like it.' He smashes the mug on the floor, shouts, 'Another!' 'Another!' is printed in block capitals beneath the picture.

She'd had the mug designed a few weeks after moving in. She'd gone for a walk through the city centre and encountered a ketchup-coloured shop that made personalized gifts. She chose the plain white mug from the shelf of blank crockery mannequins and took it to the desk. She'd shown the assistant the image on her phone, then sketched for him the layout she wanted, and the text. The shop assistant had dry skin that sat in flesh-coloured moraines along his hairline.

'You know, you could have ordered it online,' he said.

'Oh.'

'Do you want anything else on it?'

'No.'

'It won't cost any more – we have an offer on. Text on both sides costs the same as text on one. You could get, like, "Happy Birthday", and the name of whoever it's for, or whatever.' She contemplated having the mug printed with 'Happy Birthday, Lily!' but it occurred to her that when she handed over her debit card he would see that her name was Lily. That's why the mug says 'Happy Birthday, Kate!' on the other side.

She and her mother watched *Thor* on Christmas Day a few years ago. They tended not to watch films made within Lily's lifetime – the previous year they'd done *Four Adventures of Reinette and Mirabelle*; *When Harry Met Sally* the year before that. This year, though, their DVD player had stopped working the day before Christmas Eve, and because her mother refused to pay for a streaming service, they were reliant on scheduled programming.

Their Christmas Days, once there was no longer the requisite afternoon trip to her grandfather in the nursing home, always had the same itinerary. They exchanged gifts over breakfast, and that year her mother had bought her two jumpers in dark green and navy, a DVD of *Céline and Julie Go Boating*, an antique footstool she'd re-upholstered with crushed velvet, and a box of macaroons. Lily gave her mum a feather cactus that looked snow-dusted in a terracotta pot, *The Unconsoled* by Kazuo Ishiguro, a tartan blanket and a bottle of sherry. Lily never said this aloud, but she preferred their Christmases once her taciturn and bewildered grandfather was dead, once they didn't have to endure the forced jollity of the nursing home.

That afternoon, as her mother dispensed salted cashews and mini pretzels into bowls, Lily flicked through the channels. 'There's *Thor*,' she said.

'No *Casablanca*?' her mother said.

'Here's looking at you, Thor.'

The empty streets outside felt emblematic of the wider world, like nothing existed beyond the parameters of their quiet festivities. Their next-door neighbours, with whom they shared a wall, spent Christmas in Lebanon, and the usual incessant hum of the motorway, which lay just beyond their modest garden, fell silent. Her mother said they'd get bored quickly if every day was like that, but it struck Lily that variety was only desirable if you needed your life to feel lengthy. If you kept your days similarly nondescript, you left yourself with a greater capacity to keep vivid those moments which mattered. One memory of a good day, lived and relived, seemed more covetable than an indistinct life of diverse experience. Her mother had had a propensity for restlessness – she feared stagnation. After her death, stagnation was what Lily strove for, so that that which preceded it might stay with her.

When they had dinner her mother speared a Brussels sprout on her fork. Using it as a trebuchet, she shouted, 'Another!' The sprout jettisoned off the prongs and landed on the tiles with an expansive and quiet thud. When they'd stopped laughing her mother said, 'Christmas has made us idiots.'

When Lily brought the mug home she placed it next to the urn. Her mother had suggested Lily scatter the ashes, as she had done with Lily's father, but Lily couldn't bring herself to. She noticed that the nail on her right thumb had come partially detached, and she pulled at it, tearing along the perforation until she held the white, lunula-shaped tab between the finger and thumb of her other hand. She placed it in the mug, then got to work on ripping off her other nails. The mug now looked like a receptacle for flakes of desiccated coconut, and that they were bits of her – bits of dead matter, taken from her body – made it a kind of urn, too. She'd heard somewhere once that fingernails continue growing after death, and since her mother's wouldn't get to, Lily offered up her own. She performs the ritual regularly, supplementing the contents with eyelashes, toenails, skin. The remains of herself, alongside the remains of her mother.

She hears Siobhán move sluggishly from room to room. She wonders what shoes out of the five pairs Siobhán will put on today. She's always thought that trying to confront the un-knowable variables of another person's life only serves to emphasize your own solitary personhood. She waits until she hears the door upstairs open, then close. She waits five minutes, in case Siobhán has forgotten something, and when, two minutes later, she hears the door get unlocked, opened and almost immediately closed again, she muses pleasurably on the efficacy of her methods. She goes upstairs. The brown boots are missing. She turns to Caz's door and listens – inside she can hear music, alongside Caz's warbling accompaniment. She knocks. Caz opens the door in a silk dressing gown and her damp hair swaddled in a monolithic whip of towel.

'Oh! Morning, moonbeam! This is a surprise!' Her skin is slick with translucent serum.

'Hi, Caz.'

'You okay?'

'I wondered if you wanted to have breakfast together.' Lily wills their intentions to merge, for Caz to invite her inside.

'That sounds lovely, but I have work, I'm afraid,' Caz says. She thoughtfully massages gloopy fluid into her chin. 'Don't you?' she says.

'Don't I what?'

'Have work?'

'Not for a few hours.'

'Well, if you don't mind my dashing about the place while I get ready, why don't you come in for a coffee?' Caz grins. 'Seeing as you've come all this way.' She yelps at her own joke. Lily says, 'Ha ha.' Then, 'Yes, please,' and she follows Caz into the flat.

'It's nice, this,' Caz calls from the bathroom. The gravelly wheeze of the kettle absolves Lily of responding. She stands by the counter, performing a methodical itemization of her surroundings. She opens the cupboard behind her knees, then the one next to it.

'Got everything you need?' Caz peers around the doorframe, her hair dark yellow with wet, a mascara wand in her hand.

'Just looking for mugs,' Lily says.

'Cupboard above the kettle!'

'Thanks.' Caz disappears again, and Lily removes two off-white, handleless mugs from the top shelf. They look like cored-out snowballs. She resumes looking in the cupboards, the kettle ascending to its deafening death rattle. She drops to her haunches and opens the lowest drawer, finds stacks of pastel-toned Tupperware. The one up from it is full of small cylinders of paint and varnish and screwdrivers.

'Find the coffee okay?' Caz's voice is suddenly right behind her. She jumps on her heels. The kettle exhales.

'Not yet,' she says, and Caz laughs. 'What way do you arrange *your* kitchen, moonbeam?' she says, then reaches over Lily's head to the cupboard above the toaster. She brings out a jar of instant coffee. 'Milk's in the fridge,' she says. 'Give me a shout if you need help locating the fridge.' She gives Lily's shoulder a playful squeeze then pads back to the bathroom. Lily turns and watches her go, then opens the next drawer up. It's full of tea towels and padded oven mitts and a large brass corkscrew. She nudges the soft melee to one side, finds a key, nestled in the corner. She puts it in her pocket, closes the drawer and retrieves the milk. When Caz re-emerges, dressed for work, Lily hands her one of the bowlish mugs.

'Thanks,' Caz says.

'That's okay,' Lily says. They stand facing one another, sipping.

'Sure you're okay?' Caz says. 'Not like you to grace me with your presence.'

Lily shrugs, attempts a smile. 'I just thought it would be nice,' she says. Caz smiles at her, encouragingly, and it's the smile someone might direct towards an animal recently saved from an abusive captivity.

'It *is* nice,' Caz says, and rubs at her neck with one hand. A small deposit of foundation blends into her complexion. 'So,' she starts, in a cautious tone, 'any big plans for today?'

Lily shakes her head. 'Work,' she says.

'Industrious,' Caz says. 'Any plans for tonight?'

Lily considers her possibilities, says nothing. Caz laughs.

'How about you and I go for a drink?'

'A drink?'

'Why not?'

'Where?'

'Around the corner,' Caz says. 'Nothing fancy.' She commences a slow pace around the room, her long fingers and talons clasped around the mug like an eagle returning to its eyrie with prey. Lily watches her. She forces herself to abandon the suspicion that Caz is trying to entrap her.

'Okay,' she says eventually. The clock on the kitchen wall grinds towards eight.

There were arguments too, she supposes.

'Why have you done that, Lily?' her mother said once, standing by the bookcase with a duster in her hand.

'What?' Lily didn't look up from the television.

'Turned the TV on – I'm listening to music in here.'

'There's something I want to watch.'

'I was in here first.'

'But the TV's in here.'

'The point is I'm cleaning here.'

'The room doesn't need to be cleaned.'

'It does, so we don't live in filth.'

'It's hardly filthy.'

'Oh! I wonder why that is.' Her mother performed a sarcastic two-step, brandishing the duster. 'Must be the *cleaning* fairies,' she said, in a sing-song. 'The *cleaning* fairies come to *clean.*' They eyeballed each other.

'Fine.' Lily clicked the remote, loudly exiting the room.

This was the genre of most of their disagreements – little tussles of will, isolatable to their precise circumstances. Theirs were small incidents of contention unfuelled by ego, or leftover resentment, and provided one of them was willing to back down, as one invariably was, the tension of the conversation never outlived its moment.

There were other moments of disquietude, too: not so much arguments as instances of coolness. When one of them would intuit the other's ire and try not to exacerbate things; when her mother would come home from work and secrete herself behind the closed kitchen door, or when Lily would point herself, stoically, at the TV.

'What's up, Lil?'

'Nothing, I'm fine.' A cautionary snap in her tone.

'Okay, pet.' Her mother, pulling an 'O' with her face, quietly exiting the room.

Time was what solved things, rather than apologies or explanations. A show of affection from the wronged party – a head on a shoulder or a metronomic nudge with hips at the kitchen counter. A show of contrition from the guilty – a cup of tea or the laundry brought in from the line. This was all that was required to restore peace.

On the walk to work she buys a brown-bread BLT in a café and asks the girl behind the counter to heat it in the panini press, which she does, frowning slightly. Lily eats for the remainder of the walk, licking broiled grease off her fingers and blowing on the back of her hand when molten tomato slips on to her skin. It's windy and wet, and around her the foot-commuters struggle with umbrellas. Lily likes eating in transit, with the hood of her raincoat up; it feels like she's in the midst of some intrepid expedition. She wonders what Siobhán eats for breakfast, then reminds herself of the comforting weight of Siobhán's spare key in her pocket.

Before this, back during those first, initial encounters, a hypothetical scenario had replayed itself in her head.

'I can't believe this is our first time speaking properly,' she'd imagined Siobhán saying. In the scenario they are sitting outside, in the sun, with pints of cider.

'You're great,' she says. 'How has nobody ever told me before about how great you are?' There are also mutual friends, hovering on the periphery.

'Oh,' Lily says, 'I have some extreme character flaws that only make themselves apparent immediately.'

Siobhán laughs. 'Oh really? Like what?' and Lily leans in, conspiratorial, and says, 'When's the last time you saw your wallet?'

Siobhán's eyes widen, and her free hand reaches for her bag. 'My wallet's here,' she says, confused.

'I know,' Lily replies, 'but how great would it have been if I'd actually had it?'

Siobhán laughs, hard. They cheers their glasses, ebullient and bonded.

Siobhán had seemed to her like a person who could restore her to what she was before, someone with a capacity for closeness, for change. When she looked at Siobhán she'd felt the affection, charged by anticipation, that comes from sensing someone's difference from you.

She nearly collides with the woman in the rara skirt and the fur coat. She swerves at the last minute, bows her head, avoids eye contact. The woman says nothing, doesn't seem to really notice her at all. She offers an unsolicited smile to a stranger on the pedestrian crossing.

★

Her best friend at school was a short girl with a gap between her teeth named Ellen. They were grouped together one day in first-year Geography, and that was sufficient, in so far as an adult had dictated their proximity, to produce a lasting friendship. Lily liked that Ellen was always trying to predict what people were about say, so she could say it in unison. It made sense to Lily, like Ellen was trying to make herself continuous. That she invariably predicted incorrectly just made Lily like her more. Ellen was a noticeable sort of person, so Lily felt camouflaged by her; the reliable thrum of their companionship allowed Lily to float through the school days, unantagonized by her peers, and unbothered by the kinds of social quandaries that brought them grief.

When Lily left school at sixteen, she wondered if the friendship would expire, but Ellen kept texting her, and when Ellen stayed at home for university, it continued still, implacable and unchanging. It wasn't until a month after the funeral, when Lily packed up her existence and left Derry, severing ties to everyone who had known her before, that Ellen finally, resignedly, gave up.

The morning passes. She sells two newspapers to a man in green scrubs, and a balloon to a woman with a bruise around her eye socket, and a Twix to a teenager. She has a brief exchange with an elderly man in a hat who has a yellow dog on a harness. He holds out his wallet and says, 'Find the right change there, would you, love?' and she does. A girl in loose jeans buys a can of Coke, and when Lily asks about her book the girl shrugs, not unfriendly, and says, 'It's for uni.' When she walks away Lily inhales deeply, is reminded of the niceness of small talk: to have an ephemeral moment of shared existence with someone; to know implicitly that neither party attributed greater significance to the interaction than the other.

A few weeks after her diagnosis, her mother was sitting on the sofa, reading poetry. Lily was watching *Dinosaurs* on her laptop, had the Wikipedia entry for *Dinosaurs* open on her phone.

'Mum?'

'Mm?'

'Did you know that there were seven episodes of *Dinosaurs* that were never aired?'

'Yes.'

'Really?'

'No, of course not, but how great would it have been if I did?'

'So, in the final aired episode the dad dinosaur is partially complicit in ending the world.'

'Can you be partially complicit?'

Lily paused. 'I don't know,' she said.

'I think you can only be entirely complicit, but maybe partially culpable.'

'Maybe that's what I meant. Partially culpable.'

'In ending the world.'

'Yes.'

'How?'

'He contributes to the circumstances that instigate an ice age.'

'Of course. Could happen to anyone.'

'And in the final aired episode it's implied that they're all going to slowly freeze to death.'

'Right.'

'But the writers wrote an additional seven episodes. Isn't that weird?'

Her mother contemplated her feet. The chemotherapy made her feet hot, and she'd stopped wearing socks in the house. 'Well,' she said finally, 'I suppose a nuclear winter doesn't wreak its havoc in one fell swoop. For example: for lots of us there's still time for barbecues and trips to the bowling alley and the continued contribution to the effects of global warming, *before* global warming destroys our way of life entirely.'

'Does that make the barbecues more or less important?'

'I'm not sure – probably a bit of both.'

'Tragic and facile barbecuing.'

'That should be the name of your cookbook.'

'Provided I decided publishing a cookbook was worthwhile in the face of our planet's incremental demise.'

'Exactly.'

'But why not air the final seven episodes?'

'I suppose it's less neat, in terms of the narrative arc. Maybe people are less invested in tangential barbecuing.'

'I suppose,' Lily said. She put her headphones back on and her mother went back to her book. After a while, her mother spoke again.

'"I postpone my immortality for my children."'

Lily removed her headphones. 'What?' she said.

'"I postpone my immortality for my children." That's great, isn't it?'

'I'd rather you didn't.'

'Didn't what?'

'Postpone your immortality. Resume your immortality. Postpone your mortality.'

'You wouldn't like me if I were immortal.'

'I'd rather you were immortal and I not like you than the alternative.'

Her mother laughed. 'That,' she said, 'might be the nicest thing anyone has ever said to me.'

The elderly man with the dog approaches again, half whistling.

'Same again, if you don't mind, love.'

'Okay.'

'Bit miserable out there today, isn't it?'

'I quite like the rain – you're part of a current, when it's raining.'

'I like that,' he says. 'Nice to feel a part of something ancient. Preserves you in a way, maybe.'

'I like your dog.'

He jiggles the leash and the dog sniffs. 'He probably likes you too,' he says. 'What's not to like?'

'I have several extreme character flaws that only become apparent over time.'

He chuckles – a throaty, avuncular chuckle. He holds out his wallet, and she once again takes the change. As he and the dog leave she wonders what occurred between his first Dairy Milk and his second: a blood test; a discussion of biopsy results; an ozone hole widening over the ice caps, powered by a cold stratosphere.

Her mother's closest friend was an English teacher named Yvette. She wore ankle-length floral skirts and short bouclé jackets with non-uniform buttons. She had blonde, wiggly hair and dark roots.

Two years ago she organized a day for the upper sixths at school called 'It Takes a Village Day'. The students sat on the playing field in clusters, painting words on to large, flat pebbles Yvette had taken from the beach. The initiative was in response to the students' apparent moral turpitude and lack of community spirit, brought to light after a string of misdemeanours: vandalisms, fights, the kidnapping and rugby tackling of a sheep from a nearby farm. The words painted on the stones were meant to be 'kind' words: compassion; cherish; positivity; acceptance.

'Those words aren't even grammatically consistent,' Lily said to her mother.

'What do you consider a kind word?' her mother said.

Lily thought for a moment. 'Effluence.'

On 'It Takes a Village Day' Yvette paced with a megaphone, reading a parable she'd written about a stranger who arrives in a village with no money and nowhere to live. The villagers decide to give up one stone from each of their houses to build the stranger a home. At the end of the school day Yvette went to her coupé and found a back window smashed, a stone painted with the word 'Cunt' lounging on the back seat. Lily's mother helped Yvette pick glass from the upholstery, and Yvette said that if just one teenager had come away from the day less cynical, then it had been a success, and she took this to be the case later, when a student deferred university to volunteer abroad. Lily's mother told Lily that she admired Yvette's capacity for syllogistic fallacy. She took a sheet of paper and wrote 'Yvette's syllogism', then:

Yvette wants to make the students do good.
A student does good.
Yvette made the student do good.

She presented Lily with a large, flat stone upon which was painted the word 'Effluence'.

Lily hasn't seen Yvette since the funeral – there were messages left on the landline, offering to help her clear out the house, inviting her for coffee, asking if she needed anything. Lily listened to them in turn, thumbing the 'Delete' button. Once, Yvette came to the door, her yellow-topped amorphous blob of silhouette visible through the frosted glass. Lily watched it until it disappeared.

'Wouldn't be much point in my resuming my immortality if the world's not got long left,' she imagines her mother saying. She's wearing socks in this scenario, her feet no longer self-immolating.

'Wouldn't need to resume it for ever, just long enough to benefit me,' Lily would say.

'It seems that what you wanted wasn't so much my immortality but more that my expiry came about at a time more convenient to you.'

'Isn't that what loving someone is?'

Silence. 'Don't have a response?' Lily would say.

'I think you'll find it's *you* who doesn't have a response.'

When she gets home she makes pasta, covering it in olive oil and butter and Tabasco. The featureless expanse of the afternoon sprawls before her. She takes the key from her pocket, rotates it in her palm. She goes upstairs, and the hinge of Siobhán's door squeaks as she turns the key.

Hours later she is in bed, staring fixedly at the wall. She hears the key in the lock upstairs, then Siobhán's wordless, lilting cadences as she has a brief conversation on the phone. She hears a chair push itself back on the wooden floor above her. She hears the fridge door get opened, then closed. A moment later it opens again, closes. Open, close. A phone rings – the ringtone is the muffled verisimilitude of a cowbell. Then, murmurs. Siobhán starts her conversations louder than she continues them. Lily listens to the soft babbling. She thinks she hears, 'See you soon,' and then music starts. After a while Siobhán is wearing shoes, and Lily listens to her tango clumsily across the floor. Then the music stops, the door opens, the door closes. Lily goes to the window, watches Siobhán stomp down the street in a leather jacket, one hand tousling her hair. When she disappears beyond the limits of the frame, Lily goes upstairs again. There's a suitcase, newly prone in the corner, half filled. She investigates its contents, makes some adjustments.

'I don't condone what's going on here,' she imagines her mother saying.

'Your feedback is important to us. Please stay on the line.'

'Nasty.'

'Looking for me, were you, moonbeam?'

Lily encounters Caz on her way down. Caz has a yoga mat under her arm and her hair pulled away from her face. Lily can see the veins at her temples. She secretes the key in her pocket.

'Yeah,' she says. 'Hi.'

'I just need to shower,' Caz says, 'but I'll come get you in an hour?' Her leggings have daisies on them, her face the afterglow of recent redness.

'Okay,' Lily says.

'Perfect!' She sidles past Lily on the stairs. She smells of incense and armpit hair.

The bar is dark like an aquarium. It's cordoned into permeable sections with wooden frames, so it feels like being on a film set, *in medias res*.

'This place always makes me think of some GCSE student's half-finished Technology and Design coursework,' Caz says. There's a cocktail menu bound in faux leather and she opens it. 'Whatever you want,' she says. 'My treat.'

'I'll just have a cider,' Lily says.

'Bollocks to that. I insist you have something more exciting.'

Lily chooses a Blueberry Muffin, Caz a Cosmopolitan. They sit in a booth. Lily wants to ask her about Siobhán, but she's aware plausible deniability is crucial. Instead, she asks about Caz's work.

'You know, Belfast's become a real hotel metropolis,' Caz says, and every time the door opens behind Lily she looks up. 'Even ten years ago,' she says, 'there were maybe only a few big hotels in the city centre, a few smaller B & B types dotted around the place. Now, though, I don't know what visitors are doing when they leave their hotels. Are they going to visit *other* hotels?' She mimics a child. '"Oh, Mammy, let me tell you all about my great holiday to Belfast and my tour of the city's hotels."'

The cocktails arrive. Lily's tastes like a cardigan.

'And you know,' Caz says. 'Obviously, I love the hotel industry, of course I do. I started off in the shittiest little budget chain, and where I'm at now is great, but it's nothing like these monstrosities that are cropping up in the city centre, all soulless and named after wife-abusers. Prosecco for breakfast and personal concierges in the wardrobes, you know?'

Lily nods.

'You just wonder how a little boutique sort of place like mine'll manage, out in the suburbs, no five-course tasting menu, if the place just keeps filling up with hotels.'

Lily nods again.

★

They didn't take a lot of trips, but for her mother's fiftieth they went to London. They stayed in Greenwich, and their hotel room had a surfeit of pillows, and a bath, and when they looked outside they could see beehives.

'Look,' her mother said. 'They're like shrunken versions of Divis Tower.'

'Which one's Divis Tower?' Lily said.

'Jesus, Lil,' her mother said. 'Engage a bit, would you?'

The first evening they went to an Italian restaurant. Her mother had wine and Lily had an Aperol Spritz, which came in a glass shaped like a miniature football and tasted like Irn-Bru. They went to look at the *Cutty Sark*, and her mother said, 'Must have been a real bitch of a boat, to earn that name.' They watched the upside-down, wibbling twin of the city idling below the water's transparent lid – the river like a piece of cellophane separating two almost identical horizons.

'If you were a boat,' her mother said, 'what kind of boat would you like to be?'

'I'm not sure,' Lily said. 'A canoe, maybe?'

'That's a good one,' her mother said. 'And what kind of boat do you think you actually are?' Lily appraised herself, and remembered a news story about a tourist on holiday in Spain. 'I think I'm actually a pedalo,' she said. In the story the tourist took a pedalo too far out, from the provisional sea to the real sea, got overpowered by the current, had to be rescued. It was never mentioned if the pedalo was also rescued.

'What about you?' she asked her mother.

'I think I'd like to be a Viking longship,' she said, 'but I'm not sure what I actually am.'

'Maybe a houseboat,' Lily said, and her mother laughed.

'How dull,' she said, but that wasn't how Lily had intended it.

The next morning her mother had Bircher muesli and small pastries and Lily had a fry. Her mother had wanted to go to Wimbledon, but they didn't get tickets, so instead they went to the National Portrait Gallery, then to the National Gallery, saw *The Entombment (or Christ being carried to his Tomb)* by Michelangelo. The painting is an oil on wood of autumn colours, the only respite from the sand and burnt clay shades the small rash of sky that offers one eighth of the painting's whole. The planned location of the Virgin Mary sits conspicuously blank, a mottled, gold-tinged menhir in one corner. Lily had assumed paintings were created in their totality in increments, each full layer bringing an intact narrative to fruition, but instead the Virgin is left as the ochre ghost of her potential, of the artist's unfulfilled intent. Instead of a person, a space made for a person.

They walked along the Thames, and everything felt curated, like a partially animated musical set in London, rather than London itself: there were old books for sale under a bridge and a conga line of baggy-trousered people blowing bubbles, and men with saxophones on a boardwalk. Her mother bought a wrinkly copy of *Wuthering Heights* and they sat at a table outside a pub.

'This is the ultimate revenge-driven, red-blooded, sexy ghost story,' she said.

'Do ghosts have red blood?' Lily said.

'A good question,' her mother said. 'I don't know. Goblins, though,' she said, 'goblins *definitely* have red blood cells.' She smiled at Lily, coaxingly. Lily sighed, and took a drink.

'Go on then,' she said. 'Do your joke.'

'Haemogoblin,' her mother said.

'Mum.'

'It's my birthday.'

'Still, though.'

'Get it down you, moonbeam, I'm ready for another,' Caz says. Lily tips her glass – the bottom is vanilla sediment and fruit syrup, the colour of blue hyacinths. She offers to buy the next round. 'No, no,' Caz says. 'I'm just thrilled to have finally coaxed you out. Same again?' Lily nods and Caz sidles from the booth. Lily reads the drinks menu, stroking its leathery hide. After a while she turns in her seat. Caz is talking to a man at the bar. He has his whole body angled towards her. He's wide, with a wide neck and heavy eyebrows. Caz picks up the drinks and walks away, but then turns back to say something to him. The lasting impression of their exchange is that it is unfinished. Caz sits.

'Sorry about the wait,' she says.

'Do you know him?'

'Hm? Oh, no, we just got talking. He's a writer! He's writing a play about two people stuck on a boat.'

'What kind of boat?'

'That didn't come up.'

'If you were a boat, what kind of boat would you be?'

'That's a fun question.'

'And what kind of boat do you think you actually are?'

'I think I'd like to be one of those enormous yachts in St Tropez or Monaco, covered in beautiful people and Moët.'

'And what are you actually?'

'I try to think only in terms of the aspirational.'

'An aspirational boat.'

'There was a Chinese restaurant I used to go to with my dad when I was little. It had boat-like aspirations.'

'Do you think it knew it wasn't a boat?'

'If it didn't, I hope nobody ever held it up to a mirror.'

'Probably would have been too heavy to do that anyway,' Lily says, and Caz laughs. Lily's thoughts are starting to feel unbridled.

'My dad and I went there nearly every month for years,' Caz said. 'He loved their dim sum. He's a dead-on guy, my dad, you know? Real hard-working. He used to work in antique restoration, and when I was little, he'd say—'

'Want another drink?'

Caz blinks. 'Okay,' she says. 'Are you okay?'

'I'm fine,' Lily says. 'Here,' she says, and gets out her wallet. She hands Caz some notes. 'Get more drinks,' she says.

'Whoa,' Caz says, 'that's a big wad. You know, I sometimes wonder how you afford to live in Benson—'

'Same again, please.'

Caz shrugs, compliant. She walks off.

After two more cocktails exhaustion brings with it a scurf of deep melancholy. She feels unconvinced in her legs' ability to lift her home.

'I think I'm going to go,' she says.

'Okay,' Caz says, red-cheeked. 'I think I might stay,' she says. 'Maybe go find out what sort of boat it is.'

'Okay,' Lily says. They stand, and Lily submits to a hug. Caz now smells of ginger and damp polyester.

When she gets in she goes up one flight of stairs too many. The automatic lights come on. She sways on her feet. She can hear a hob extractor fan going inside, then another noise. A woman's moaning: short gasps, then a long bray, like a sheep. Then silence. Lily stands there for a few moments, then returns downstairs.

In her flat she contemplates the residual tubes of pasta lying, sickly, in a pan. She pours a glass of water and sits at the table. At her left hand is the small blue exercise book she took from Siobhán's. She opens it at its centre, starts reading. The handwriting has great looping tumours and uneven crossbars; occasionally a word's second half gets truncated, folded like a concertina to make it fit within the page's parameters. The sentences proliferate with spelling errors. Lily works her way methodically through a tangential and excitable depiction of ten years in the future, and the words, written as phonetic, alien versions of themselves, in meandering sentences about yoghurt tubes and floating buses, combined with the thick smog of drunkenness, causes a kind of schism in her consciousness. She finds herself becoming angry, angry that children are being permitted to entertain these idealized frescos of how life will be – better, Technicolor – and angry that anyone might think words have any semblance of unimpeachable meaning, that it isn't all so stupid, that it isn't all so easily dismantled, that these marks on a page have anything to do with existing. She looks at the annotations and marginalia – a small depiction of a smiling face, 'What great imagination!' in green pen, ticks and corrections. They seem complicit in something. Her face starts leaking, gently, on to her hands. She abandons the book on the table and curls on to her bed. The pendulum of her mood, which has spent the day oscillating between extremities, frightens her. The rivulets of tears conjoin on the fabric of her pillowcase, the dark patch widening. Eventually she runs dry.

★

The next day her head hurts. She takes a can of Fanta from the fridge and drinks it, then gives a man in a white coat too little change to cover the cost. He looks harried, doesn't notice, and doesn't say thank you. 'People will always find ways to justify their own selfishness,' her mother said once. As he turns, his stethoscope swings around him, like a cow's tail batting away flies. Lily drinks her purloined Fanta. When she short-changes people she invariably spends the change in the shop, and through this she feels that she is creating a self-sustaining economy.

'I'm not sure you have a tenable grasp on economics,' her mother might say.

In the Hope office Marian gives her a sheet with addresses, a pile of letters, a pile of envelopes. Hannah walks in from her lunch break, says, 'So, you would not believe what happened last night.' She's wearing a T-shirt that says 'Commiepolitan'. Marian is doing complicated-looking things with a spreadsheet, attempting to create some dynamic formula, but she still says, 'Tell us, love?' and Lily wonders if her inexhaustible generosity preceded her son's death, or arose subsequently.

'Well,' Hannah says, 'you know my friend Laura? MDMA, *Antiques Roadshow*? Her boyfriend tried to get off with me? Well, last night they invited me for a drink, to clear the air, as it were.'

'That right, love?' Marian's top has white stripes on a burgundy background.

'I know – weird, right? But I figured, why not go and try to salvage things. Plus, I'd done nothing wrong.'

Hannah is a full-time employee – she commences her day at 9 a.m., finishes at 5 p.m. And yet Lily often seems to be present for her most personal anecdotes. Lily isn't sure if Hannah reserves them for when Lily is there, and what that means, if she does.

'So,' Hannah says, 'we meet up, right? And yeah, it's a bit awkward: I kind of wondered when we were going to broach the subject, but then, we just – didn't. Weird, right?'

'A bit weird, love?' Marian glances at her computer. Lily watches her click Save, then click Save again, then click Save As, then retype the document's pre-existing name, then click Save again.

'But, right, I figured if that's how they want to play it, chill with me. So, we have a really lovely night, and they both get a bit steaming – I was taking it easy because I need to finish that newsletter thing today – and at one point he goes to the toilet, for, like, a really long time, and Laura tells me, and get this: she tells me that when he's really drunk, he shits on the kitchen floor.'

'Hannah?' Marian's tone has a grimace in it.

'I know, it's gross, I'm sorry. But yeah! Apparently he's done it, like, three times, and the day after he accused me of trying to get off with him, Laura found a little turd, wrapped up, in the kitchen bin, and that's how she knows he was probably too wasted to remember what happened.'

Marian clicks Save again.

'So, I've been exonerated! By a turd! In a bin! I mean, Laura says she's not going to break up with him, but I think the trust is pretty much gone, so who knows how long they'll last. Sure, shitting on the floor, *that* she can countenance, but trying to get off with your mate might be just a bridge too far.' Hannah leans back in her chair, exhales. 'Poirot-level stuff, isn't it?' she says.

Marian swivels in her seat, gives Lily a half-apologetic look. Lily wonders why Marian thinks she requires an apologetic look, why Marian thinks she wouldn't enjoy Hannah's anecdote, wouldn't have similar anecdotes of her own.

'Hannah?' Lily says, and Hannah swivels, surprised.

'Yeah?' she says.

'When I was at school there was a girl who hid used sanitary towels all over the place.'

Hannah raises an eyebrow. Marian frowns, confused. Lily wonders if she's miscalculated. The silence hangs baggily.

'Holy shit,' Hannah says. Marian says, 'Hannah? Language?' and Hannah says, 'Sorry, Marian, but no, holy shit. That's so weird, and goth. Where did she hide them?'

'Behind radiators, under desks, the stairwells sometimes.'

'Wow. Hardcore. What happened?'

'Someone caught her doing it and told on her.'

'Was she expelled?'

'Just suspended. Then there was a copycat for a while.'

Hannah whoops a little, bounces on her chair. 'No way!' she says.

'Way,' Lily says, beginning to feel something akin to enjoyment.

'A copycat phantom menstruation distributor: that's incredible.'

'The copycat wasn't as good, though.'

'I guess to be the original is to have artistic vision, and integrity, whereas impersonation is a bit hackneyed. But also: how do you be *less* good at hiding sanitary towels?'

'They were always rolled up.'

'That's definitely subpar execution. Like when you go see a

play and you can tell one of the actors is embarrassed. It ruins the whole thing.'

'Exactly.'

'Girls?' Marian says, and Lily wonders if she's different now, in Marian's estimation – if she's more girl, more rascal, more in need of curbing. Less whatever she was before. Hannah says, 'Sorry, you're right, sorry, back to work.' She cracks her knuckles. She rotates back to her computer, then stops herself, turns back, grins at Lily, turns again. Lily pictures the two of them in a beer garden, Hannah saying, 'How has nobody ever told me how great you are?'

SIOBHÁN

She wakes at six thirty to a message: *Shit – I'm sorry. Ellie wiped me out. I love you xxx.* She replies: *Love you*, then puts her phone on mute. Everything in her bathroom seems to be in a non-intuitive position, and she ends up harried, running late. She can't find her toothpaste, so instead she scrubs at her teeth forcibly with the brush, trying to resurrect some froth from the fossilized white, caked to the bristles. She swills twice with mouthwash to compensate. Another day starts.

'I think I'm going to take a holiday somewhere next week,' she tells her mother, when her phone rings at lunchtime.

'What's that?' she says, and Siobhán can hear the clicking of her computer mouse. 'You called *me*,' she wants to say.

'I might go away, for a couple of a days, over half-term,' she says instead.

'Why?'

'I'm kind of wiped out.'

'What's wrong?'

'Nothing, just work's been a bit hectic.'

'Are you all right?'

'I'm fine.'

'I hate that word. Tell me what's wrong.'

'Nothing. I'm fine.'

Her mother sighs. 'By yourself?'

'What?'

'Are you going away by yourself?'

'Yeah.'

'Where?'

'Somewhere I can get cheap last minute. Spain, maybe.'

'Shall I come?'

'I was thinking it might be nice to go by myself. I haven't been anywhere alone since TEFL.'

'I'll come – save you travelling alone.'

'It might be nice to go alone, though.'

'You don't want me there?'

'It's not that.'

'I could use a holiday, to be honest.'

'A holiday from *what*?' Siobhán wants to say. 'Oh,' she says instead.

'Where are you thinking?'

'I'd like to go to Seville.'

'Seville is inland, though. Wouldn't it be nicer to be by the sea? If we go to the coast it'll be warmer.'

'But I—'

'I can look it up tonight, save you the trouble. Four nights?'

Siobhán picks at the top of her desk, which has been sanded down and glossed to a rink, with occasional pointillist ridges of aspiring splinters. She rests her forehead on her palm. 'Fine,' she says.

'If you're worried about the price, I can make up any extra cost,' her mother says.

'Right, fine.'

'Okay, I'd better go reply to this email. Was there something else?'

'You phoned me.'

'No need to get grumpy!'

To get the job, for there to even be a job to get, was miraculous. Northern Ireland was producing more teachers yearly than it knew what to do with, and the majority of those on her course had failed to get permanent teaching positions – they'd decamped to England or Australia or had resigned themselves to substitution work for the foreseeable. She was set on not leaving, because how could she leave him? She didn't speak Irish, so teaching in the Republic wasn't an option. Instead, she directed all her energies to making herself a glittering desideratum, an indispensable, pedagogical marvel. When she was offered the permanent post she texted Andrew first, then Tara, then her mother, who replied with four consecutive messages that evening:

Just back from hospital visiting hours.

Andrea had her gall bladder out.

Not sure how she'll cope now that Jim's gone.

Will you be paying into a pension?

Her mother didn't seem to grasp what an unlikely thing it was, to find a permanent teaching job in Belfast, a year out of training. She has always seemed to hold the opinion that if Siobhán has done it, it can't have been that difficult.

That afternoon she goes to redistribute the exercise books she marked that weekend. Callum's is missing. She scrabbles in the tote bag, as though it might be concealing unseen depths. She runs her hands over her desk, lifting pages. She casts her mind back to marking the books, wonders what aberration in thought led to one going missing. Her mouth makes the shape of a soundless 'Fuck'. She walks to his desk, bows her head in contrition.

'I'm so sorry, Callum,' she says. He gazes at her, blankly. 'I promise I'll get it back to you as soon as possible.'

'It's okay, miss.' He had a speech impediment when he was younger, largely resolved now, but on especially sibilant words a lisp creeps in. He smiles at her, and she feels a swell of affection in her chest. She knows she can be unduly mawkish when it comes to her students, but their guilelessness occasionally overwhelms her in a way that makes her regret ever taking the job for granted. She doesn't deserve their inexhaustible capacity for forgiveness. That afternoon she explains to Callum's mother why he doesn't have his English book, and the woman's face is a mirror of her son's. The three exchange smiles, and the untarnished goodwill of the moment makes Siobhán laugh out loud.

That evening she still can't find it. She messages Andrew: *Shit, I've lost one of my kids' exercise books. Fuck, I'm such a shit teacher.* She stares longingly at the screen, willing him to appear, willing him to dispel what she's thinking. She searches her flat, scouring tote bags she hasn't used in months; checking under the radiator and in her knicker drawer, getting progressively more worked up. She owes a duty to these children, owes them a level of pastoral attentiveness, wants to imbue them with a sense of worth that will withstand the bombardment that's to come. She commences packing for her holiday as a means of tidying up – she throws in sandals and dresses and the weighty truncheon cans of hairspray and dry shampoo she bought on her way home. The small suitcase looks fun-sized and laughable, does nothing noticeable to improve the appearance of the flat. She messages Sophie: *I've lost Callum's English book.* Sophie replies immediately: *Don't panic – it'll show up. I've lost kids' books before – you just rejig the h/w schedule a little till it reappears. Worst comes to the worst, you throw yourself at the mercy of their parent. It'll be grand xx.* Siobhán stares at the message, then flicks back to the conversation with Andrew, which remains one-sided. She finds her toothpaste in the wardrobe.

An hour later she quashes her anxieties about missing a response from him and agrees to a drink with Mark. They met on her PGCE, but now he does freelance transcribing and works on a hypothetical novel. His novel is about the American political landscape, and one day he deigned to let Siobhán read the first page. It opened: 'One day, in a room of the White House.' Siobhán said, 'Do you not think you should set it somewhere you're familiar with?' and Mark replied, 'I think it's going to be stylistically similar to *On the Road* – have you heard of Kerouac?' Siobhán likes flirting with him because he has a girlfriend she's never met, which absolves her of any duty of care. 'I love my fellow creature . . . but he doesn't exist!' she read in a book Andrew gave her last year. The girlfriend is named Marie, which Mark shortens to Mar. He doesn't seem to realize how ridiculous this is – Mar and Mark, like it's the same name spoken by two people, one of whom is severely congested.

She arrives, late and flustered. 'Sorry sorry sorry,' she says. Mark raises an eyebrow, amused. 'You all right?' he says. 'You're a bit red.'

'I'm grand,' she says. 'I just need to go to the toilet and then I'll grab us some drinks, okay?'

'Mine's an IPA.'

On her walk to the toilet she sees the two women from the other evening – the blonde girl is teary-eyed and gripping the hands of the other, who is wearing an 'Eat the rich' T-shirt. 'Where *does* she get those T-shirts?' Siobhán wonders, then nearly slips on a patch of wet floor.

'I think I might be a Carlsberg convert,' she says to Mark, holding their drinks aloft. He says, 'Steady on, Kev.' They perch on high stools at a shallow ledge stuck to a pillar. Siobhán can never coax Andrew in here. She supposes he thinks it's unbecoming for a man in his late thirties, with his income, to drink £3 pints. Or maybe he's more worried about somebody seeing him. The bar he likes them to meet at, when he visits, is on the far edge of the city centre and Escher-like in its arrangement. If she gets him on a good day they'll make out in one of the booths. On a bad day she'll lean in and he'll offer her his cheek and she'll excuse herself to scream in the toilet.

'What do you think of this?' Mark says, and there's a picture of a black shirt with white piebald on his phone screen.

'Cute,' Siobhán says. 'If you want to look like a Friesian cow.'

'You don't think I could pull it off?' He frowns at the screen. He pushes his brown, curly hair off his forehead with a shiny forearm. Siobhán suspects he uses self-tanner, but has never asked.

'Oh, you could absolutely pull it off,' she says. 'It's the putting it on that's the problem.'

'Fuck you.'

'You won't get a chance if you're wearing that shirt,' Siobhán says, which she knows doesn't really bear scrutiny, but she also knows he'll let it slide because she's steered the conversation into the encrypted waters of their hypothetical fucking. He laughs, and lets his hand rest on her knee for a couple of seconds.

'Salty bitch,' he says.

'What do you need a new shirt for anyway? You work from home.'

'I go out sometimes, you know.'

'So you're going to get all dressed up like Garry Essendine for the big shop?'

'Who?'

'Doesn't matter.'

'If I buy it, can I get it delivered to yours?'

'Why?'

'Mar says we're saving to buy a house.'

'Ew.'

'Right?'

'Why the fuck would you want to buy a house?'

Andrew spends most nights on property websites, then tells Siobhán about the houses he's looking at, as though it's not upsetting for her to think about him buying a forever home for his wife and daughter. When they're messaging in the evening and he disappears for prolonged stretches she knows what he's doing – hunting for an affordable two-bedroom in Ballyfermot. It's made her preternaturally opposed to home ownership, and she'll now occasionally refer to property as a 'fundamentally unethical commodity', or say that landlords are the scourge of the earth. She suspects these opinions could be argued convincingly, if she were to explore them with a shred of critical reasoning, beyond their immediate pertinence to her, but who has the time? Sometimes when she's drunk she spits on the estate agents' up the road.

'Property is a fundamentally unethical commodity,' she says.

'Mar thinks it's important to get on the ladder.' Mark shrugs.

'Mar must be a riot at dinner parties,' Siobhán says, and then knows she's gone too far by mentioning her name.

Mark backpedals, sheepish.

'No, no,' he says. 'I mean, it makes sense. Stability and all that – better use of your money. Plus, she works bloody hard, so she deserves a house more than most people.'

'Okay, Ayn Rand.'

'Who?'

'Doesn't matter.'

They drink deeply. Siobhán leans forward to scratch at her ankle. Mark looks down the gaping neck of her top.

Siobhán notices the man approaching too late to suggest any evasive manoeuvres. Next thing his hand is landing on the table like a gavel. The crevices of his knuckles are grey.

'Sorry to disturb you both,' he says, in an accent it takes her several sentences to acclimatize to, 'but do you mind if I ask you a question?'

'Yes, I mind,' Siobhán thinks at him. She says nothing.

Mark is three quarters of his pint deep. 'Go on, mate,' he says. He has never said 'mate' in Siobhán's company before.

The man peers at Siobhán. 'Have you ever been to the National Gallery in London?'

On the screen behind his head, Graham Norton is rubbing his plaid thighs assiduously in delight. She keeps her eyes on his big, white teeth. 'Yes,' she responds, sullen. Mark is leaning forward on his stool, hungrily, and Siobhán can almost see the inner workings of his mind, wondering if the exchange that's about to take place could be borrowed and then transposed into a bar 'next to the White House'.

The man thrusts an arm behind him and seizes a stool from another table. He whirls it like a matador's cape and lets it land next to Siobhán. He's balding, with wire-rimmed glasses and a navy sweatshirt. He clambers on to the stool and lets the phlegm cook in his throat for a moment.

'There's a painting, right?'

'No shit,' Siobhán thinks. 'Okay,' she says instead.

He peers closely at her. 'There's a woman in it,' he says. 'Looks like you.'

'Oh!' Siobhán allows herself to be cautiously flattered.

'Yeah!' he says, enthusiastic. 'Same sad expression. Same big nose.'

There's a brief silence before Mark starts laughing in a slap-stick way, like a cartoon weasel. He nudges her and says, 'There you go, Shiv. You're a classic Pre-Raphaelite sad woman.'

'Yeah,' Siobhán says. 'Thanks a lot,' she says to the man, flatly. She wishes she had the confidence to tell a stranger to fuck off.

'So, what are your names?' the man says, and at this she permits herself a small, audible groan. Mark nudges her with his foot. He asks them what they do and Mark describes himself as a writer. Siobhán thinks, 'I hate you,' at him.

'A writer?' the man says, and he cracks his hatched knuckles. Siobhán knows what he's going to say before he says it. 'I could be a writer,' he says, and Siobhán wishes that there were someone else in her head to bear witness to her insightfulness.

'It's pretty hard going, mate,' Mark says with an indulgent smile.

'You sent me six videos of children on anaesthesia yesterday,' Siobhán wants to say. She says nothing.

'I bet you wouldn't find anyone in this room with a bigger vocabulary than me,' the man says. He looks around with a sneer. 'Yeah,' he says. 'Bet there's not a soul in this place as well-read or loquacious as I am. See?' He gives Siobhán a nod. '*Loquacious*,' he masticates.

'That right?' Siobhán says, and now that she knows her disdain for proceedings is going either unnoticed or ignored, the meagre fun of it fades.

'Caliban,' he says abruptly. 'Bet there's not a fucker in here knows who Caliban is.'

'Maybe go find out,' she says, meek.

'I've had a hell of a life, you know,' he says. 'If I wrote the book of my life it would need to be in three volumes.'

'Go on then, mate,' Mark says. 'Give us the main plot points.'

Forty-five minutes later they're still there – newly intimate with Dai's childhood landscapes of Port Talbot and Carrickmore. Dai pauses for a moment to burp. Mark says, 'Don't stop now, mate – I want to know about the girl from Woolworths with the gammy leg.'

'Ahhh, Mary,' Dai replies, rapturous. Siobhán divides her attention between watching her phone vibrate occasionally and watching Michael Sheen on Graham's sofa.

Dai wedges his fist behind his glasses and rubs his eye. 'Before I continue, few more drinks, maybe?' He prods Siobhán's upper arm. 'What are you having, love?'

Siobhán looks at Mark. He doesn't look at her.

'Actually,' she says, 'we need to be heading on.'

'No we don't,' Mark says.

'Well, I do,' she says.

'No you don't,' he says.

'One more won't kill you, love,' Dai says. 'Give me a hand, will you, mate?' he says to Mark.

'No bother, mate,' Mark says, and as he gets up he lifts Siobhán's phone from the table. 'So you can't leave,' he says, then winks. Siobhán glares after him. 'I'm a doormat flimsy shitbag,' she mouths at her thighs. Spittle lands on her tights. The men return.

'Here you go, love.' The man sets a pint in front of her. She drinks half of it in seconds.

'Thirsty girl,' he says, and Siobhán pictures dropping a plugged-in toaster on top of him in the bath. 'Well,' he says, 'let me tell you about my guinea pig.'

'Christ,' Siobhán says under her breath. Mark nudges her again.

'She killed herself,' Dai says.

'What?' Mark says.

'Yeah,' Dai says. 'Threw herself into a fire. She lived in a little cage in my room, and one day I let her out to roam about the place, and she ran straight into the fireplace. Little body looked like a croquette by the time I got it out.' He sniffs. 'Guess she'd rather die than be with me.' There's a crack in his voice, and Siobhán realizes he's going to cry. 'Just like everyone,' he says. 'Just like my ex—' He breaks off, and the tears come, loud and wet. Now, Mark looks at Siobhán with an appalled expression. Dai smears his face with his hand, then places it on top of Siobhán's. Siobhán stares at the clammy mitten.

'Sorry,' the man says, thickly. 'It's just, my wife. Or my ex-wife, she just—' He loses his words again with another bout of crying. Mark is looking at him like a pathologist. He drains his pint. 'Mind if I go grab another?' he says.

''Course, mate,' Mark says.

'Back in a tick,' Dai sniffs, then leaves. Mark leans forward, squeezes Siobhán's knee, hisses, 'Want to go?'

'Fuck, yes,' Siobhán says, and she grabs her bag from the floor. On their way out she sees the girl in the communist T-shirt and the blonde woman, now joined by the shorn-headed man. All three grin at one another in silence, the awkwardness palpable.

'Well, that was something,' Mark says as they walk home.

'Yeah.' Siobhán pauses. '*Mate.*'

'Don't be a dick.'

'Fine.' They say nothing for a moment.

'Still,' Mark says, 'he had some vocabulary.'

'Most loquacious man in the room.'

'Could be a writer if he wanted to,' Mark says.

'Bestselling author of *The Guinea Pig Suicides*,' Siobhán says.

'Doesn't think anyone has heard of the Taliban,' Mark says.

Siobhán stops. 'What?' she says.

'Remember? He said nobody in the pub would know who the Taliban is.'

'Caliban, Mark. He said Caliban.'

'Who?'

When she gets in she boils the kettle, then fills a pan, adds pasta. She has another cursory, defeated look for the exercise book, then sits on the floor and pulls her shoes off. Her phone vibrates.

Hi sweetheart. Did you find the book?

No, I feel like such a dirtbag. I don't know how the fuck I could have lost it.

It'll show up.

I hope so.

Did you have a good night?

No.

Oh sweetheart.

Met an absolute lunatic in the pub and Mark encouraged him to annoy us for an hour.

Oh God.

His pet guinea pig killed itself.

Whaaat?

Threw itself into a fire apparently.

Wow. Just like Jerome Morrow.

Siobhán is too tired to google this. *Hahahaha!* she says. Sometimes when she makes a joke he'll respond with laughter so quickly that it almost coincides with the joke. She wonders if this is the logical conclusion of human communication – a reiterative format of reactions corresponsive to prescribed stimuli.

'Babe: *Self-immolating Pig in the City*', she says.

Hahahahaha! he says punctually. *Are you home now?*

Yeah.

I think you should touch yourself.

Okay.

She remembers the pasta after he has sent her a video of him ejaculating. She runs into the kitchen. The water is gone and the pasta is blackened and bulbous and stuck to the sides of the pan like pebbledash. She runs some cold water into it, throws in some Fairy Liquid, goes to bed.

In the playground her hangover revs gently at each temple. Audrey, who teaches P7, is looking at her, and Siobhán wonders if she can smell the beer squeezing its way out of her pores and oxidizing.

'All right, Siobhán?'

'Hi, Audrey.'

'Ready for half-term?'

'Like you would not believe.'

'Not like you not to look bright-eyed and bushy-tailed, Siobhán – normally you put the rest of us to shame. You're not coming down with something, are you?'

'My bright eyes have conjunctivitis and my bushy tail's got stuck in some farm machinery.'

Audrey takes a step back. 'Do you actually have conjunctivitis? Did one of the kids give you that?'

'No, just a joke. But seriously: I *do* have myxomatosis.'

Audrey frowns. 'Another joke?'

'Yes, Audrey.'

Audrey laughs like she's taking it for a test drive. 'Sorry,' she says. 'I'm off to Edinburgh with the husband. Don't want to risk catching anything.'

'No worries,' Siobhán says. She stares resolutely at three kids running in and out of the path of a skipping rope.

'Are you going anywhere nice?'

'Spain. Few days.'

'Lovely! With a boyfriend?'

'No. Mum.'

'Well, that'll be great. Nice to get away, isn't it?'

'Yeah,' Siobhán says flatly. One child misjudges his departure time from the centrifuge. He falls on his face, commences wailing. ''Scuse me,' Siobhán says. She crosses the playground and peels him off the ground. She takes him by the hand and leads him inside. He bleeds on her skirt – she doesn't begrudge it. She lifts him on to a table. He sneezes on her head while she bends over his legs. 'Bless you,' she says. She dabs at the various grazes with an antiseptic wipe and applies plasters to both his knees. She lets him hug her afterwards, and he smells like laundry and bananas. After he's scampered back outside she gingerly wipes the dew from the top of her head.

One thing they don't prepare trainee teachers for is the impending ill health. Children are virus incubators. Siobhán suspects that, in lieu of largely useless things, like how to write in cursive, or how to identify an oak leaf, they should be teaching them to apply hand sanitizer after sneezing and not to lick each other like rampant cats.

She has a track record of letting men infect her. Before Andrew she dated a cowboy, in aesthetic terms only, named Frank. They dated for five months, and three months in she overheard him referring to himself as single. This struck her as especially galling, considering that after a fortnight together he'd given her ringworm. He was an avid hiker, and prior to their coupling he'd gone schlepping around the wet Hebrides. He had a low sex drive, and their dates would usually culminate with them sitting in her bed – her palpitating with unsatiated lust, him yawning demonstrably and delicately removing her hand from his thigh. When he told her he had ringworm and showed her the taupe blobs around his crotch, she said, 'I don't care,' and straddled him. He preferred it with her on top, which she now thinks was less an enjoying-the-view thing and more a path-of-least-resistance thing. For the next six weeks they passed their ringworm back and forth like a logbook. At the beginning of their fourth month together he told her that, while he was attracted to her, he wasn't *that* attracted to her, that he didn't want a relationship with her, and that he didn't love her. Somehow, they continued to date for another three weeks. A week after that, he moved to Cork.

When she was twenty she let a physicist called David take the condom off, mid-sex. A month later she had six weeks' worth of antibiotics on the shelf by her bed.

Nine months into knowing Andrew, he took her to Paris. They stayed in a flat that had an anachronistic, alpine feel – when she looked out of the window she expected to see snow bunnies, not Notre-Dame. She said to Andrew, 'Do you think literal snow bunnies know that the sexy women in salopettes are also called snow bunnies?' And he said, 'They probably think it in French.' She said, 'So they're *neige lapins*.' She pronounced it 'nedge lap-pins', and he laughed.

On their first evening they walked for an hour and a half in torrential rain, trying to find the Eiffel Tower.

'This is the second time I've lost the Eiffel Tower,' she said, and he gave her waist a squeeze. 'You know I plan to die by throwing myself off a tower.'

'Oh yeah?'

'Yeah, so everyone will think that *I fell*.'

He laughed. He bought some cigarettes from a supermarket, and they huddled under her ineffectual umbrella and smoked. This was when the EU was introducing deterrent cigarette packaging, and they laughed at the smouldering bazooka wound where the man's genitals had once been. They had dinner in a restaurant darker than a planetarium. He had mussels and she had chicken, and three hours later his vomiting started. The next day they lolloped biliously around – they saw the Twomblys in the Pompidou Centre and the Picassos in the Picasso museum. They sat for a long time in front of *Deux femmes courant sur la plage*. For him the blue sky was an antiemetic, while she felt something bordering on obsession, looking at the women's hammy feet. He puked in a bin off the Champs-Élysées.

The second day he stayed in bed and she went to Shakespeare & Co. and bought a copy of Chekhov's *Three Sisters*. She went to a cosmetics behemoth and bought a lipstick in a shade that didn't suit her pallid complexion. She sat on a bench and watched a bulbous male pigeon try to rape some female pigeons. She ate a slice of pizza the size of a traffic cone, drank a pint of Stella at a wind-blown table in Place Edmond Michelet, then gave a homeless man five euro as recompense for her speaking bad French at him. When she returned to the flat Andrew was asleep, so she wrote *l'amour* on her wrist in new eyeliner and sent a photo to her mother – *Got a tattoo!* Her mother tried to call her immediately. She switched her phone off.

The next morning they woke early and had perfunctory sex. She was slightly worried he would puke on her face, but he didn't. They arrived at the airport late and she had to bargain with the beautiful woman at Security to let them skip the queue. '*Excusez moi*,' she said, '*notre departure est en une heure*.' She thought of Hugo Diamond, how much more proficiently he would have handled the situation.

They slept on the flight home, her head on his shoulder. On landing he had a text from his wife saying she'd decided to pick him up from the airport, so they walked into Arrivals separately. She'd elected to fly from Dublin, so they could travel together, so while he followed his wife to the multi-storey she trudged to the bus stop. She got home, ordered two portions of cheesy chips, ate them in bed. An hour later she was throwing up beige into the sink in her bedroom, and when she told him he realized that what he'd had wasn't food poisoning at all; it was the norovirus Ellie had had the week before. The next day she lurched, sallow and shaking, to her 11 a.m. lecture. At eleven thirty, she shat herself.

The inverse of this is she once had a man cease all contact because she gave him a cold sore. She hadn't realized, initially, that it was a cold sore – she thought it was a combination of premenstrual acne and dry skin. She'd been liberally applying Sudocrem and moisturizer, feeling attentive and virtuous. The day after their date, she realized her error, when the lump had grown flaky and threatening. She texted him, saying, *Oh my god I'm so sorry I've had this thing on my lip I thought it was a spot but I think it's actually a cold sore I'm so sorry I really hope you don't get one.* Two days later he replied with, *I've got a cold sore.* It was the last time she heard from him.

She wonders, sometimes, if her willingness to accept men's diseases is a marker of her desperation: if she will endure any indignity to feel wanted. She wonders if this willingness contributes to the ultimate inevitability of them not wanting her, whether, if she prioritized her health over pleasing them, maybe they'd stick around. She also wonders what it says that a man will not even suffer a cold sore for her.

She told Andrew about the cold sore, one evening when they were divulging the most ridiculous moments of their romantic histories. He said, 'I'd take a cold sore for you,' which was exactly what she wanted him to say, although, given his perpetual unwellness, a cold sore was probably a drop in the ocean. Sticking a pebble to the side of Sisyphus' boulder with Blu-tack.

On Friday evening, she and Sophie stay late again. The caretaker is disappointed to see them huddled in a corner of the classroom with steaming mugs. 'I implore you not to stay late tonight, girls,' he says. 'I've got a life, you know.' They promise not to, and he shuffles past the open door.

'Poor Colin,' Sophie says, arranging printouts into different piles. 'Reckon we're the bane of his existence?'

'I reckon he has much bigger, badder banes beyond the walls of this school,' Siobhán says, methodically working her way through a packet of colouring pencils, sharpening the blunt ones.

'Seeing your mystery man over half-term?' Sophie asks, cautious.

'Less said about that the better,' Siobhán says, inspecting the dull edge of a white pencil. 'Who on earth was using this?' she mutters. 'The white should always be left alone.'

'They should put that on your grave,' Sophie says.

'"The white should always be left alone"?' Siobhán says. 'Bit Enoch Powell, is it not?'

'No. "Less said about that the better." That's your credo.'

'Let no man write my epitaph, because they should be minding their own damn business,' Siobhán says.

'Okay, prickly,' Sophie says.

'Sorry,' Siobhán says. 'What are you doing next week?'

'Oh, not much,' Sophie says. 'Probably marking, crying, wanking.'

'Why crying?'

'I'm getting ghosted by Alex.'

'Fuck sake.'

'I know.'

'Wanker.'

'Yeah.'

'What happened? I thought things were going well?'

'We killed a dog.'

A mouthful of coffee capsizes in Siobhán's throat. She coughs. 'Jesus,' she wheezes. 'You what?'

'On Saturday.'

'Whose dog?'

'His mate's.'

'How'd you kill it?'

'Lex wanted to take the dog up Cave Hill – he was dog-sitting, and apparently the dog's owner was all for it. Lex said we could let her off the lead, so we did, and she was sniffing about the place, and then she sat down, and then she just, sort of' – Sophie grimaces – 'rolled off.'

'Rolled off.'

'Right over the fucking edge.'

'The dog rolled over the edge of Cave Hill?'

'Yep.'

'Christ.'

'I know.'

'So, then what?'

'So then we had to spend about three fucking hours looking for the body. Lex called the owner, so he showed up, and eventually we found her.'

'And she was—'

'Stiff as an ironing board.'

'Fuck.'

'The owner was fucking inconsolable. He started weeping, and that set Lex off, and then I was just, sort of, there.'

'Oh my God.'

'Like, I don't know the guy. I was just the bitch complicit in his dog's manslaughter, and I—' She breaks off, looks at Siobhán's face. 'Don't you fucking dare,' she says.

Siobhán tries to stop, but the smile comes. 'No, no,' she says, 'no – I'm sorry, no.'

'Don't you fucking dare laugh.'

'I'm sorry, it's just—' And then she starts laughing.

'It's not fucking funny!' Sophie says.

'Is a bit.'

'It's *not*!' she says.

'Life's a bitch,' Siobhán says, and then Sophie submits, letting out a yelp of a laugh. They each cross their arms over their chests, shoulders galumphing.

'Then it—' Sophie can't speak. 'And then you—' she tries again.

'Then it what, Soph?'

'Then it—' Her face is purple and the skin below her closed eyes is shiny with wet.

'Dies?' Siobhán ventures.

'*Dies*.' Their laughter reverberates off the walls of the cold classroom, seems to shake the single-glazed windows in their frames. The Iron Man, glistening with his second coat of paint, remains impassive.

Sophie gives her a quick and cursory hug at their parting spot. 'Thanks, mate,' she says, gruffly. She wraps her trench coat around herself tightly. Siobhán is envious of how French she looks in the greying light.

'If he ghosts you over a dead dog then he's an arsehole,' she says.

'Aye,' Sophie says, her jaw clenched. 'But hard not to feel like *you're* the problem, you know?'

'Christ, do I know.'

'Have a good half-term.'

'Bye, mate.'

The rain is gentle, almost therapeutic. The failing sun turns the puddles into strobes, bursting from the world's centre. It's the early-evening period when the Belfast dress code is inconsistent – there are girls migrating to the bars on Malone in heels, with legs that have been watercoloured with fake tan; others emerging from the library with bulging tote bags and empty water bottles. Siobhán contemplates sitting on the wall outside the Lanyon Building for a while to watch them, to let the damp atmosphere refresh her skin, but she doesn't want to look like someone who thinks they're enjoying a moment of epiphany, so she walks on, permitting herself the occasional glance at the Neapolitan sky. She buys a net sack full of oranges in the supermarket and swings it gaily, like a cudgel.

★

It's become increasingly hard for her to frame someone else's pain as anything other than trivial or, at best, manageable, in comparison to her own. Sophie having been held as an infant by a convicted murderer; her being made to feel inadequate by a man – Siobhán can see, in an abstract way, how these things might be upsetting, but ultimately they feel like superficial, glancing blows. They seem incomparable to her pain, which is malignant, chronic. That she knows this inability to legitimize others' experience is a failing on her part does nothing to alter the state of things. It's just one more niggling concern that she tries to ignore.

LILY

She loses the next two nights to the morose, sealed-off oubliette of her bedroom. Then comes the weekend, undeserving of its title. She drifts in and out of a dream with no visuals, just the pitch-black sensation of some new cognitive void having asserted itself within the parameters of her skull, inaccessible to her but sequestering her consciousness to one corner of her mind. She wakes up, disorientated and anxious, then succumbs to it again. Siobhán gets a food delivery, and Lily hears her thanking the delivery man at the door. She pours beans and Tabasco on top of bread and wodges the whole messy chimera into the old toastie maker she liberates from its box for the first time. She eats the seeping parcel by the sink and looks at the blank tiling of the calendar.

On Friday evenings they'd have people for dinner. Often Yvette and her husband, Peter, before they separated, and Ellen. Lily's mother would make Bolognese or carbonara or roast chicken with rosemary potatoes. She and Yvette would drink Sauvignon and lapse into their childhoods.

'I'm so *happy* your generation will never have to know how it *was*,' Yvette would say repeatedly. Ellen and Lily would roll their eyes at each other, conspiratorial, and Lily's mother would purse her lips at them in false reproof. Often, Lily and Ellen would occupy themselves with Ellen's phone while the older women talked, listening in spurts.

'I was eleven when the Abercorn bombing happened,' her mother said once, 'and it was my first proper understanding of the ramifications of a tragic event. I remember it so vividly – Mum and I were sat at the table, listening to the coverage on the wireless. Her face was just grey.'

'Your generation will, I *pray*, never have to experience something like that,' Yvette said, leaning over the table. 'I hope you never have to know how *strange* it was to live through it,' she said. 'How *frightening*.'

Several months before this particular dinner party Lily and her mother had called in at Yvette's on their way home from the supermarket to return a casserole dish. From a distance they could see a solitary figure, sitting cross-legged on the roof of the portico. It was Peter, who had attempted to get in through an upstairs window, only to find it locked; unable to climb back down, he had been sitting there for two hours. When they got out of the car he shrugged at them, bashfully. Yvette's sobs could be heard from inside, and Lily's mother informed her later that Peter, who was the deputy head of another school, had been sleeping with a sixth-form student.

Yvette poured more wine into her stubbily stemmed wine glass. 'It was all just so *terrible*,' she said. Ellen suppressed a snicker, and Lily saw the smallest itch of a smile on her mother's face, followed by a compensatory guilty frown.

'I remember my friend Lindsay and I took the train to Belfast so we could see *Grease* at the cinema,' her mother said. 'The Curzon on the Ormeau. I would probably be a bit wary of you doing that, Lil, by yourself, but there we were, doing it in the eighties, younger than you are now, because you learn to assess risk on a curve, I suppose. You learned to live around what was happening. It's strange, how partially inured to it we were, because neither of us had lost anyone to it, and because it was just the backdrop of our normal. It was how our whole lives had been, but we were also so jumpy, about being in the city, seeing the soldiers – we were kind of giddy. You lived on a knife-edge, you know? Things had the potential to change, like that, not just in terms of big events, but in the way a conversation could turn, if the wrong subject came up, if you had the wrong answer to certain questions.'

'I hope you'll *never* know how that was,' Yvette said, again, and the progressive mawkishness of her tone, the growing wildness of her eyes, finally made Lily's mother laugh, which made it okay for Lily, and Ellen, to laugh too. The mood abated in intensity; Lily's mother placed an arm around Yvette's shoulders and gave her a squeeze, then went to fetch dessert.

At the end of these evenings Yvette would administer great, gubernatorial hugs to everyone. She'd call a taxi and Ellen's father would pick her up. Lily and her mother would return to the table to scrape the last of the pavlova shrapnel or errant profiteroles from the oval, cream dish, the dredged-up histories once more relegated.

She rarely engaged in self-examination, though she was accustomed to her mother's regular musing upon her nature. Sometimes Lily would catch her eyeing her from across the living room, a sort of post-prandial half-smile on her face.

'Please stop scrutinizing me,' she said once.

'I'm just enjoying the fruits of my labour,' her mother said. 'As well as pursuing that quest of all mothers to understand their children as something partially distinct from themselves, and partially the same.'

'Okay, but do you have to do it so loudly?'

Her mother laughed.

'With a view to what?' Lily said.

'Absolution, I suppose. I want to perceive you as distinct enough that my mistakes could conceivably leave you unscathed, that you aren't doomed to some tragic, palimpsestic repetition, but also enough the same that your happiness is partially mine to take credit for. If you're part me, then it makes sense that I will tirelessly strive for your happiness, but if you're *also* distinct from me, then I can convince myself that I didn't live a selfish life, that I wasn't prioritizing my own needs because they coalesced with yours.'

Lily looked at her for a while. 'There's bound to have been a simpler way of saying that,' she said.

Her mother laughed again. 'I don't know,' she said. 'I'm just thinking my way through the thought. Did it make sense?'

Lily shrugged. 'Sure,' she said. 'I don't object to the practice, in theory. But maybe do it where I can't see you.'

She wonders now if it's the nature of human desire to seek from other people what was deficient in your parents' perception of you, if aspiration or lust is fuelled by that first fundamental misunderstanding. At school, Lily would listen to people complaining about their parents; on Friday evenings she would hear Ellen's father leaning on the horn of his Vauxhall, too important to fetch Ellen at the door. Ellen would scramble for her possessions, then scurry to the car with her apologies pre-prepared, as though he were some deity requiring tribute. Lily's mother didn't need anything from her, didn't need her to be anything. Lily didn't need to build a life beyond the shadows of her mother's expectations, and so was happy to reside in them. Now that she's gone, Lily has no ballast for her own sense of self, and her recourse is to an anger that she doesn't fully understand.

Lily thought they should take a taxi to the hospital, the day they went to speak to the consultant.

'Get you, Little Lord Fauntleroy,' her mother said. She was on the sofa, lacing her boots. Lily was pacing in her coat.

'I just don't think you should have to drive,' Lily said. 'And *I* don't want to drive us there.'

'Bit like Odysseus steering the boat straight into Scylla, right?'

'What?' Lily said, accelerating her pace. 'What are you talking about?'

'Did you know,' her mother said, scratching her head, 'that apparently you can say "stuck between Scylla and Charybdis" instead of saying "between a rock and a hard place"?'

'Why would anyone say that?' Lily said, taking her hands in and out of her pockets. 'How is that a better expression? Expressions are supposed to be succinct.'

'I know, right? Although,' her mother said, 'presumably you were educated at Eton, Fauntleroy, so perhaps you're willing to forgo brevity in favour of an appellation to your classically educated sensibilities. After all—'

'Oh my God, can you shut up?' Lily said. 'Can you please just shut up? Stop talking, please.'

'Hey.' Her mother stood up, went to where Lily was wringing her hands by the sink. 'It's okay,' she said.

'It's not,' Lily said.

'No,' her mother said. 'But it'll be okay that it's not.' She put her arms around Lily.

'It'll be okay that it's not okay?'

'Yes.'

'You're so stupid,' Lily mumbled into her shoulder.

Her mother laughed.

SIOBHÁN

She wakes with a streaming nose and a sore throat. She texts Mark – they had tentative plans to go to the gym. He texts back, *Lazy bitch*, and she lets that sit. She checks when Andrew was last online – twelve minutes prior. 'Twat,' she thinks, then feels bad for thinking it. She unpacks the suitcase, looking for Callum's book, then repacks it. She goes online and orders a fry from the café around the corner. While she watches the horizontal bar on the screen pulse with the progress of her order she masturbates half-heartedly. She takes two decongestants and a multivitamin, then puts on the 2006 version of *The Omen*. The delivery man comes upstairs and delivers it to her door, and she puts a hash brown in her mouth as Julia Stiles dies of an air embolism.

She spends Sunday checking her phone and leafing through yesterday's mental-arithmetic tests. She texts Mark, *Weird that 9 squared is 81, when 8 plus 1 equals 9. I can't explain this, but 81 is the Irn-Bru of numbers.* He texts back, *You drunk?* And she lets that sit. When she finishes marking she opens the net bag of oranges and arranges them delicately in a bowl, next to another bowl with a solitary green banana inside. She stares at the still life for a while. The colours are disconcerting in their vibrancy, dichotomous with everything else around them. She messages Tara: *Is an orange called an orange cause it's orange or is orange called orange because of an orange?*

Tara replies: *Bit early to start getting worked up about the 12th. Lol.*

Tara messages again: *You all right? Want to catch up soon?* She doesn't reply. She goes to the shelf and retrieves the copy of *Three Sisters*, still with the complimentary bookmark from Shakespeare & Co. inside the front cover. She pours herself a glass of wine and takes two more decongestants, then stops herself, with much cajoling, from sending pictures to Andrew of Vershinin and Masha's conversation about Vershinin's unhappiness: 'when my daughters become ill a great anxiety takes hold of me, and my conscience tortures me that their mother is like the person she is. If only you had seen her today. It was so shameful.' She reads and rereads the line, 'I adore, I adore, I adore ... I adore your eyes, your movements, which I dream of ... You're a wonderful, a marvellous woman!' She wonders if it renders her suffering, her desires, unremarkable, to see them depicted so accurately, or if it substantiates them. She wants Andrew to be here, to be sharing this moment of connectivity with a great piece of literature – she wants him to be witness to the injustice of their situation. She wants him to understand that the characters have forgone their happiness so that he and Siobhán don't have to. At nine thirty he messages: *Hi sweetheart, how are you?* and, now too drunk and maudlin to stop herself, she replies, *Reading Chekhov*, and sends him a picture of Masha's Act 3 confession to Olga.

Oh sweetheart, he replies.

I love you, she says.

I love you.

I wish it were you, coming to Spain with me.

Me too, sweetheart.

It's my birthday soon. Can we see each other?

I hope so.

LILY

On Monday morning she half enters the foyer, spots her, then retreats, unseen. Siobhán has the suitcase – small, grey, with four wheels – and a large, squashy holdall. Lily stands in the stairwell, peeking around the doorframe. Siobhán checks her phone, taps her foot. A taxi pulls up and she struggles to open the door, drops her bag. Lily watches her disappear, go somewhere beyond Lily's sphere of influence. A few minutes after her departure, Lily exits, her mood plummeting with each step.

It began with her turning yellow, like someone had adjusted the exposure on her skin, like she'd been plucked from an ageing photograph. With the jaundice came itching, then nausea. 'Bile salts, which help with the emulsification of fat, accumulate under skin and cause itching,' Lily read online. There was no pain, though. In the beginning there was no pain, which was worse than if there'd been pain. Jaundice with no pain was a bad sign.

An MRI scan proved the pancreatic mass, then an ERCP provided a tissue sample and a stent, put in to fix the jaundice. The diagnosis came, then the prognosis, swift and exacting: maybe six months, they were told, with the caveat that there was no way of knowing for sure. The treatment would be palliative, they were told, rather than curative. There would be chemotherapy, but no surgery, no radiotherapy. There was no point, they were told. It had spread to the blood vessels. Lily felt the floor disappear, then the walls, then the ceiling. Her mother's hand manifested in hers – the only thing that survived the dissolution of the room.

That afternoon Hannah is wearing a T-shirt that says 'Believe Women'. She says, 'Hey, ladies, want to hear a joke?'

Marian says, 'Hannah?' softly, then glances at Lily, who is staring fixedly at the filing cabinet, earphones in but disconnected.

'Oh, not in the mood, is she?' Hannah asks. 'Last week's good humours were a blip, were they?' Marian makes a short hiss of a shushing noise, the screw cap on a fizzy drink turned for the briefest instant. Hannah shrugs. 'Fine,' she says. Lily slams the drawer too hard and Hannah jumps in her seat. 'Lenny strikes again,' she mutters. Lily scowls at the back of her head. When she gets up to leave, later, she says, 'I'm sorry, I can't come in Wednesday, Marian,' and Marian says, 'That's fine, love? We're grateful for all the help you give us?' On the walk home she clenches and unclenches her fist.

Her mother wanted her to go to a support group. Following the diagnosis, her mother occasionally went, would come home with an artificial smile and pink eyes.

'Can't I just come to yours?' Lily said.

'We need different kinds of support,' her mother said.

'It seems counterintuitive for us not to get our support together.'

'You need long-term support, though. UHT-milk support. What I need is more short term; yellow-sticker support.'

'Don't say things like that.'

'I'm sorry.'

She made Lily promise to give the support group a go, after she'd died, and Lily did, once. She sat in a room full of people who looked like the stock images that come inside new photo frames. She felt aggressively a-empathetic, as though survival and generosity had to compete for space in the same vessel. A woman with a too-nice face asked if anyone wanted to share, and several people did, and by the end of it Lily had other people's names and experiences threatening to dislodge her own, as well as a new, vitriolic derision for a group of strangers. She didn't go back.

SIOBHÁN

The Mediterranean morning heat lands like mascarpone as they exit the plane. A quarter of the way down the staircase, her mother realizes she left her jacket in the overhead locker.

'Nip back up and get it, would you?' she calls over her shoulder, flustered.

Siobhán is trying to thumb her book into her overstuffed holdall. 'What?' she says. 'No – let's wait till everyone's off and then I'll go back.' The throng carries them gently downwards.

'No,' her mother says. 'Go now – go back and get it for me now. Please. Go on. Go on, now. It's not too busy. Go, Siobhán, go.'

'Jesus.' She fights her way back up the incline like a salmon, muttering apologies to scornful expressions. She gets the jacket.

In the hotel room her mother decides there aren't enough hangers, that the view doesn't have enough sea in it. Siobhán is in the bathroom, flipping her parting to one side so she can spray powder on the roots, which are already greasy from the heat. She presses on the nozzle – it makes a thin exhalation.

'Did you bring dry shampoo?' she calls.

'No, of course not. I don't use that stuff. Did you request a sea view? I told you to.'

'I said if possible.' She tries another can. 'What the fuck?' she mutters to herself. 'Did you bring hairspray?' she calls.

'What?' Her mother is experimenting with the air-conditioning.

'Hairspray, did you bring any?'

'No, I don't use that either. If you need these things, why didn't you bring them?' She disciplines the fan – it commences a gentle hum. 'Did you pay the extra for the sea view?' she says.

'I *did* bring them, but the cans are empty. I bought new cans the other day. I don't understand what's happening. And no, I didn't pay the extra.' Siobhán applies pressure to the protruding nose of the mousse canister. It gurgles, and half an inch of white seeps out, then nothing. '*What* is going on?' She hums pitifully to the mirror, her fingers embedded in her hair.

'Why didn't you pay the extra?'

'Because the hotel is literally *on* the sea. Why would we pay extra to see *in*side what we can see *out*side?'

Her mother emerges in the mirror behind her, her hands laden with too many meticulously folded knickers. 'Don't get snippy with me just because *you* didn't bring the products you need. That's not my fault.'

'I *did* bring them, but they're empty!'

'Well, that's just incredibly silly.' Her mother shakes her head, disappears beyond the doorframe. 'I *asked* you to get us a room with a sea view,' she calls. Siobhán stares at herself in the mirror, puts her fingers into her mouth and bites them.

They leave the first restaurant they choose for lunch because the waiter takes too long to offer them drinks. 'You know I can't abide poor service,' her mother says, as they meander impotently down a side street.

'Okay,' Siobhán says.

'Where shall we go instead?'

'I don't care – you choose.'

'Is there anywhere you like the look of?'

'Wherever.'

'You know, Siobhán, *you* could make a decision for once.'

The tops of Siobhán's feet get sunburned around the straps of her sandals, leaving red stripes on her puffy, exposed skin. Her half-term has coincided with his university's reading week, so Andrew has taken his family to Shropshire, where his in-laws live. He warned her in advance that the signal would be bad, and she doesn't hear from him all day. At 11.50 p.m. her phone vibrates. *I love you*, he says. She replies immediately: *I love you. How's Shropshire?* He doesn't reply. Her foam earplugs are ineffectual. She lies awake to the sound of her mother's snoring and the glottal grunt of the moribund air-conditioner.

LILY

Kate Middleton is wearing a dress that matches William's shirt. Her sunglasses look like they were photoshopped in subsequently. They applaud differently – his hands curve like baseball mitts; hers remain flat and severe, like cymbals. Djokovic and Federer jog on the spot, kicking their heels out of time with one another.

Lily has always had an innate suspicion of Federer. She suspects his gregariousness is overset with smugness – that he's the kind of person who would offer to lend you money while telling you how much money he makes. Her mother didn't share this aversion.

'Everyone loves him!' she said.

'Because he has everyone fooled.'

'He's gracious in victory and defeat – he's a gentleman on the court.'

'It's a carefully curated public image. I bet in real life he's kicking dogs and re-gifting Christmas presents.'

As time went on Lily honed her objections, and her mother her adoration. It became a routine they performed throughout Wimbledon.

'I heard Federer gave a kidney to a Latvian orphan,' her mother said.

'Probably to compensate for having caused the orphan's kidney failure in the first place.'

'How did he cause the orphan's kidney failure?'

'Punching.'

'He punched an orphan in the kidneys?'

'Yes.'

In contrast, her mother couldn't stand Djokovic. She thought him disproportionately aggressive, while Lily liked that he wasn't reticent about showing his anger – that his desire to win superseded his desire to be popular. She liked when he lost a point and threw his racket on the ground, his sinewy legs bent and jouncing. Her mother thought his aggression made him a poor sportsman, while Lily suspected that people's dislike of him stemmed from a larger problem of ingrained anti-Serbian sentiment.

'Expand on that,' her mother said.

'No thanks,' Lily said.

Her mother laughed.

On his second serve of the first game Federer sends the ball to the tip of the net, then over. The three linesmen crouch behind him like small, sky-coloured pylons. The screen reads 107mph, then 119mph on the second serve. Djokovic returns it into the doubles alley. A linesman indicates with his left arm. When Federer faults on the third point the applause wanes – the audience had expected a different outcome, commenced reacting one way then was forced to correct it. This seems a fundamental truth of tennis: the dichotomy between the anticipated and the realized, how a spectator's temporality is shaken when they respond wrongly. To react on time requires you to react in advance. How embarrassing, to get it wrong.

The female linesman behind Djokovic lowers herself to a

squat for live play. Federer plays an ace. The white knot of his bandana is a cotton physalis. Outside her flat Lily can hear the February wind berating its adversaries, the trees and houses and pockets of air in stasis. A church bell struggles to be heard, but in July 2019 Federer secures his game point after a three-shot rally. The clock in the corner of the match says ten past two; the clock on Lily's phone says five to one.

Federer commences serving for the third game. Djokovic returns – leaping backwards. Prior to each return the ball seems to slow, making itself available. Then, there's the cork pop of impact and it re-penetrates the atmosphere. The camera captures the stands: a sea of sunglasses and arrhythmic clapping. The people are arranged in vertiginous diagonals across the screen, innumerable.

Patches of grass are worn to sand-coloured, scored lesions. Nothing about the match happens in a vacuum – the immediate moment has no primacy over what's come before. Lily thinks of the blue sofa of their house, the way it retained the shape of them. The camera circles Federer's calves. Djokovic pirouettes, hits the ball into the net.

It takes longer than she imagines he would have liked, but Federer wins the game on Djokovic's fault. Mirka Federer is dressed like a birthday cake. 'You can't beat time,' a commentator says. Djokovic palms his racket like a tambourine and the umpire says, 'Time.'

'I don't think the first set is vital for Novak, but it's vital for Roger,' Boris Becker says.

'Unfortunately, with this type of cancer, early diagnoses are nearly always impossible,' they were told. 'Time wasn't on our side,' they were told. Djokovic serves his first and second serves with the noise of plastic film being peeled from a ready meal. He double-faults.

'I have a theory that you play better tennis, the more noise you make,' her mother said.

'Is that sarcasm?' Lily said.

Her mother laughed. 'No! I think being good at tennis is 80 per cent noise.'

'What's the other 20 per cent?'

'Twelve per cent is a sense of adventure.'

'And the last eight?'

'Protein.'

'So, none of being good at tennis comes from playing or practising tennis?'

'Christ, no.'

There's a long rally, then an ambiguity. Federer's return is called out; he challenges it. The simulation of the court tilts on its axis – the ball simulacrum leaves its incriminating residue imprint beyond the line. It's out.

By the tenth game of the first set, Federer looks exasperated. He serves, Djokovic challenges; it's in. Federer serves, Djokovic returns, Federer returns. Out.

'If you can get Federer scrambling off the return, you know you've done something right,' a commentator says.

'Look,' Lily said. 'Federer's scrambling.'

'Don't be nasty.'

'He put all his eggs in one basket, then scrambled them, then threw them out the window.'

'Poor Roger.'

'Poor Roger nothing – he broke Andy Murray's leg.'

'That was probably just to bring him good luck.'

'Or he was making an omelette.'

'Can't make an omelette without breaking a few legs.'

'Exactly.'

'Get your sick mother some more wine, would you?' She shook her glass in Lily's face.

'Should you be drinking?'

'At this stage I can't imagine not drinking would make a damn bit of difference.'

Another long rally happens. Federer has Djokovic covering huge swathes of ground. The silence in the stands is colossal. One of Djokovic's returns is so gentle it produces no sound. Federer taps the ball and it lilts over the net, staying close. Djokovic tilts forward and sprints. Federer comes close, expectant. Djokovic makes it, sends the ball past Federer, into the furthest corner. It bounces, departs the court. The crowd moans, orgiastic, then applauds.

'Oh, lovely!' her mother said.

'What did I miss?' Lily said, handing her the wine.

'Here.' Her mother reached for the remote. 'I'll take it back.'

'But then we'll be out of sync with real time.'

'Real time is a construct.'

'We'll be out of sync with the construct.'

'We'll just make it up later, when they're doing a slow-motion replay.'

'So, we'll go forward while they go back, like Paula Abdul.'

'Exactly. It's a complex and harrowing grapple with our own linearity, tennis.' She took the match back to one minute prior. Djokovic made it, sent the ball past Federer, into the furthest corner. It bounced, departed the court. The crowd moaned, then applauded. Federer was nestled by the net.

'That was good,' Lily said.

'Great tennis,' her mother said. She took a sip of wine. 'Great wine,' she said.

When the match ends, Lily looks up and sees dark. She gets out of bed, turns the heating on, takes a box of Jaffa Cakes from the cupboard. She gets back into bed, drags the red ball on YouTube back to the far left of its track. Kate Middleton is wearing a dress that matches William's shirt. Her sunglasses look like they were photoshopped in subsequently. The match starts.

She calls in sick to work for the rest of the week. Her supervisor is curt on the phone. She doesn't bother contacting Marian. She hovers. She turns on the radio and the noise is an unwelcome distraction from her stasis, so she turns it off. She eats noodles with oil and Tabasco, takes antihistamines to induce a nonsensical half-sleep, idly following thoughts that mutate midway through, as though on a cryptex. She cleans the shower and abandons the sponge in the stall; it becomes turgid and cakey. She goes to Siobhán's, which remains abandoned. She wonders where she is, stares at the vibrant arrangement of neglected fruit on the counter, makes some rearrangements.

'Sometimes I wonder if *I'm* the dead one,' she imagines saying to her mother.

Her mother would laugh. 'You're awfully dramatic.'

'Pain is relative.'

'Pain is other relatives.'

'Shut up.'

'Pain is relative up to a point. Besides, there's an urn full of my prior corporeal form that would beg to differ.'

'I think I'm dead and this is my hell – you being gone.'

'What did I say about invoking arbitrary ideas of hell?'

'Don't do it?'

'Exactly.'

SIOBHÁN

Her mother shakes her awake at half seven.

'C'mon, lazybones. No point coming abroad to stay in bed all day.'

She checks her phone. No response.

They go to a market. Siobhán leaves her mother fingering crocheted sarongs and wanders up and down the produce, looking at the fish on ice, their bodies cheese-grater grey, their matte eyes like grout. She spots a *farmacia* across the square and goes in, picking up cans and inspecting them. When she emerges from the icy smog of the shop she hears, 'Siobhán! *Siobhán!*'

'Where did you go?' her mother says, too loud, when Siobhán reaches her. People look over.

'I just nipped over there to get some hair stuff.'

'Let me know next time! I couldn't see you!'

They go to a café for a drink. Siobhán checks her phone. No messages. She googles 'Can heat make hairspray dissolve in the can?' She feels sick.

'Are you going to spend all day checking your phone?' her mother says. 'Here, put a little bit of suncream on my shoulders, would you, and then I'll do you.' Siobhán reaches out her hand. 'You really should invest in some hand cream,' her mother says. 'That elephant skin on your knuckles is horrible.'

★

They go at her mother's pace, wandering slowly up the esplanade, stopping to contemplate the stands selling plates and handmade jewellery. Her mother asks what she thinks of the rings – chunky and clay.

'Yeah, they're nice.'

'Would you like one? I'll get you one.'

'No, it's okay.'

'C'mon,' her mother says, happy and cajoling. 'Choose one, I want to buy you a little holiday present.'

'No, seriously,' Siobhán says, shrugging. 'I don't need it.'

'What about the earrings then? Is there anything you fancy?'

'Not really. It's fine.'

'Not even a necklace? That one would look lovely on you.'

'No, Mum.'

Her mother sighs, disappointed. 'Okay,' she says. 'I think I might get something.' She lifts one, squiggled with burgundy and ivory, says, 'Can I?' to the woman sitting beyond the stall. The woman nods. Siobhán watches her shove the ring firmly over the swollen joint of her eczema'd middle finger. When it's installed at the base, below the knuckle, the flesh above looks turgid. 'What do you think?' she says.

'Looks good.'

'It's not too zany? Not a bit young for me?'

'Not at all.'

On the wall next to them a haggard orange cat arranges itself in a pocket of blistering light. Siobhán watches its multilidded yellow eyes close. Then she hears: 'Siobhán. Shit, Siobhán.' She turns and her mother is trying to wrest the ring from her finger; the skin that emerges beneath it with each upward tug is white, and the skin offering resistance bunches

149

up like a concertina. 'Shit, Siobhán,' her mother is saying, panicked.

'It's okay,' Siobhán says. 'Just give it a minute.'

'It's not coming off, Siobhán. *Shit.*'

'Calm down – just do it slowly. It'll come off. It's okay.' Siobhán keeps her tone low and level, trying to affect a posture of non-committal relaxation for those walking past and glancing over.

'It's not coming off. I can't get it off. Shit, Siobhán, help.'

The woman behind the stall hasn't noticed what's happening – she's flipping insouciantly through a newspaper.

'Give me your hand. I'll have a go.'

Her mother ignores her, keeps pulling at it. 'Shit, shit, shit.' Her face is pink. Siobhán looks at the cat – its ribcage protrudes from its flank. It stretches, opening itself to the warmth.

'Siobhán, could you help me, *please.*'

'Right, okay.'

Siobhán moves round to the side of the stall. The woman looks up, raises an eyebrow.

'Hi, sorry – um, the ring, it's um, stuck, on her finger.' Siobhán mimes putting the ring on, then failing to take it off. The gesture is faintly obscene. The woman raises herself from her seat slightly, peers over her wares to watch Siobhán's mother's exertions. Siobhán's mother looks at her, apologetic. The woman returns to her seat, reaches one hand to the ground and produces a small spray bottle. She hands it to Siobhán, saying nothing, her other hand never losing her place on the page.

'Thanks,' Siobhán says. 'Thanks so much.' She spritzes the pale, soaping liquid on to her mother's finger. Her mother resumes working at the ring. It slides off.

'Thank God,' her mother says. 'Here.' Siobhán hands the bottle and the ring to the woman. 'Thank you so much,' she says. The woman lifts one corner of her mouth, gives a half-nod of acknowledgement.

'Should I ask how much they are?' Siobhán says to her mother.

'God, no. I'm not buying anything after that ordeal. If you don't want anything, let's just go.' They walk on, Siobhán saying, 'Gracias, gracias,' over her shoulder.

'Lovely this, isn't it?' her mother says. They're sitting under an umbrella with the La Casera logo. Siobhán pulls her chair in to shield the back of her neck from the encroaching sun.

'Yeah,' she replies, nudging bodies through her paella. There's a pitcher of sangria on the table between them.

'By the way,' her mother says, bifurcating a slice of beef tomato, 'keep July free, will you? I want to clear out the attic and I was hoping you would come home and help me.'

'July?' Siobhán spears a shrunken croissant of prawn.

'Yes – you won't be working, sure.'

Siobhán frowns. 'I can come home for some of it,' she says.

Her mother's tone turns slightly hostile. 'Why just some?'

Siobhán shrugs. 'Tara and I will probably go down south for the Twelfth, if she's back from Bangladesh.'

'What nonsense.'

'It's not nonsense – I hate being in Belfast for the Twelfth. You know that.'

'I don't see why – my father used to take me to the parades when I was little and it was perfectly family friendly.'

'They burned tricolours last year, Mum. There were signs up saying "Kill All Taigs".'

'I think you're playing the victim here a bit, Siobhán. You haven't been to Mass since you were a child. You're hardly devout.'

Siobhán stares fixedly at her plate.

'I must say,' her mother says, 'this picking and choosing of when you wish to identify as Catholic is very silly, Siobhán, and part of me wonders if it's just to upset me, to show how little you respect *my* history. You went to an integrated school, you *teach* at an integrated school, your mother is Methodist—'

'Barely,' Siobhán mutters.

'Don't be cheeky. Don't you think this disdain for the Twelfth is a little self-indulgent?'

'It's not about that,' Siobhán says. 'I have Protestant friends who want to be as far away from it as possible too. If I were Protestant, I'd still want to be as far away from it as possible.'

'Seems more like you want to be as far away from actually helping me do some housework.'

'I've literally just said I'll come for a bit and help you.'

'While framing it to make you seem like some grand martyr, risking persecution by the state.'

The waiter arrives and asks in a thick accent if everything is fine with their meal. Siobhán offers him a wan smile, her eyes heavy behind her sunglasses. Her mum says, 'Yes, thank you, señor,' and when he departs she does a little laugh. 'Anyway,' she says, 'no point falling out over it. I'd appreciate any help you can give me.' She shakes the basket of individually wrapped breadsticks in Siobhán's face. 'Little breadstick?' she says. 'They're free.'

She worries sometimes that she does unconsciously think of her claim to Catholicism as having cachet. She certainly likes that Andrew views her as exotic, her exoticism tethered to that abounding perception people have of Northern Ireland – a place as binary, a place as two incompatible cultural homogenies squashed together. He's intrigued, not just by her difference but also by her ostensible membership of a group that has known oppression recently enough for it to be interesting. He spent a whole evening in December quizzing her about tactical voting in South Belfast, expressing a disproportionate amount of sympathy for her admission that she would have to vote for a nationalist MP she didn't agree with, purely to challenge her constituency's historic majority of a unionist MP she agreed with even less.

'Are you all right, Siobhán?' her mother says, sipping primly at her gazpacho. It's their final evening, and they've decided to dine at the hotel.

'What?' Siobhán says, watching the bubbles in her sparkling water cascade upwards. 'Of course.'

'You've seemed a bit down recently.'

'I'm grand.'

'You know I hate that word.'

'I am, though.'

'If there was something going on, you should tell me. I know you think your old mother doesn't know anything, but I might be able to help.'

'Seriously, I'm fine.'

'You just seem a little chaotic at the moment – a little moody. Has something happened at work?'

'No.'

'Have you fallen out with Tara?'

'Jesus, of course not.'

'Is it a romantic issue, then?'

'Stop asking. I'm fine, seriously.'

'Just tell me – what's wrong?'

'I'm. *Fine.*'

Her mother shakes her head slightly, purses her lips. They resume their meals in silence, until:

'You haven't been bitten by anything, have you, Siobhán? I have insect spray in my bag.'

'Oh my God, would you stop fussing?'

'Yes, yes, okay,' her mother says, looking wounded.

Siobhán sighs. 'Seriously, Mum, I'm good!' She feigns exuberance. She lifts her glass and they cheers. Siobhán glances around. At other tables people are scrunching ten- and twenty-euro notes into the maître d's hand. Siobhán watches him smile with his swarthy, generous cheeks. A great egg of a man.

'Do you think he's still referred to as a maître d' in Spain?' Siobhán asks.

Her mother twists in her seat. 'Do we need to tip him?' she says.

'I don't think so – those people have probably been here longer than four nights, plus this is the only night we've had dinner here.'

'Do you have any cash?'

'No.'

'How can you not have any cash?'

'I've been paying for everything with a card.'

'How can you be an adult in the world and not carry cash? You should carry cash.'

'Why, though?'

'So you don't rely on me for things like this.'

'I don't think we need to tip him.'

'Other people have.'

'So? Like I said, they've probably been here a week, are probably on half-board.'

'Do you think we could piggyback on someone else's tip?'

'What? Jesus Christ – no. We absolutely could *not* do that.'

'That girl at the next table – you're mates with her, right?'

'We spoke a couple of times at breakfast. Please, just leave it.'

'We could go in on her tip and then buy her a drink later.'

'This is insane.'

'We can't just not do anything, Siobhán!'

'Of course we can!'

'Oh, grow up.'

'But that's—'

'Shit. He's coming.'

'Don't worry about it!'

He delivers a bright blue drink to the table closest to theirs. The tables are tightly crammed together, to avail of the benefits of the outdoor heaters. Siobhán can see the veins on the orange segment floating on the blue liquid's surface. The drink's recipient says, '*Gracias*,' really leaning into the t-h of it, then says, 'Thank you for taking such good care of us all week,' and hands him a note.

Siobhán's mother catches him with an enquiring smile as he turns. He approaches, says, '*Si, signora?*'

She gestures at the table with the blue drink, then at the money in his hand. 'That was from us as well,' she says. He frowns, confused.

LILY

She hears the door open above her on Friday evening. She hears the washing machine trundle like a horse and cart on cobbles. She hears the *ding* of the microwave. She looks at the lurid pink cans of hairspray and dry shampoo and mousse on the counter, the ones she swapped out for empties she found in Siobhán's bin. After a long period, she thinks she hears crying.

SIOBHÁN

On the bus back from the airport her mother takes a tea towel printed with *'¡Olé!'* out of her bag.

'Here,' she says, handing it to Siobhán. 'I got you this at the airport. For your flat.' She pokes at the flamenco dancer in a red dress, smiling blithely. 'She looks a bit like you!' she says.

'Thanks.'

'Good trip,' her mother says.

Siobhán takes her phone off flight mode and it starts reverberating with emails, messages from Tara, Mark, Sophie. Andrew was last online an hour ago.

Her mother nudges her with a newly freckled elbow, says with pantomime enunciation, *'Good. Trip. Thanks. Mum.'*

Siobhán looks at the head of the person in front of her. 'Good trip. Thanks, Mum,' she intones. Her mother nestles happily in her seat.

When she has loaded her clothes into the washing machine she messages him again.

Are you okay?

The stack of last week's unfinished marking sits on the counter. She ignores it. Her phone pings with emails from parents. She ignores them too. She toasts some bread, puts a cheese slice on top, opens the microwave, remembers the unrectified brownie explosion, swears. She takes a picture of the mess and sends it to Sophie: *Diorama of the dirty protests*. She cleans it, then microwaves the cheese-atop-toast. She squeezes ketchup on top and eats it in bed. The edges of the bread are stiff, the middle soggy. She watches *Saw V*, takes a bite out of her toast as Scott Patterson performs a tracheotomy on himself with a biro. Sophie replies: *Ew*.

Two hours later, her phone vibrates.

Hi sweetheart.

She stares at it intermittently for three minutes, then lets herself reply.

Hi.

Good trip?

Exhausting.

Oh sweetheart.

You all right?

Yeah. Sorry.

It's okay.

I've been feeling guilty.

Oh.

I'm struggling to justify the risk I'm taking. What I'm doing to them. I'm threatening their happiness every day.

Yeah.

This is the worst thing I've ever done. If she found out, I don't know what she'd do. I couldn't forgive myself.

You know, Andrew, people separate. My parents separated, then he died. It was largely fine.

That's not an option.

Okay.

I love you.

She doesn't respond immediately, and is gratified when he says, *Siobhán?*

I love you too, she says, hoping that he feels like he had to coax the response from her.

But this is wrong. I'm doing something so wrong.

But us, together – it doesn't feel wrong.

I'm struggling to know if the risk is worth it.

Her chest feels tight, then static. *Oh*, she says.

I need some space to think about things. I promise I'll message when I get back on Sunday, and I promise I'll try and see you for your birthday.

Okay.

Speak soon, sweetheart xxx

She opens a bottle of wine, dropping the cap. It falls on to one of the chairs at the kitchen table.

'Bollocks,' she says, sliding it out. Next to the cap, on the seat of the chair, is Callum's exercise book.

'Oh my God, what?'

She picks it up and stares at it.

'I'm losing my fucking mind,' she informs the room. She places the book on the table and takes the wine to bed. The washing machine beeps and her laundry stays abandoned in the drum. She cries at the volume of her loneliness, pictures herself as a widow in a turret. She texts Mark.

Hey, Markess of Granby. Fancy a drink?

He replies half an hour later.

Sorry, mucker – at Mar's parents' house. Smashing it at Cluedo. Tomorrow?

She doesn't reply.

LILY

On Sunday the air is mildewy. Damper than actual rain. A broad open window in a house front makes a terrarium of the living room: she watches four people rearranging themselves on sofas, lifting cans of Heineken from a box on the floor. She catches errant snatches of sound, a cheer from the lit television, showing football; an expletive as a can expels foam; a braying laugh in response to a joke. In Botanic, groups of university students gravitate towards the glass-panelled monolith of the library. The flower bed by the white carapace of the glasshouse is conspicuously flowerless. Light finds its occasional way around the grey cloud and competes with the air, then gets subsumed again. A man runs laps of the lawn in a pair of jeans.

At a café there isn't competition for the outdoor tables, so she pulls her raincoat over her hips and thighs and sits. The apple juice is the colour of ambergris and the same temperature as the rain.

'Hi,' a voice says. The woman in the rara skirt is standing at the edge of the café's raised forecourt. Lily shrinks into her hood, ignores her.

'You, love – hey, you.' Her knees reveal themselves among the heavy and matted fur of her coat as she climbs the two steps, the skin blueish.

'Hey, you, love.' She permeates the invisible boundary of the patio, approaches. She sits in the empty seat next to Lily, then leans forward. Lily keeps her mouth wrapped around her straw.

'Can you help me, please?'

She runs the word 'you' into 'help'. It sounds like 'whelp me'. Her hair is dyed pink-red and there are lumps along the fraying threads of her parting.

'Do you live round here?' she says. 'I'm supposed to be getting the bus to my sister's. She lives not that far from here. I'm supposed to be getting the bus to hers but I've lost my ticket and I don't have any money. I know it's stupid to have lost my ticket, but I have, and I thought, that girl looks nice, so I thought I'd come over and ask you for help and – would you mind? Please? I just need to get to my sister's.'

Lily looks around – the students pass in their clusters, glancing into the forecourt and then away, desperate not to be implicated. Her apple juice is starting to taste like chewed straw. She sets it down and reaches in for her wallet. The ripping noise of the Velcro is too loud. She takes out a 50p and a 20p and a pound coin, tries to hand them over. The woman looks at her hand like it's a non sequitur.

'See,' she says, sniffing a droplet back into her nose. 'The thing is, my bus is in a little bit, yeah? And nobody else will speak to me and I need enough money for a new ticket to my sister's. I need to get to her, you know? Do you live near here? I used to live not far from here – nice place. Me and this other girl – she was a bit of a head case, but she was a really good cook. She'd get the discount beef from Tesco at the end of the day – you know, when they mark the price down on the yellow stickers? So, she'd get it dead cheap but it tasted class, you know? It was dead on for a while but she had issues, you know? Like, she thought I was slagging her off to people, but I wasn't, because I'm not like that, and my sister really isn't like that. She's lovely, my sister. I just need to get the next bus to her, you know?'

The rain is light but incessant, like tinnitus, and the woman's fur is turning darker. Lily stands, and the woman stands too, symbiotic. They walk each other to the cashpoint, and at the kerb Lily trips on the wide legs of her trousers and goes down. The woman tries to catch her, but she's not strong enough, and she is pulled over – one hand on the ground next to Lily's torso, the other still gripping Lily's arm. Lily thinks they must look like two soldiers in a war film, sprawling in wet mud, possibly about to kiss. The woman laughs, nervily and scratchily, and they get to their feet. The sleeve of the woman's coat has slid up, revealing her forearms, and Lily can see loose scar tissue and clusters of red spotting. The scar tissue is pink and wormy. At the cash point Lily hands over two ten-pound notes, and the woman balls them in her palm, then lunges forward and hugs her. It's like having an empty birdcage held to her chest. They separate, and the woman teeters away, and Lily feels the rain get heavier.

She does a circuitous route to nowhere – the length of the Dublin Road, past the cinema which has been threatening its own closure for the last year, past the great gnomon of a hotel that Caz hates. She loops back on to the towpath. The river moves along, well plotted, and people walk past in their archipelagos. As the path opens up on to the Ormeau Bridge she can see a crane lurking among the reeds, like a telephone mast among trees. She passes the swimming pool, the student gym. An old woman on a bench balances food on her thighs and Lily thinks about the great poverty of her future.

As she walks through the Holylands she glances down a

dark, wheelie-binned alley – a gloomy aperture between con-
tiguous houses – and sees a sparrowhawk fighting with a
pigeon. She stops to watch, and when the hawk sinks its talons
deeply into the pigeon's neck it makes a noise, then goes silent.
She walks on, and when she passes the university cinema she
buys a ticket for the documentary about tickling. She settles
into her aisle seat in the dark, wonders if living will ever feel
again less like something to be endured in the service of attain-
ing something better, if it will ever reveal some new facet that
isn't so unbearable.

The rain has stopped, properly, for the first time in days. The
sun is out, and the paving stones are split with triangle-shaped
shadows, making them half grey and half yellow with light. The
memory of the rain makes the air fresh. The early evening has
brought people out, and she avoids looking at their faces
through the glare of the low sun. She walks through and around
campus, the old bricks emitting warmth. She crosses University
Street then heads up the Lisburn Road, eyes still fixed on the
ground. It isn't until she hears a voice saying, 'Oh my God,' to
the right of her that she looks up, sees the expensive beige
trench coat that has manifested beside her and then the woman
in it, who speeds past. A man hurries over from across the
street, and Lily proceeds slowly, still unsure of the catalyst for
the growing congregation. Soon, Lily is at the edge of a sizeable
crowd. She peers over the head of the woman in the raincoat
and stares at the centrepiece.

The thin body is bent, the pink rara skirt crumpled. Blood
springs from a gash on one knee and soaks into the balding fur
coat. A thick graze is visible on one side of the face, pressed
into the ground. The flesh around the eye is swelling. One

hand is bent backwards, wrongly – there is a broad knob of bone pressing through the skin of her wrist, trying to make its way out.

The woman in the raincoat has a hand clasped over her mouth, and Lily has always wondered what situation might incite a person to hold their face together like that, to stop whatever might leak out; the same way she wonders what news would drive a person to slide down a wall in anguish, like they do in films. Who's capable of dynamism in response to desolation? The man from across the street is balancing on the balls of his feet, his body hovering close to the ground. He's on his phone.

'Hi,' he says. 'Hi, I need an ambulance. A woman's been assaulted, I think. Yes. No. Yes. Her wrist is broken and she's hit her head. No, I – I don't think she can walk.'

From above, the woman's shape might look like she's sprinting. Her eyelids flutter madly and saliva runs from one corner of her mouth and mixes with the streaks of blood on the pavement. The man on the phone is struggling to get his arm out of his jumper sleeve while keeping the phone clasped to his ear. He speaks urgently and softly. 'No,' he says. 'No, nobody's moved her. She's breathing, but she's not responsive.'

Trench-coat woman de-coats, revealing a chest covered in freckles. She arranges the coat in a horseshoe shape around the wrist, a makeshift protective perimeter. Lily wonders about offering to go buy some chalk, if it might be worth outlining the woman's shape for posterity.

The woman on the ground is finding consciousness; she emits a couple of high-pitched whimpers. The man on the phone says, 'She's coming round. What should we do?' The trench-coat woman has a silver bracelet on one arm, clanking with charms: a dog, a cherub, a high-heeled shoe. They dangle over the broken wrist like a mobile over a baby. She says, 'Give her some space,' but nobody is listening. The woman on the ground turns to face the sky, her face newly asymmetrical. She flicks her eyes back and forth as though searching for an invisible assailant, as though still trapped in the moment of whatever happened to her. She goes to sit up, and the man on the phone and the de-coated woman realize too late what is going to happen. They tell her to lie still, too afraid or too disgusted to touch her. She looks at them, fearful, and places her one good hand on the ground, presses down, rises slightly. She tries to do the same with her other hand. She puts weight on it. 'No, wait,' trench-coat woman says. The cars speed past. A manhole cover on the road rattles. The woman looks at her broken hand. The blood sits on her kneecap in dried, ferrous streaks. She starts to scream.

The sanitary towels could be smelled before they were seen, usually. Lily caught the perpetrator in the act, once – she walked into the bathroom and saw the girl leaving a cubicle, a pad freshly smeared with dark red in one hand, a wrapped one, purloined from the bin, in the other. They stared at one another. 'Hi,' Lily said. The girl said nothing, and that afternoon, Lily went to the school office.

She doesn't know, precisely, why she did it. When she thinks about it now, she wonders if she wanted a moment of influence in a stranger's life, to be able to see some coalescence between the two of them – to know that for a moment their lives overlapped in some tangible way. Something about the way the girl looked at her as she stood there, the bloody totems in her hands, made Lily think she wanted that too. Maybe sometimes the pursuit of an idea, and its dogma, will run interminably, will risk consuming you, if there isn't someone who'll offer you the chance to give it up, who'll say, 'It's okay, you can stop being this now.'

When the scream starts the crowd leans back as one organism, as though choreographed. The woman's scream eclipses all other noises and sensations – the smell of a worn-out clutch, the molten glare of the late sun, the chill in the air. The noise subsumes it all. The woman pulls her broken wrist abruptly into her lap and cradles it, looking at her limp, violet fingers. She glances up at her audience-in-the-round, then goes silent. Trench-coat woman finally steels herself to touch her, and places a hand on her shoulder, says, 'It's okay – you're going to be okay.' The man talks into his phone: 'Yes, she's awake, but I don't know the extent of her head injury.' Another man dislodges himself from the crowd and places his palms on the woman's blue, veiny legs. He moves his hands back and forth along her shins and the veins disappear and reappear with the pressure of his thumbs, like earthworms poking their heads out of the ground. Lily wonders at this tacit arrangement in which these strangers are now seemingly responsible for this woman's safety.

After a moment, as though sensing her looking, the woman on the ground finds Lily's eyes. They look at each other for a protracted moment. Her expression is plaintive. The woman with the trench coat and the freckles twists on her thin ankles. She looks at Lily, then back to the woman on the pavement, then back to Lily.

'Do you know her?' she says, and Lily notes how different her tone is from the one she used to say, 'It's okay – you're going to be okay.' Lily must seem as conniving as anyone, more so. She could say, 'She has a sister – you need to get in touch with her sister.' She says nothing. She shakes her head and backs away, the crowd closing as she retreats, like blades of grass.

Back at the café, she buys another apple juice. She sits at the same table, and this time there is a couple at the table next to her. The girl is wearing dirty and expensive trainers and corduroy trousers that sit in capacious folds around her thighs and knees. The boy has brown hair – curly, messy – and shiny forearms. Their heads are close, like two cherries on a stalk. Lily works to hear them over the sound of an ambulance in the distance.

'Mark?' she says.

'Yep?'

'You know Interrail passes?'

'Yeah? What about them?'

'They should be called "You're Up" cards,' she says.

He laughs, then places a hand on the back of her head. 'No, Mar,' he says, 'they shouldn't.'

Her mother always gave change to people who asked. Her generosity existed without the corollary of convenience, of wanting, primarily, to be left alone.

On Monday, Siobhán rises later than usual. Lily wakes with her at six, staring at the ceiling, trying to detect vibrations in the uneven lumps of plaster that rim the walls, the bubonic cornicing. She tries to imagine the atoms of Siobhán's world above her moving – all the matter, all the small ways Lily has exerted herself upon that matter, interacting with Siobhán's form to rouse her. When footsteps do happen, they're harried, and then there's the low wheeze of a hairdryer. The door slams at six forty-five. Lily scratches at an itch on her thigh and the skin starts to bubble with agitated welts as she persists. In the shower the skin stings, and afterwards she trims her macerated nails over the mug. It sits, full of bits of her.

Outside the students' union a girl with orange plaits wiggles a clipboard in her face.

'Hi!' the girls says, cheerful. 'Would you like to sign this petition? It's to stop—'

'Okay.' Lily holds her hand out for the pen.

'It's to stop them from closing the needle exchange on Botan—'

'Here you go.' Lily returns the pen. The girl blinks.

'Great!' she says, and she frees a flyer from the clipboard. 'You can find out more about it here,' she says. 'The service is super-important and without it drug users will be at greater risk from—'

'Thanks,' Lily says over her shoulder, already in transit. She arrives at the hospital and deposits the flyer into a bin at reception.

In the office Hannah is talking about her childhood, about the time she got her arm stuck in a tube door on a trip to London, about the Mr Blobby theme park that 'destroyed' the seaside town in Lancashire where she grew up.

'The council sued Noel Edmonds,' she says. 'It was known as Blobbygate.'

Marian chuckles. When Lily walked in earlier Marian said, 'We missed you last week, love?' but didn't probe. Now, Lily is tracing the baroque curlicues on a custard cream with her finger, change from a donation box sitting in front of her in small plastic sacks. Hannah talks for a while longer and eventually stops. Marian gives a contented hum of peroration.

Lily's mother grew up on a farm in Antrim. When Lily was thirteen years old, three years before her grandfather was diagnosed with Alzheimer's, five before he became unfit to live alone and the farm was sold, she and her mum stayed for a week during the summer. The farmhouse was a raised bungalow surrounded by flattened expanses of green and, beyond that, the meagre protuberance of Slemish. On shelves there were ceramic cows, some mimetic, some anthropomorphized. The paintings on the walls of verdant landscape were indistinguishable from what was visible through the windows. Next to the house was a concourse lined with bockety, derelict stables, filled with animal feed and hay and galvanized farm equipment. Next to the stables was a barn of corrugated steel, from which lowing could be heard.

Her grandfather reared beef cattle, and on their first afternoon Lily saw a calf being born. It was raining lightly, and her grandfather gave her a coat to wear. He was stooped and muscular, like a cauldron. The labouring cow was lying in an empty, hay-filled enclosure. Her grandfather pushed his sleeves up his arms and circled the prostrate cow like a vulture. Lily's mum edged her way around the gate and lowered herself to the ground, stroking the cow's fist-sized and slippery grey nose.

Before there was any calf visible there was the beginning of a half-inflated balloon, undulating in and out and in. It was part red and part brown and part the yellowish shade of frozen milk. Her grandfather stood back, frowning, and waiting. The latex texture of the bag hung flaccid, and the cow moaned. A moment passed, and Lily climbed to the penultimate rung of the gate to get a better view. Her mother nose-stroked assiduously, saying nothing. After a few moments Lily's grandfather sighed: 'Bollocks.' He reached his arm in, found something, pulled. The cow made a noise like a rusted hinge, and he kept pulling. The calf came out the colour of mackerel – silent and floppy.

On the second day Lily and her mum walked up and down the narrow country road. They stopped for a while to look at the sheep and the goat that lived in the field behind the farm, and Lily's mum told her that when a sheep is reared with a goat, the sheep will behave like a goat.

On the third day another calf was due. The barn smelt like pellets and diesel. The cow's pupil was an inkwell, its nose the colour of Calpol. Lily stroked the coarse hair between its ears. Her grandfather, bent-kneed and planted at the open end of things, said, 'Here it comes,' and he and Lily's mother massaged out the erupting head and hooves, magnified and distorted by the amber caul. The membrane split and the calf landed on its side, commenced an uncoordinated jerking. Lily swallowed a ball of nausea and her grandfather said, 'Well, thank Christ for that,' and she laughed through her distaste. Her mother's hands were slimy with blood and mucus, and she waggled her fingers in Lily's face. 'Stop acting the lig, you two,' her grandfather said.

'Hey, Dad,' Lily's mother said, wiping her hands on her thighs.

'What?'

'What do you call fizzy milk?'

Lily's grandfather sighed. 'What?' he said.

'Lait Fizzérables.'

The calf was quick to stand. The cow put its pennant-sized tongue over her child's face and ears. The calf blinked, just larger than a child's bicycle.

On the fourth day Lily asked if she could name the calf.

'You could,' her grandfather said, 'though not much point. He'll be gone in a few months, once he's weaned.'

'Gone where?' Lily said.

'I rear beef cattle, sweetie,' her grandfather said. 'Where do you think?'

A topic that went unmentioned during that week on the farm was her mother's younger sister, who drowned three years before Lily was born. Seven years later, as they sorted her grandfather's clothes into two bags, 'charity' and 'recycle', Lily's mother mentioned her.

'No doubt Joanne would think I made an absolute hames of selling the farm,' she said. 'She was always the one with any business acumen.'

Lily's grandfather had been buried three days prior in Portglenone, in the family plot.

Lily said nothing, sat cautiously in the silence as she unsplit the stitches attaching a name label to a bally old jumper with her thumbnail. Her mother contemplated a pair of fraying beige trousers.

'After your father and I graduated we came straight here,' she said. 'We wanted to start our lives, and I'd had enough rural isolation and agriculture for a lifetime. Then a year later Mum died, and Joanne was pressured into staying on the farm to help run things. I'd just got engaged and didn't want to go back to that house, which had became a bit of a mausoleum. Any time I went, your grandfather was just maudlin and bitter, so we didn't visit much, and Joanne – she fell in with this loyalist dickhead. He pressured her into hiding weapons, in one of the old stables. She shouldn't have said yes, but he was threatening enough, and that's what they did – they pressured you – and also for some reason she thought she loved him, so she did it. Anyway, your grandfather found them, and he had her arrested.'

'He had her arrested?'

'Yeah, he said he wasn't going to tolerate any paramilitary involvement, so yeah, he turned her in. Nothing came of it, though. It was pretty obvious she'd been coerced.'

'What happened after?'

'Well, the dickhead fucked off to Tyrone to pursue murder full time and I think did eventually wind up in prison. After that, though, your grandfather kept Jo pretty much under house arrest. She didn't get to socialize much before that, anyway – she couldn't drive – but after that debacle she didn't leave the farm at all, really, except to go get groceries. She stayed home and ran the business side of things, and then, sure, you know what happened.' She looked to the wall, her jaw set. 'And we don't know if it was intentional, or not,' she continued, 'but yeah, she washed up at Ramore. After that you'd be hard pressed getting your grandfather to say two words about her.' She laughed hollowly, 'And then twenty years later he couldn't have remembered her if he'd wanted to.'

Lily lifted a comb from the box and inspected it, then set it down. Her mum sighed.

'We weren't close, growing up,' she said. 'And probably if

you'd said to me, "If you leave, Joanne'll get stuck," I'd have replied, "Rather her than me."' She lifted an unopened box of incontinence pads from the box, looked at Lily with a grim expression. 'We suppress our moral imaginations sometimes, I guess,' she said, 'to let us get what we want.'

'Where are you from again, Lily?' Hannah breaks Lily's reverie. 'Derry,' Lily says reluctantly, and she watches Hannah's eyes go wide.

'Shit, what was that like?'

'What do you mean?'

'Was there all sorts of mad stuff going on? Bomb scares, police checks, stuff like that.'

Lily shrugs. She turns her eyes to the money in what she hopes is a demonstrative way.

'Hannah?' Marian says, casting Lily a sympathetic look.

'What?' Hannah says. 'It's a totally normal question.'

Lily shrugs again. She doesn't care.

Her childhood was a calm one, worthy of being mythologized not for what was happening beyond the walls of their house but for what was happening within them, for the specificities of her small, resected world. Her parents moved to the glob of their cul-de-sac during a period in which the city was haemorrhaging people. Their street was populated through a combination of necessity and altruism: newly married couples flocking to affordable housing; young professionals from elsewhere coming to bolster the emergency services. Lily and her mother's neighbours were a Lebanese doctor and his wife, a nurse from Cullybackey, who tended their garden on the weekends till it was verdant and stately. One biblically warm summer in Lily's early twenties, their fig tree brandished an impossible haul. They'd suspend cellophane bags of green, oleaginous fruits from Lily's mother's door handle, which Lily would chance upon in the evenings when she visited. They'd eat them in the garden, squelching their way through wet, sweet sinew.

'Figs!' Lily called, letting herself in one evening. She held the bag aloft.

'What's that?' her mother replied, exiting the kitchen, a half-eaten fig in her hand, its innards anatomical-looking – tawny alveoli among juicy interstices. 'Bloody hell,' she said. 'That's the third bag this week.' She chomped down the remainder of the fig in her hand, and they had figs and chips for dinner.

'More figs,' Lily said, two days later, proffering the laden sack as if it were a kitten. Her mother moaned.

'Hello!' Lily said, the next day.

'Hi, love,' her mother called out. Lily hung her jacket on the banister and walked into the kitchen. 'Hope you're hungry,' her mother said. 'We'll be having—'

'Figs?' Lily said. Her mother turned slowly, saw the bag.

'Dear God,' she said quietly.

'That'll do, fig,' Lily said.

'Maybe let's get on with work, girls?' Marian says.

Hannah rolls her eyes. 'No room for discourse in this office,' she mutters.

Marian smiles at Lily before turning around, and Lily wonders what tragic back story Marian thinks she just rescued Lily from divulging.

SIOBHÁN

She sleeps until twelve on Saturday afternoon. She re-washes her crumpled and stagnant laundry, then flicks through assignments, correcting spelling errors arbitrarily, giving ticks and double ticks and occasionally a triple tick and a smiley face. She reads an article about learning techniques, then forces herself to read it again when she decides she didn't really read it the first time. She looks for the oranges; three of them are fermenting in a bowl under the now mocha-coloured soft banana.

'Why the fuck did I do that?' she says to herself. 'I'm an idiot.' She retrieves the least crispy-looking orange, eats its least grey, decrepit segments. She puts on her running shoes and leggings and realizes she left her headphones on the plane. She puts her pyjamas back on.

She'd like to be someone who takes a book to a bar – who sits with an afternoon glass of Sauvignon and sips it slowly – but she knows that she'd just be itching for someone to approach her and flirt, to make her feel pretty and desired. She'd be worse than those women she hates who go out in solidarity throngs, hoping to attract attention. She'd spend an hour arranging her hair and putting on mascara just to go unnoticed, just to return home, irascible. Instead she masturbates joylessly, checks her phone, orders a takeaway, checks her phone. She pushes the hoover around and contemplates going to see Caz, instead goes nowhere, speaks to no one. She checks her phone.

The next day she forces herself repeatedly into sleep, finally leaving bed, groggy and congested, at 2 p.m. She has a message.

Hey, you. Just got home. Are you free Tuesday? I have a meeting in town and I'd love to take you for dinner.

She's ashamed at the perceptible and immediate shift in her mood. She almost wishes that she still felt miserable – that the causation wasn't so obvious. She replies straight away.

Of course I'm free. I'd love that.

He replies quickly. *Excellent! So excited to see you, sweetheart.*

Her bones feel lighter.

On Monday morning she leaves her hair dirty, gathering it up in a bun on top of her head, two greasy tendrils irritating her cheeks. The mass of it feels dense and moist, like a baked potato. An advantage of her situation is that she doesn't feel the need to commit to vanity when she's not with him. She puts on earrings, though, to balance things out. On her walk to work she scrolls through the birthday messages people have left on her Facebook page. She has a lengthy email from Tara.

She's at her desk by 7 a.m., planning her marking schedule so she can feel unencumbered tomorrow evening. Sophie comes in at eight and peers around the door. She stands with her body out of sight and sets her head at an angle, making it look disembodied, sliding up and down the doorframe. Siobhán watches her and wonders how long this part of her life will go on for, then realizes that there's nothing to suggest that any of this is temporary, and just what is it she's expecting to follow it, exactly?

'Happy birthday, mate!' Sophie says, then plants herself, bodied, in the doorway, producing a gift bag from behind her back.

'Do you ever worry that you're just waiting for a better part of your life to start?' Siobhán says.

Sophie laughs, circumnavigates the desks. 'Jesus, Shiv, one of those birthdays, is it?'

'Seriously, though: I think I'm putting undue pressure on the future.'

'That's the kind of thinking that winds up getting you hit by a bus.'

'Why?'

'Bad karma, to not appreciate what you have.'

'Oh – I thought you might know a bus driver who has homicidal tendencies towards those who don't live in the moment.'

'That's an insane thing to say.'

'But "bad karma" isn't?'

'Shut up and open your present.'

It's perfume, and a card with a parrot on it.

To Shiv,

Here's to more years of lesson planning and trying to keep our sanity intact.

Big love,
Sophie xo

Siobhán stands, and they hug. 'Thanks, Soph,' she says. She sprays them both – the room fills with ylang-ylang. Sophie sniffs the sleeve of her jumper. 'That's probably exactly what this needed,' she says. 'I'm too scared to wash it.'

'It new?'

'Yeah, but already well worn. How do you wash cashmere?'

'Ask the murderous bus driver if he knows a murderous dry cleaner.'

'I'm leaving now.'

The rain sounds like a grain silo filling, and when the kids arrive they are spattered and dejected. Siobhán gives the radiator dial as extreme an anticlockwise twist as she can manage, even though Colin has warned them against interfering. Everyone is lethargic after the week off, so she has them do out-loud reading rather than anything too strenuous. When it's Siobhán's turn she puts on different voices and gesticulates wildly, and they laugh. She returns Callum's exercise book with an expression of contrition, and he looks delighted by the attention. Ayesha spots the gift bag by her desk and they sing 'Happy Birthday'. Siobhán has to think of quotidian things – lasagnes and staplers – to stop herself from welling up. By lunchtime the rain has stopped. The bell is due to go in three minutes and Siobhán can see the kids fidgeting, reluctant to commit to starting a new question or sharpening a blunt pencil. Kimberly is brazenly empty-handed and staring vacantly into space; Kyle is pretending to contemplate his fifteen-centimetre ruler; others have begun to cautiously feed their books, one at a time, into their bags. Normally this would irritate her, but right now she feels impish and benevolent. She twirls on her heels and they freeze in various poses of departure. She smiles.

'Go on then, you absolute rascals. Pack up.' The bell rings and the poised kids jettison themselves from their desks.

'Try not to break anything on your way out,' Siobhán calls after them. She brings out her phone and reads Tara's email, realizes she knows nothing about Tara's job or hydrogeology or Bangladesh. She can't motivate herself to write an adequate response, so she messages: *Thx for the email T, will reply properly soon I promise xxx*. She feels a flicker of guilt, suppresses it.

When Tara and Siobhán were twenty-one they went to Paris in August. They spent an evening trying to find the Eiffel Tower; never did. They got to the Louvre after it had closed, so they ran around the shrunken pyramids, cackling, pretending to be giants. Tara was always being told she looked like a young Bernadette Devlin, so Siobhán took pictures of her in black and white. 'We can sell these as historical artefacts,' she said. They found a bar full of elderly, garlicky-looking men with suspenders, and they ordered copious amounts of a canned drink they couldn't identify. 'This is incredible,' Tara said. 'Why do we not have this at home?'

'This is my new favourite *boisson*,' Siobhán said.

'*Moi aussi*,' Tara said.

They cheersed so aggressively that Siobhán's glass exploded in her hand. They stared at the mess on the floor, Siobhán gripping the still-intact handle. 'I'll sort it,' she said, then went up to the bar and said, teetering, '*Une person à fracasé une verre là-bas.*'

The girl looked at her for a long time, then nodded.

Tara and Siobhán moved to another table, and Siobhán said, 'If *you're* the one to report it, they never suspect you of being *le culprit.*'

Tara shook her head. 'You're *une idiote*,' she said.

They discovered later that they'd been drinking cans of pre-mixed shandy.

She's on playground duty, so she meanders around the perimeter, trying to bury her hands deeper in her pockets. The newborn sun is making the tarmac glimmer, and the chalked-on shapes of hopscotches and grids look vibrant. She waves maniacally to Sophie, who's guarding the disobedience wall.

She watches a few from her class playing Kiss Chase, the ethical implications of which she hasn't got round to explaining. She notices the absence of Kimberly, Kate, Amy, Ayesha, and something like unease begins to assemble itself in her mind. Rebecca runs towards her, pursued by Christopher. He grabs her arm and she slows, stops, turns. Her face is sullen. He kisses her on the cheek and she blushes, then he darts off. Before she can commence her pursuit, Siobhán steps forward.

'Rebecca?'

She smiles, embarrassed. 'Yes, miss?'

'Where are your mates?'

She's nervous, and Siobhán feels the grim satisfaction of suspicion vindicated. 'Miss?' Rebecca says.

'The other girls – where are they?'

Rebecca looks visibly uncomfortable now. 'Don't know, miss,' she says, avoiding eye contact.

'Okay,' Siobhán says. 'Thanks anyway – go on.' Rebecca absconds, and Siobhán makes her way across the flat rectangle.

'Keep an eye on things, will you?' she says to Sophie. 'I need to go check something.' She leaves the playground, heads in the direction of the Portakabins. Behind one is a small, soggy levee of fallen leaves and unmown grass, untouched by light. When Siobhán turns the corner there is frenzied activity as the girls slide on the slick marshland, trying to conceal a small grey box.

'Hi, girls,' Siobhán says. They look at her – Ayesha and Amy worried, Kate already on the verge of tears, Kimberly defiant, but not so much that Siobhán can't see the wariness underneath.

'So.' Siobhán keeps her tone measured, strives for neutrality. She doesn't feel good; there are too many of them to look at, and her authority feels stretched too thin. She thinks about tomorrow evening, about the prospect of sitting across from Andrew in a restaurant, his pistachio-eyes and full lips, his hand brushing hers under the table. She takes a breath. 'So,' she repeats. 'Who feels up to explaining to me what's going on?' At this Kate does start crying. Siobhán knows she won't have wanted to be out here, sucking ineffectually on an unlit cigarette.

'Okay,' Siobhán says, and she arranges her face in judicial contemplation. She imagines the feeling of Andrew's lips on her neck. She doesn't especially care that they have cigarettes, but now that she's gone to the trouble of catching them, she has to do something.

'Okay,' she repeats. 'First of all – give me those.' She steps forward, and the incline of the earth keeps her at a lower level – Kimberly reaches down to relinquish the box. Her face is indifference atop apprehension. Siobhán turns and walks, calls back, 'Come. Now.' When the natural height hierarchy is resumed she feels more confident.

'I'm going to give you all the benefit of assuming that you're not idiots, okay? I'm not going to lecture you about smoking because one, you don't even have a lighter, by the looks of things, and two, I know you all know how harmful it is, and how stupid.'

Kate's nose is running, visibly. Kimberly is evasive – her gaze is directed somewhere just beyond Siobhán's shoulder. Siobhán stays silent for a moment, then, acting on impulse, she steps forward and claps. Kate and Amy flinch, Ayesha's eyes go huge, Kimberly jumps.

'Great, okay – you're paying attention. Good start.' Siobhán directs this at Kimberly, and her anger gives the air a substantive, unsavoury edge. There's protocol in place for situations like this – incident report logs, informing the head, summoning the parents. The girls would be sent home today, then there'd be a tedious and unduly lengthy meeting to discuss suspension. To set the ball of her responsibilities in motion would be to resign herself to a week, if not more, of inconvenience. She'd probably have to stay late tomorrow. She weighs up the risks. 'You know,' she says, and she thinks that what she'd really like to be doing is sleeping, 'in situations like this I'm supposed to phone your parents.' She feels a spasm of guilt when Kate's shoulders start heaving, when Amy and Ayesha look at each other, panicked. Kimberly remains barbed with humiliation.

'But,' Siobhán says, and she wonders what she might say next. 'Presumably,' she says, 'whichever parent you stole these from will have noticed already, so maybe I'll let them have their own chat with you. Maybe this time I don't contact them.' Four pairs of shoulders relax a little. 'Provided,' Siobhán says, 'you guys stop being so stupid, stop messing me about, and stop embarrassing yourselves.'

Now that she's given them a reprieve, she feels justified in

being more acerbic. 'Catch yourselves on,' she says with a slight sneer, and Kimberly finally looks like a child.

She bans them from the playground for a fortnight. Kate cries at intervals for the rest of the afternoon, and by the end of the day she looks like an anaphylactic pool inflatable. Amy and Ayesha are humbled and meek, reluctant to draw attention to themselves. It's hard for Siobhán not to placate them, to earn back their joy and enthusiasm – it's hard to remember that she doesn't owe them an easy time. It's less difficult to have resolve when there's an obvious villain. Kimberly picks at her bracelets for the rest of the day, yawning audibly. Siobhán wonders if she might hate her.

By the time the school day is over she feels rattled, and her grimy scalp is itchy. When Sophie wanders into the room she is ignoring the exercise books stacked high on her desk, is scrolling through her phone.

'You see that they're closing the needle exchange on Botanic?' she says.

'Oh yeah?' Sophie sounds tired. 'Why?' she says.

'Doesn't say, but probably the bouji cunts are upset at the prospect of addicts encroaching on their gentrification.'

'Like closing the exchange is a solution to anything,' Sophie says, leaning on a table and rubbing her temples.

'Right? This city is a fucking shitshow when it comes to class-blinkeredness.' Siobhán grimaces at her phone, then looks up, notices for the first time Sophie's navy puffer coat. 'Hey,' she says. 'What happened to the trench?'

'You wouldn't believe the afternoon I had yesterday,' Sophie says, and she moves her scarf to one side and scratches at her freckled chest.

'What happened?' Siobhán says, her eyes roving back to her phone screen, where a message from Andrew has appeared: *Happy Birthday, sweetheart! Hope today has been okay. Can't wait to see you tomorrow xxx.* She replies, *I'm SO excited to see you*, and he says, *I've made a booking for 7, but my meeting should be over by 5, so drinks before?* She says, *Perfect*, and he goes offline. She hears Sophie say, 'And by the time the ambulance got there, she was completely hysterical.' Siobhán hasn't heard anything that preceded it.

'I hope she's all right,' Sophie continues. 'Eventually she said something about a sister, so maybe they were able to contact her. Like you said, mate, Belfast has zero infrastructure for the vulnerable.'

Siobhán tries to come up with something that will imply she's been listening. 'Jesus,' she says, eventually.

'I know,' Sophie says. Another pause.

'And the coat . . .' Siobhán says.

'The rip isn't too bad, thankfully.'

'I'm sorry.'

Sophie laughs. 'It was the *least* of my worries,' she says.

'Still, it's a great coat.'

'Yeah, well, the guy in the repair place said they should be able to fix it, so hopefully it'll be all right.'

Outside, the wind is a high-pitched cacophony.

'I'm going to head home,' Sophie says. 'You coming?'

'I might grab a taxi.'

'Sure, why not – if not on your birthday, then when?'

'Exactly.'

Sophie leaves, and Siobhán loads the exercise books, one at a time, taking note of each name in turn, into a carrier bag. She tips the taxi driver half of what the brief journey costs, and when she gets into the foyer she realizes she left the gift bag containing Sophie's card and present on the back seat. 'Fuck,' she says, but is too lethargic to phone the taxi firm. There's a parcel propped against the wall under the postboxes. She takes it upstairs and finds a pair of gold earrings, John Ashbery's *Collected Poems 1956–1987* and a card. She opens the book several times at random, reads a line then reads it again, then again, forces herself to try and grasp each word as it happens, tries to retain that grasp as the next word comes. She tries to find herself in the poem, can't; can't find much of anything in the poem. She wonders if maybe she's not meant to understand it, then wonders if wondering this is an easy way of exonerating herself of stupidity. She's never really known what to do with art that doesn't have at least a glancing familiarity. She feels like an idiot, feels like she's disappointing him. 'You're a fucking idiot,' she says aloud. She reads 'Idaho', then takes the book to bed, falls asleep with angry tears in her eyes.

She wakes at 7 p.m. with a headache. Her sheets have that day-slept smell. She loosens her hair from its rhizome and takes two paracetamol and two ibuprofen. She stands still under burning water and waits for the tablets to kick in, then sits at the kitchen table in her knickers and two jumpers with sodden hair and an enormous glass of red wine. She shoves her hair down the neck of her jumper to let it dry against the broiled skin on her back, and to stop it dripping on her laptop keys, which betray their years of accumulated finger grease under the kitchen lights. She downloads some worksheet templates, groans aloud at their tedium, and starts to make her own, manoeuvring awkward clip art around text boxes and grids. She tries to achieve an automated, hive-mind industriousness. By the time she's finished her hair is dry and the flat is warm – she pours more wine and bounces around, then puts so much moisturizer on her legs that her skin feels like panna cotta. Her phone vibrates.

My wife is being really difficult – she's giving me a hard time about leaving her with Ellie tomorrow.

Siobhán stops bouncing. She contemplates putting her phone in the microwave. She contemplates not engaging.

Oh, she replies, engaging.

Sorry, sweetheart. I'm just whining.

'Yeah, you are,' she thinks. *No, you're not*, she says.

I feel bad leaving Ellie with her when she's like this. I know she'll just sit her in front of the TV.

'Why'd you have a child with someone so difficult?' she thinks. *Yeah*, she says.

He's typing. He stops. He's typing. He stops. Siobhán goes again.

We could postpone if you want? If you need to go home after the meeting. 'I'm a stupid, weak, obsequious wanker,' she mutters aloud.

He's typing. He stops. He's typing. *I'd really like to see you*, he says, and she adores him again. She'd forgive him anything; take anything he was willing to give her.

Me too, she says.

I'll figure it out, he says.

I love you, she says.

A pause.

I love you too, he says.

She sets her phone on the table and yells into her sleeves.

Something she's discovered is that when a relationship functions primarily through messaging a sensitivity develops to intuited signs and signals, newly perceived to be coded or sinister. Early in their relationship Siobhán discovered she had a new attitude towards the word 'too'. It became something malevolent. If she said, 'I love you,' when they were equally jubilant with adoration, she could expect in response, 'I love you, Siobhán,' or 'I love you, sweetheart.' If they'd had a difficult conversation, she'd say, 'I love you,' but receive 'I love you too.' 'Too', for Siobhán, became representative of coercion – of words said with reluctance, words forcibly extracted. She's never told him about this – he'd deny it – but she knows. She knows what 'too' means. It's a monument to the threat her presence poses; a threat to his once-held perception of himself, to his daughter's nuclear-family happiness. A threat to the life he's built.

She folds a short black dress into a tote bag, throws on top the earrings he bought her and a nude-coloured bra that looks like a birthday cake. It's a good day at school – the lugubrious weather has broken. The air is fresh, rather than brothy. The kids are in high spirits and after first break Siobhán brings out the papier-maché Iron Man and they coo over it. They've brought in their own dolls and she splits them into groups for embalming. Amy and Ayesha and Kate are ingratiating and deferential, and when they return from eating lunch to resume their sentence in the classroom Siobhán chats to them, keen to show that she doesn't like them any less. Kimberly hasn't shown up today, and there's an atmosphere of relief.

When school ends she locks herself in the staff toilet and goes over her armpits with a razor and dabs between her legs with a damp paper towel. She changes into her frilly bra and her black dress. She gets the bus into town rather than walking, gets out at City Hall and stops for a moment to watch the light catch the great windows and the mullions. She strolls into the Cathedral Quarter, which bears an eclectic mix of walking tours and hen parties on beer bikes, young professionals in office attire and students in padded coats. She installs herself in a bar off Hill Street, trying to maintain good posture on a stool in a crevice. She orders a vodka soda and flips through Elena Ferrante. At half four her phone vibrates.

Leaving the meeting now. See you soon, sweetheart x

This is the moment she wishes she could live in.

Things go fast, like always. He arrives, fidgety and affectionate. The bar and its contents beyond their table collapse and shrink till their moment feels solipsistic and spotlit.

'Hi, sweetheart,' he says, sitting down. Siobhán smiles at him.

'Know what I really love about this book?'

He laughs. 'Tell me,' he says.

'That bit at the end where she references the title and it's set up as a twist – psych! It was the other one! The other character! *She's* the brilliant friend. Not the one you thought! Twist!'

'I think that actually happens in the second one too.'

'No way.'

'Yeah, although it's less brazen.'

'I love it when films do it. Like at the end of *Mission Impossible*, when Tom Cruise says, "Turns out some missions truly are impossible."'

He decides to participate. 'Or in *Con Air*, when Nicolas Cage says, "I thought I could con anything, but the one thing I couldn't con was air."'

'Or in *War of the Worlds*, when Tom Cruise says, "Turns out some missions truly are wars of the world."'

When they finally stop laughing he puts his hand on her knee for a moment and she feels it everywhere.

'I always get Nicolas Cage and John Cusack mixed up,' she says.

'Nicolas Cage is the one in the Bad Seeds.'

'Oh – and John Cusack is the one who wrote *On the Road*.'

'Spot on. John Cusoac.'

She tells him about Mark's novel, and he laughs. She feels a little guilty, but not enough to counteract wanting to be entertaining. 'God,' Andrew says. 'Young male arrogance is truly astounding.'

'I think he thinks I'm less capable because I decided to actually teach. I think he, like *so* many people, thinks teaching is a conciliation when your dreams come to nothing rather than an actual aspiration in and of itself.'

'Then he's an idiot, because you're the one doing an objectively arduous and worthwhile job while he's writing what, to be honest, Siobhán, sounds like a truly execrable novel.'

Siobhán likes it when he disparages other people, when he makes her feel like she's better and more special than they are. She tries not to make it a topic she deliberately leads him into, but sometimes she can't help it. Sated, she moves the conversation on.

'I've been rereading *NW*,' she says.

'You know, I still haven't read it, which is awful of me,' he says.

'Oh my God, it's incredible,' Siobhán says, and she does a deep inhalation. 'The way she experiments with form to explore the relationship between, like, the female body and time is just so clever. The pressure Leah feels to get pregnant, and how Smith halts the flow of the narrative, which becomes, like, mimetic of time itself, like, passing. I guess if you think about it, the thingness of a novel is indebted to forward motion, so to try and thwart this there are these moments where Smith does these, like, visual corruptions of, like, the propulsion of a paragraph.' Siobhán pauses for breath. 'I don't know,' she says. 'Maybe that's nonsense – I might be talking nonsense.'

She's always meticulous in undermining her own opinions, especially when she's the less knowledgeable one. If *she* raises the possibility of her own stupidity, there's no satisfaction for the person thinking it.

'You're not talking nonsense at all!' he says, and he rubs the palette of her knee with his thumb. 'I'm really interested,' he says. Newly bolstered, she continues.

'And,' she says, 'then there's this whole bit for Natalie's section that's, like, an embedded Bildungsroman, and it's all tethered to Kierkegaard's idea of the Moment, because Smith labels one of the sections with, like, a Google url, and the result is Kierkegaard, and the Kierkegaard thing is so interesting, because instead of a moment of religious epiphany, Natalie's moment is her achieving orgasm on a train, and it's all just so cleverly done and . . .'

She trails off. The hotness in her cheeks starts to dissipate. She thinks she's delivered an at least semi-coherent précis of the undergraduate dissertation she found online and committed to memory. She wants to demonstrate that she's not reducible to young and silly – she can engage with him on a professional level. She's not just a holiday from the serious demands of his life, she can be everything to him, a source of sexual pleasure and intellectual edification. She glances coyly up from her glass. He's smiling at her, beatific.

'I'll have to read it,' he says. 'I love different takes on the Bildungsroman.'

'Me too,' she says, trying not to think about how she'd tried, on his recommendation, and failed, to read *Tristram Shandy*.

They're drinking too much. She feels her head becoming bleary, but with the bleariness comes invincibility, an unwillingness to slow down. At dinner they have a bottle of white wine, and cocktails. They ad-lib about Mark's novel, growing increasingly cruel, laughing wetly. He leans over to place his forehead on her shoulder. She loves their smugness – how they devolve into callbacks and self-referentiality. She likes being part of an entity that would irritate her were she not in it – it makes her think that most irritation probably stems from jealousy, wishing you had someone to be cruel with. She forgoes the last morsels on the plates. He pays the bill.

On the walk from the restaurant to another bar he pulls her into the aperture between two buildings and they kiss like thirsty dogs. He puts his hand up her dress and she puts her hand between his legs. He moans audibly. It starts to rain and he pulls away. They pant.

In the bar they order another bottle of wine. Siobhán pays this time. He lets her kiss him, even though the bar is well lit and busy. At last orders, they leave. It's a half-hour walk back to Benson Tower, but the rain has stopped. She's unsteady on her feet, and he takes her hand.

Five minutes from her flat, she turns.

'Would you have come to see me today if you hadn't had a meeting?' she slurs.

His face goes anguished.

'Sweetheart,' he begins.

'Why does it take for you to have a meeting for us to see each other? Why wouldn't you come just because you wanted to – why do you need an excuse?'

'Siobhán, you know why; you know how difficult this is for me.'

'Do you not want to spend time with me? Is that it?'

They argue in the street. She raises her voice – he half raises his. He's less drunk, more coherent. He shows her that she's being unreasonable, so she backs down. She cries, then apologizes. She apologizes again, and again. He forgives her. They stumble into her flat. They have sex that she can only half remember as it's happening: blurry stills of him on top; the indistinct canvas of his forehead as he leans over to kiss her neck; the cilia fibres of the pillow as he enters her from behind.

LILY

On Tuesday night she listens out for Siobhán's return. After midnight, she hears shouting in the street. She rises from bed like a marionette and opens the curtains. Siobhán is on the footpath below, with a man. Lily wriggles the ill-fitting window in its frame to ease it gently upwards. Siobhán's voice is high-pitched and plaintive.

'You make zero effort to see me,' she's saying. 'If it weren't for little fluke gaps in your schedule you just never would, and I don't think it would even matter to you if you didn't.' She's slurring her 's's, and Lily watches the top of her head sway as she takes corrective steps back and forth. She's wearing a low-cut dress, and Lily can see the jutting twin promontories of her cleavage. The man takes a step towards her and she raises an arm and plants it on his chest. He says something, but the hushed depth of his voice doesn't carry.

'This is *so* hard,' Siobhán says, and her voice breaks. The man's voice resumes its low buzz and he reaches out a hand. Siobhán gives him her bag, then hugs herself while he rummages in it.

'No, I don't *want* to go in there with you,' she wails. He puts his hand to his hair and rearranges it, his other hand hovering with the bag, ill at ease in holding it. Siobhán is sobbing. He moves the mass of his hair from left to right, then drops the bag and puts his arm around her. She acquiesces, and her cries get absorbed by his chest. After a while they both speak inaudibly. He lifts her chin with his hand and kisses her forehead. She allows him to herd her into the building. Lily closes the window but continues to stare out. Her reflection sits atop the view, a dark dough of night with her face pressed on to it.

Siobhán's front door opens and closes twice the next morning. Lily goes to work and sells a teenager with stretched ear lobes an expensive teddy bear and another teenager a Twirl. In the Hope office she files to the soundtrack of Hannah and Marian's typing and sporadic chatter. She wears the same, uncomfortable outfit she wore yesterday, and the day before: too tired to deflect her encroaching thoughts, she commits entirely to the unwavering aesthetic of stagnancy, hoping it will make her feel less. At home she covers the mirrors with tea towels and bed sheets, and it looks like she's in mourning.

That evening she sees Siobhán from across the street, returning to Bnson Twer in her running shoes and leggings and a top that has ridden up and sits in an unflattering loose bubble around her waist. She looks unhappy. Lily watches her tug at her top again and again, then readjust the scrunchie holding back her hair. She disappears into the building, and Lily proceeds to the supermarket. She buys an enormous cabbage, which she realizes she doesn't know what to do with. In the dusk of her kitchen she sets the cabbage on the table, next to the vase with the limp polyester flowers and the porcelain jug. She ruminates over the tableau for a while. The fake flowers' blooms are coral and umber. They nod their flaccid heads. She lifts the curly-paged edition of *Wuthering Heights* from her bedside table.

Her mother said art was a means of experiencing connect-ivity. The idea that your pain could be, if not universal, then at least not totally singular, was comforting, apparently. She said there was an easing to be garnered from shared experience. 'Wait,' she said once. 'Not shared per se, but experienced simi-larly, separately.' She thought the capacity of another person to have depicted a pain similar to your own, to have transmuted it into language, implied that eventually there might be the means for you to process it. 'Oh God,' she said, then, 'I sound like an arse.'

As she moves listlessly from page to page, Lily doesn't feel comforted. She feels aggrieved. The book makes her think of her mother, not just because it was her favourite, but because of Heathcliff's grief. If art makes you think of a per-son but fails to deliver you that person, then where's the comfort?

'I want to be able to tell you that this book's making me think of you,' she imagines saying.

'That's an impossibly high burden to place on art,' her mother would say.

'Sorry, didn't realize you were in the pocket of Big Art.'

'Don't be churlish.'

She wants to tell her mother that she was wrong about art, about its putative comforting properties.

'There's no homogeneity of response to loss,' she'd say.

'Good word.'

'Shut up. I'm still the only one experiencing it, inside me. There's nobody else in here to share the burden.'

'How very solipsistic of you.'

'Shut *up*.'

She throws the book on to the floor, then picks it up and

apologizes to it for having done so. She appraises the yellowed pages.

A real person, asking for empathy, is always going to stay unknowable, because no matter how hard you try to comprehend their pain, you'll always be limited by the mechanisms of your own experience. This is where her vitrol came from, that day with the support group – trying to understand, failing, and losing her own experience in the process. At least the images and characters in a novel don't have a life beyond the one she gives them – the book is hers to understand and control. She hears Siobhán's door open and close above her. She waits a few minutes, then goes upstairs.

SIOBHÁN

Her alarm goes at six thirty. He groans, then stretches, then mutters, 'Hi, sweetheart,' then rolls on top of her. She feigns orgasm as he ejaculates. Her abdomen feels like a cast-iron moulding of a bloated abdomen, and she struggles not to fart. Her head is a cacophony. They don't discuss the argument. He leaves at six fifty-five; they kiss briefly at the door. He says, 'See you soon, sweetheart.' She cries in the shower.

It takes her too long to get ready – she devotes considerable effort to arranging the birthday cards from Andrew and Tara and her mother on her bedside table, placing Andrew's at the forefront. She abandons the others in a stack on the kitchen counter, feeling another pang of guilt at having lost Sophie's. Everything she needs seems to be in the wrong place. She locates a shapeless jumper in her underwear drawer. 'What the fuck was I doing last night?' she mutters, finding her copy of *Charlotte's Web* behind the toilet. She takes a taxi; is rude to the driver; doesn't tip. Her phone stays silent, and she keeps it on the desk, where she can monitor it. At the first break she goes to the staff room and makes coffee. There are no clean mugs.

'All right, darlin'?' Sophie leans against the counter next to her. Siobhán grunts.

'Not monitoring the prisoners today?'

'I asked Theresa to supervise.'

'You a bit down?'

Siobhán grunts again.

'Oh no – what's happened?'

'Nothing.'

'Something's happened.'

'I'm fine.'

'You're clearly not.'

Siobhán scrubs harder at the mug to get the overnight stains out. The water from the staff-room tap becomes suddenly scalding.

'Jesus – fuck!' Siobhán jerks her hand away and cradles it to her chest.

'You okay?' Sophie leans closer.

Siobhán hisses. 'I said I'm fucking fine, all right?'

Sophie raises an eyebrow. 'Okay,' she says. 'Whatever you need.' She sidesteps away, lowers herself to one of the depressed armchairs, eyes Siobhán. Siobhán ignores her and runs her fingers under cold water. When the threat of her tears has dissipated, she turns. Sophie pats the cushion beside her and Siobhán sits. When Sophie produces a packet of custard creams, she takes three. They sit, silently, while others move around them. Siobhán taps her heels against the chair legs to keep the bad thoughts at bay. Too soon, the bell goes.

'Now, my little circles – how did we get on this week?'

The class is split for reading exercises – the circles are the highest level, have been tasked with the first three chapters of *The Lion, the Witch and the Wardrobe*. They sit in a ring on the library floor, and Siobhán watches them frown at the questions on the sheet.

Siobhán has never wanted children of her own, has never

felt the inclination. She loves teaching kids, and she loves *her* kids, because she gets to watch them become cleverer; she gets to watch them learn and achieve and become less half formed. It feels monumental; a privilege to be involved in that. It's less about the children as stationary matter and more about their becoming. To have one of her own, though; to have her body made slack and vascular; to feel it get ripped open by all the grizzle and effluvious straining of childbirth; to sacrifice sleep to constant wariness; to put her own wants second, for ever. She has no doubt that she'd love a baby, if she had one, but it wouldn't be a choice, really. Maternal love strikes her as a kind of parasitic submission – it renders your own unhappiness unimportant, and why would she want that?

She wonders what stage Ellie is at in her reading – if she's a proficient reader. If she's like Andrew, she will be. Siobhán has seen photographs: Ellie's skinny, pale with round cheeks. Neat, chestnut hair like a Benedictine monk. A downturned pout. Siobhán gets the impression that she's clingy, and sensitive. Could Siobhán take that on? Could Siobhán hold Ellie's little sticky hand and lead her to school and pick her up afterwards? Could Siobhán be a weekend mum? Siobhán knows from Andrew that Ellie still wets the bed – could Siobhán get up at 3 a.m., bundle putrid sheets into a washing machine, strip Ellie and bathe her damp little arse? Could Siobhán let Ellie sleep in *her* bed, weepy and grasping?

Kimberly's pencil case is full of lip glosses and Starbursts. Siobhán watches her riffle in Rebecca's for a rubber, her blonde hair sliding across the desk like a street sweeper. Siobhán glances at her phone: nothing. She rubs the back of her neck.

'How old are you, miss?'

199

'Christ,' Siobhán thinks. 'Old enough, Kim,' she says.

'Are you married?'

Siobhán imagines locking her in a cupboard. She inhales, exhales.

'No, Kim,' she sighs. 'I'm not married.' Kimberly smiles, and Siobhán wonders if their dynamic is becoming dangerous.

She buys new headphones on her way home and forces herself on a run that evening. Her lungs turn acrid almost immediately, her muscles lactic and painful. Her Lycra sports top rides up repeatedly till it flaps like a lamprey around her waist. She ceases movement every time her phone vibrates, but it's an email about cheap flights, then a text from Sophie, then a warning that she's low on data. She gives up on speed long before she reaches the embankment, slows to a walk instead, grateful for the dark's concealment. When she gets to the theatre she turns and heads home. On her street she can see someone on the opposite pavement, watching her. She keeps her eyes downcast and tugs at her top, ashamed of herself. The wind is a kettle trapped at the boil.

'Fancy a night on the town, angel?'

Siobhán answers the door ensconced in various towels, her skin still blotchy from her not-run. She feels like shucked Spam. Caz is wearing a long and diaphanous dress that simultaneously conceals and prioritizes every part of her. She fills the hall like citronella.

'I have school tomorrow, Caz,' Siobhán says.

'We'll keep it breezy. A couple of glasses of wine; maybe a nut bowl.'

'You're a nut bowl.'

'If you're resorting to insults, I've already won.'

Siobhán sighs. 'You're not wrong,' she says.

'Yay!'

They arrange to meet in the foyer in twenty-five minutes. Siobhán blow-dries her hair, hastily applies make-up and a dress.

She doesn't remember if her moods were more stable, before Andrew, and if they were, was it preferable? Was the pale life she had before better than her current peaks and troughs? Some days every bit of her feels like it's being ground away against some immoveable surface; others she feels like she would scoop a drowning wasp from a bird bath and feed it sugar water, sing a song about the glories of living. For the first few years, what they had seemed conducive to her success – their love was compatible with her life. Now, increasingly, something is changing. She feels like she's unravelling. In the stairwell she sidesteps the lacuna of walked-in rainwater, buries her phone deep within her handbag.

LILY

She reads the triumvirate of birthday cards on Siobhán's bed-side table.

Dear Shiv,

Happy Birthday, dreamboat! I hope this arrives on time/at all. I definitely haven't mastered the nuances of international post-age yet. I miss you lots, wish I could be there to celebrate. I'll update you on everything in an email (can barely remember how to hold a pencil at this stage) but for now I'll just say: I love you loads.

Tara xoxo

My beautiful Siobhán,

Happy Birthday, sweetheart. I hope you know how much I adore you: you are the cleverest, funniest, most gorgeous woman I've ever met, and I feel so lucky to know you. I hope you like the earrings: in the jewellers' I was asked what kind I was looking for and I replied, 'The kind for someone with holes in their ears.' I'm a real philistine, Siobhán. This book is one I go back to often. 'The switches had been tripped, as it were; the entire world or one's limited idea of it was bathed in glowing love, of a sort that need never have come into being but was now as indispensable as air is to living creatures.' I love you.

Yours,
Andrew xxx

To Siobhán,

Happy Birthday!

Love, Mum

In the kitchen, there are other cards, in a stack. Ones Siobhán hasn't afforded the dignity of uprightness. Lily flicks through them – generalized well wishes from myriad names. She reads them with a growing dearth behind her eyes: an inability to decipher feeling that presents as a hollow feelinglessness. She can't process the information newly available to her. She wonders if Siobhán appreciates her situation, her privilege to turn in any direction and find someone there, arms outstretched. She starts to feel angry, tries to transform it into passivity. She returns downstairs, tries to resume *Wuthering Heights*, feels the waves of her inchoate fury build. She throws the book on the floor again, then eyes the mug with all the bits of her in. An idea arrives. She checks the time, then takes the mug in both hands and slinks back upstairs.

'Promise me you'll make an effort with people,' her mother had said, a week before she died.

Her room in the hospice was softly lit – it got the sun in the evenings, when there was sun in the evenings. Her pain had become unmanageable at home, and the bathroom was too far from her bedroom. From the window you could see the slow progress of the Foyle, its milky edges and cerulean middle. The hospice sat on a grassy hill next to the new bridge, the bridge's apex far above the river's surface. People at school used to say that if you threw yourself from it, it would be like landing on concrete. Once a year Lily would hear the *thwips* of a helicopter and know that someone else had encountered water as solid. In the corridor outside her mother's room she could hear the soft hum of wordless conversation.

Her mother had joked, when it was recommended that she be admitted, that it was for Lily's convenience.

'If I die at home you'll just have to lug me to the kerb on bin day,' she said.

'It feels rude to say this because you're dying,' Lily had replied, 'but please shut up.'

'What do you mean?' Lily said, now.

'You know what I mean,' her mother said. She was sleeping a lot, was tired when she was awake. 'We've had each other, and it's been divine, and maybe I let us get too wrapped up in each other, because we were having such a good time, but when I'm gone you're going to need other people.'

'Other people are terrible.'

'Maybe don't start with that.'

'Fine.'

'Seriously. Don't stop tending to your life, just because I'm not there any more.'

'You're being quite demanding right now.'

'Such is the purview of a dying woman.'

'Poor view? Shall I open the curtains some more?'

'Shut up,' her mother said. 'Promise me,' she said.

'Okay.'

'Good,' she said. 'And that concludes my dying wishes.'

'You should have held out for more. You could have got a jet ski.'

'Gosh, you're right. Hold the promise, bring me a jet ski.'

'Okay,' Lily said, and they said nothing for a while. They watched the shadows in the room grow and shrink and move.

SIOBHÁN

'You're a smokeshow,' Caz says when they're standing at the bar.

'I don't know about that,' Siobhán says. Caz has changed into high-waisted green trousers and a black blouse – she's all bouffant and high glamour in a way Siobhán suspects wouldn't translate into attractive anywhere but here.

'Seriously,' Caz says. 'You look great.'

Siobhán laughs. 'Thanks, Caz. I'm going to nip to the loo, okay?'

Caz winks.

In the toilet she checks her phone. One text from Mark.

What's a gorge's favourite musician?

Siobhán replies. *Go on. Tell me.*

Avril Ravine.

Siobhán groans under her breath. *And he sticks the landing,* she writes.

Nothing from Andrew. She buries her phone again and goes to the sink. The bathroom lighting is gold-tinged and flattering. She puts on more lipstick.

She finds Caz at a table with four men.

'Look! I made some friends!' Caz slides a glass of white wine in front of the one empty seat. Siobhán sits down.

'Hi,' she says. The men smile to various degrees. One already has an arm draped across the back of Caz's chair. Siobhán inspects him – he has a thick neck and thick eyebrows and a slight squint. She'd guess he's in his early thirties. A moment later he and Caz are whispering conspiratorially and the others seem like intruders. Siobhán sips her wine.

'So, what do you do?'

She looks away from Caz, whose hand is now resting on the man's bicep. The man who spoke is sitting next to her, has a small hoop earring and stubble and a tight black T-shirt. The other two are a bald man in a checked shirt and an especially hirsute blond in a bally fisherman's jumper. As a collective they seem incongruous.

'I'm a teacher,' Siobhán says, vituperative.

'Oooh,' Earring says. 'Out on a school night?' The over-familiarity sets her teeth on edge. 'Calm down,' she thinks to herself.

'If you view time for what it is,' she says, 'which is an inherently arbitrary construct, then the assignation of a time frame as being night, or not night, school or not school, is pointless.'

Earring says nothing for a moment, then does a laugh that suggests he wasn't listening. 'Yeah,' he says.

'What's your name?' Bald says.

'Siobhán.'

'With or without a fada?' Hairy Fisherman says.

'Jesus, what are you trying to prove?' Siobhán thinks. 'With,' she says.

'Does it bug you when people spell it without?' he says.

'Of course,' Siobhán says. She pauses. 'Because as the Bible dictates,' she says, 'honour thy mother and fada.'

Bald laughs, and a second later Hairy Fisherman and Earring join in. Siobhán suspects they're already bored of her

207

trying to be funny. She looks over at Caz – Eyebrows is whispering something in her ear. She makes eye contact with Siobhán and preens. Siobhán returns a bemused look. A moment later Eyebrows announces, 'Just going out for a smoke here, lads,' and he and Caz rise, hand in hand. The four remaining at the table watch them go.

'So,' Siobhán offers, 'how do you all know each other?'

'We studied together and now we work together,' Hairy Fisherman says, then names one of the monolithic insurance companies that occupies air space by the water. Hairy Fisherman and Bald work in human resources; Earring in customer service. 'Big Balls out there with your mate works in HR too' – Hairy Fisherman gestures in the direction of the beer garden – 'but he just got a big commission and a grant from the Arts Council, so he's packing it in to be a full-time fucking playwright.'

'Oh, cool,' Siobhán says, and there's a lull. 'So,' she says, 'do you like working there?'

'It's a job.' Earring shrugs, and Siobhán can sense them directing signals to one another, wondering whose approach will win the conversation, and, by extension, her. She settles back in her chair, apathetic enough to be desirable.

They're all in the company book club, they tell her, and she wonders what reaction this piece of trivia is tailored to elicit. She listens to them argue for a while about *Blood Meridian*, and she tries to arrange her face in a way that implies that she's read it but considers none of their opinions worthwhile. She then wonders why she's bothering.

'So,' Earring says, wrenching her from her reverie, 'what's your favourite book?'

'Christ,' Siobhán mutters, under her breath.

'What?' he frowns.

'Nothing.'

'No – what did you say?'

'*NW*, by Zadie Smith,' she says. 'That's my favourite book.'

Earring frowns. Bald smiles. Hairy Fisherman emits neutrality.

'Who's that?' Earring says.

'Jesus, don't embarrass yourself,' Bald says, and Siobhán laughs.

'Have you read *Utterly Monkey*?' Hairy Fisherman says. Before she can say anything Bald interjects again: 'Fucking hell,' he says.

'What?' Hairy Fisherman is defensive.

'You realize you just responded to her telling us her favourite book, written by a woman of colour, by asking if she's read a book by the author's *white* husband?'

'Okay, what are *you* trying to prove?' Siobhán thinks, but instead of saying anything she laughs, in spite of herself. Hairy Fisherman's face goes purple. 'No, but—' he starts, and then he and Bald are shouting at one another over the table. Siobhán sips her wine, tries to keep her face impartial, avoids turning to look at Earring. Suddenly his voice is hushed and humid at her ear.

'You know,' he says, 'I've always found teachers sexy.'

She checks her phone. No messages. She drinks the last of her wine. Earring suggests another. She looks at her phone again, then leans a little closer. She nods.

'Does that feel good?' he says.

She can't really feel anything – the angle is wrong. 'Yeah,' she says, and she turns her head and bites his ear lobe. He groans, and his hand starts moving faster. She adjusts her coat so the movement underneath isn't visible. Groups of girls in stilettos troop past, trying to summon the taxis that roll along the road.

'You're so fucking sexy,' he says.

She purrs into his ear. She's starting to get cold – the stone windowsill they're sitting on is icy and damp. After a while she modulates the tone of her breathing. She jerks her knee and exhales into his ear, makes a whinnying noise.

'Good girl,' he says, and she almost laughs.

At Benson Tower she puts a fiver into his hand.

'Here,' she says. 'Take this.'

'Wait,' he says, and he unbuckles his seat belt. 'Am I not—'

'Oh, God, no – you're not coming in with me,' she says, and she opens the door.

'But—' he starts.

'Thanks so much,' she calls to the driver.

'All right, love,' he calls back.

'Bye,' she says, and she gets out and slams the door and walks hurriedly. She turns back only when she's reached the foyer. The taxi pulls away from the kerb – he stares at her from the back seat, the automated open-door light still illuminated. His bald head is refulgent, glistening at her as the taxi turns the corner. Between her legs feels raw and kneaded.

From bed she phones Andrew. It rings, but no answer. She tries again – no answer. She tries again, and this time the ring gets cut off halfway through. She tries again. This time, there's no ring.

'Hi, this is Andrew O'Kane – I can't come to the—'

'Hi, this is Andrew O'Kane – I can't—'

'Hi, this is Andr—'

She phones Mark.

'The person you are calling is unable to take your call. Please leave a message after the tone.'

'Hey – what you at? Let's party.'

The clock by her bed flicks to 01:28. She meticulously removes her tights then rolls on to her front. She burps.

LILY

'You can't begrudge her having people in her life who love her,' she imagines her mother saying.

'I know. I don't.'

'Really? Because it seems like you do.'

'I just think it's gratuitous. To have that many people. I bet she takes them for granted.'

'I think maybe you know a love is a proper one when you *can* take it for granted.'

'Did you read that on a coaster?'

'No, but maybe *you* did,' her mother would smirk.

'Don't be smug.'

She's woken early by the chaotic spin of the washing machine overhead, and finds herself wondering, for the first time, if Siobhán is all right. She wonders if her ministrations are having too great an effect.

After leaving school she got a job in a bakery. It was owned by a local man who was rumoured to have killed a child in a hit and run. Lily couldn't speak to the veracity of these rumours, but he was always perfectly cordial when she encountered him, and rarely drunk, or in a car. She answered primarily to his wife, Kelly, a woman with cropped red hair who taught her how to use the till, count the float, wave the card machine around when it was malfunctioning. The food was baked off-site, so in the morning Lily would decant pastries into the display case. Occasionally someone would order something bespoke – a lurid blue Victoria sponge for a christening, a lemon drizzle for a retirement.

'Why *always* lemon for retirement cakes?' she posited to her mother one evening.

'You know what they say: when life gives you lemons—'

'Retire?'

'Precisely.'

School for Lily had always been a necessary bureaucracy. She approached it with the singularity of mind necessary to get through her exams unscathed and unpestered, deriving neither enjoyment nor misery from the experience. School was a means of making herself life-compliant, rather than instrumental to some nebulous idea of success. When she told her mother she planned on leaving after her GCSEs, her mother had not tried to persuade her otherwise. 'If I thought this was symptomatic of a poor work ethic, maybe I'd intervene,' she said. 'What matters to me is that you're relatively self-sufficient.'

'And happy, obviously,' Lily said.

'Okay, *greedy*.'

Ellen was more indignant.

'You'll regret not doing your A levels,' she said.

'Why?' Lily said, and because Ellen could only provide a list of things A levels facilitated, things Lily did not want anyway, and things which seemed to have as a primary by-product a greater entrenchment in the system of more exams and debt, Lily considered herself vindicated. What she had always sought, rather than academic success, was an expansive acquisition of meandering knowledge, unlocalized. This seemed preferable to the strategic conscription of information. 'So, what you're saying is,' her mother said, '*maybe* the mercenary narrowing of the great expansiveness of existence makes people blinkered and ensures that everything becomes moored to the meagre circumference around their own narrow mindset?'

Lily looked at her. 'Sure,' she said. 'Why not?'

She loved the quiet order of the job – the tangible gratification of successful serving, the brevity and positivity of customer interaction. She liked the reliability of her wages and the post-lunch lulls she could spend reading articles on her phone.

'La Mancha what?' Kelly said one day.

'Negra,' Lily said. 'It's a black ooze. It's been recurring in Venezuela since the eighties. Before 1992 it was responsible for around eighteen hundred deaths.'

'Goodness me.'

Lily had a penchant for talking to women over the age of fifty. She suspected she lacked the aggression her peers seemed to direct towards middle-aged women, which she attributed to a fear of becoming them. Having no especial attachment to her looks or youth, nor goals that felt time sensitive, she didn't see older women as bleak portents of the future, and therefore didn't resent them. She suspected older women liked *her* because she was clean and quiet.

When Lily was twenty-one the bakery expanded, subsuming the dusty and rebarbative unoccupied retail space next door. It became a café – new staff were brought in and Lily was made Assistant Manager. With her new income she moved into a small rented flat in a newbuild fifteen minutes from her mother's house.

Following the diagnosis, Lily gave up the flat and moved home again. Ellen offered to assume responsibility for the Friday-night dinners, but Lily kept her at bay. To permit Ellen continued access to their lives would have been, in Lily's mind, a betrayal of the situation's gravity. Yvette still came over, delivering lasagnes of increasingly avant-garde flavours ('Is that *duck*?' her mother said once, peering into it), but the dinner tradition fell away. When her mother went into the hospice, Kelly held Lily tightly against her body, told her that she was welcome back when the time was right. The time was never right, because to return would have been to resume a life now missing its key component, to leave the house with only one shoe on, to not know where the missing shoe had gone, to know the missing shoe was gone for ever. Her relationships with the people around her had been made expansive by the prism of her mother's influence. Without her, she lacked variation – she was a concentrated projectile, searing blankly towards nowhere. After her death was a kind of apostasy, which Lily followed up with a new, disconnected existence: one so featureless as to permit her to retreat, undisturbed, into her increasingly indistinct memories.

Those initial encounters with Siobhán had felt like the first nascent steps towards what she'd promised her mother. Perhaps, had her mother not asked it of her, she would have managed the commencement of a new life more elegantly, or even managed to resume her old life. The weight of her mother's posthumous desires seemed deserving of something prodigious, but when it turned out Siobhán had made no space for her in her thoughts she felt even less like a person, and regressed to something curdled, pursuing this course of action that doesn't seem to be fixing anything, that she's struggling to clarify.

SIOBHÁN

She peels her eyelids apart with her fingers, one at a time. The clock says 05:46. She groans, readjusts herself on the mattress, realizes.

'Fuck fuck fuck fuck fuck.'

The blinds and curtains are open. The sky outside is flat and impenetrable. She bundles her foetid dress and wet sheets into the washing machine with uncoordinated movements, puts them on the fast cycle. She takes a shower, leaning heavily against the wall, thoughts waxy. She sits on her knees on the bare mattress, naked, pointing a hairdryer at the tectonic, yellow-toned stain, watching its edges retreat. When it's dry she sprays it with Febreze, then flips the mattress and puts on clean sheets. Tara told her once that adult bedwetting is a sign of abandonment issues, and she can't decide if this fixes anything. She takes the washed sheets out of the machine and drapes them over the kitchen chairs and the too-small jalopy clothes airer. She takes two paracetamol and two ibuprofen and puts on some pasta. It becomes 07:13. Her phone is dead but she avoids charging it. Her hair is still wet when she puts on make-up and a pair of elasticated trousers that make her look bottom-heavy. By the time she gets to school her head is numb from her wind-blasted wet hair and the painkillers. Her mouth tastes like stale wine and toothpaste. She prints out worksheets and draws a grid on the board, fills it with words that have their prefixes missing. Her shoes are hurting. The kids arrive and she smiles widely. Another day happens.

When she gets home she clambers on to the bed on all fours. The clean sheets smell like lavender. She sleeps.

At 6 p.m. she wakes up and charges her phone. It commences a violent mutiny. Four messages from Mark; three missed calls and fifteen messages from Andrew. She opens Mark's first.

On the sauce were you then, mucker?

Sorry, was dead to the world when you called.

You not have school today?

Keep out of trouble, mate x

Then:

Siobhán.

What the hell was that, last night?

You can't do this, Siobhán.

Your calls woke Ellie up.

I had to turn my phone off.

Jesus – why were you calling me?

Were you drunk??

Siobhán, why aren't you replying?

This isn't fair.

I don't have the energy for this – it's not fair of you to worry me like this.

My wife came in and asked who wouldn't stop calling me. Jesus, Siobhán – it's not fair of you to force me to lie to her face like that.

What's going on?

Siobhán for God's sake why aren't my messages delivering – where are you?

Are you okay? This is really selfish.

Where are you?

She replies: *I'm sorry.*

He opens it immediately. *Jesus, Siobhán.*

I'm sorry, she says.

You can't do this.

I know, I'm sorry.

I didn't know if you were dead or not. I didn't know if I should call the police.

I know.

You put me in a really difficult position, Siobhán.

I know. I'm sorry.

You can't just call me when you're drunk.

I know.

You know the risk I'm taking. You know how dangerous this is for me.

I'm sorry.

Are you okay? Did something happen?

No — I was just drunk. I'm sorry.

Christ.

I'm so sorry.

I have to go sort out Ellie's dinner.

Okay.

I'll message you later.

Okay.

He goes offline. She replies to Mark: *Hahahaha — sorry, pal.*

He replies: *You're a rascal, you are.*

I know. Sorry.

Nothing to be sorry for — sorry I wasn't awake to answer. Love me some drunk Siobhán chat.

I'm relieved you were asleep. I definitely would have made a tit of myself.

Ah sure, we've all been there. You hanging today?

Like you wouldn't believe. School was a mission.

Hahahaha, I bet. You about tonight? Mar's away till Monday and I'm bored. We could just do coffee if you're not feeling the booze?

She thinks about Andrew's message – *I'll message you later. Can't do tonight*, she says. *But what about Saturday?*

Beautiful.

At 10 p.m. she's at the kitchen table, staring at book reports and annotated maps. Her phone sits, undisturbed. He was last online twenty minutes ago.

By eleven thirty she has finished lesson plans for the end of May. He was last online fifteen minutes ago. She falls asleep.

She wakes to a message: *My wife's in Derry this weekend with Ellie – I'll call you tomorrow x*. She resists the urge to say: 'If she's in Derry, then why aren't you here, with me?' Instead, she says nothing.

In her classroom she scrolls through the news on social media. A young journalist has been murdered on the Falls Road – caught between freshly radicalized young republicans and the PSNI. She reads the various attempts by British journalists to pathologize the environment, feels the horror of the event's specificity get flattened with each smug and meaningless generalization. This is where Andrew would normally message to say, *You okay, sweetheart?* and she could assume some authority on the matter, some authentic, localized wisdom. Her phone stays silent. She looks at pictures of the journalist, finds that her eyes are getting wet, puts her phone away.

The day passes in some impossibility of frenzied and slow. In the morning Ayesha sets her hand down too heavily on a pencil that has rolled on to her chair. She says, 'Miss?' searchingly, and Siobhán turns just in time to see the tears start – tears of alarm, rather than pain. The bright blue HB dangles from her palm. Amy has both hands clamped over her mouth.

In the vestibule between classrooms Siobhán attempts to remove the pencil. The tip breaks off. Ayesha sees this, cries harder. 'It's okay, it's okay,' Siobhán says. She wipes the small palm with an antiseptic wipe, searches for the embedded graphite with a pair of tweezers. Ayesha flinches. 'It's okay, it's okay,' Siobhán says. 'Keep still for me.' She grasps the dark grey point between the two prongs. It disintegrates further. 'For fuck's sake,' Siobhán thinks. Ayesha peers over her head, her pigtails tickling Siobhán's ears.

'Keep your head up for me, would you, Ayesha? Just so I can get more light.'

Ayesha lifts her sniffing head, then lowers it again. Light arrives on the abrasion, then leaves. Siobhán ignores the irritation of the pigtails at her helix, deposits the shrapnel on the table. She tries, and fails, to get the last piece.

'I can't get it all, Ayesha, okay? Not without hurting you. It's okay, though, all right? It won't do you any harm.' Siobhán straightens up, unfurls the stiffness in her lower back.

'What if I die of lead poisoning, miss?' Ayesha says, and Siobhán stops herself from laughing.

'It's graphite, not lead, Ayesha. You won't die of lead poisoning, I promise. See? It's already healing up.'

Ayesha inspects her hand, suspicious. She looks disappointed.

'Want a plaster?' Siobhán says. 'Just to be safe?'

Ayesha nods, and while Siobhán is digging in the first-aid kit for one sufficiently pretty, the classroom assistant barrels down the hall with Robbie, who has a fresh, wet, chunk-laden stain down his jumper. They disappear into the toilet, the assistant rolling her eyes at Siobhán as they pass. The stiffness in Siobhán's back encroaches on her neck, starts to manifest at the base of her skull. Ayesha says, 'Thanks, miss,' and Siobhán manages a smile.

LILY

Uniformed children board a bus across the street, and she wonders what Siobhán is doing. She crosses over, finds herself among a throng of short people with backpacks and clarinets. They're demure, and happy, like kittens. She understands the appeal of being around people like this. She emerges from the fog of small acolytes.

'Happy Friday!' Hannah says.

'Happy Friday,' Lily intones tonelessly. She's proofreading a newsletter. 'Weird, isn't it,' she offers, 'how language is so mutable and terms so generalized that you wouldn't know most of these words had anything to do with charity work?'

Hannah laughs. 'You hungover or something?'

'No.'

'I have painkillers in my bag.'

'I'm fine.'

Hannah rolls across the floor, fluvial on four wheels, plants her elbows on Lily's desk. She balances her chin on her cupped hands. 'Would you do me a favour?' she says.

Lily doesn't look up. 'Probably,' she says.

'If I email them through to you, would you submit some permit applications?'

Lily turns. 'That's not so much a favour as it is literally one of my responsibilities,' she says.

'So' – Hannah sucks out the 'o' – 'is that a yes?'

'Yes.'

'Thanks, pal.' She scooches, then reverses. 'Actually, though, would you *actually* do me a favour?'

'Still, probably.'

'Eat some of these.' Hannah sets a packet of fairy cakes on Lily's desk. 'If you don't, I'll just eat them all, and I have some very serious plans to become beautiful before summer.'

Lily liberates a fairy cake. It has marigold sponge and rose-coloured icing. 'You're already beautiful,' she says flatly, inspecting the individual pixels of cake. Hannah squeals. 'Thanks, mate!' Lily looks at her, then returns her eyes to the screen. When she opens her browser there's news of an actor's wife's untimely death, and she clicks on the piece and scrolls through the various saccharine soundbites.

When she reads a tribute online from a person's spouse or relative lamenting their death, she wonders at the almost surprised tone of it all, wonders why people aren't thinking more throughout their lives about the outcome's inevitability. Why get close to someone who will only leave a them-shaped chasm almost as soon as you've decided to place them at the centre of your life? People's blithe capacity for love, in spite of their appalling, built-in obsolescence – it's infuriating. She closes the article.

'Awful, isn't it?' Marian is saying. 'So young, such a waste?'

'I reckon this is a sign of what's coming,' Hannah says. 'Activity like this is never a one-off.'

'I hate to see young people getting caught up in it?' Marian says. 'As either victims or perpetrators?'

'It's all going to kick off,' Hannah says. 'I bet you. It's Brexit – it's throwing this place right back into conflict.'

'He was so young?' Marian says softly, and Lily can hear wetness in her voice.

'This is how it starts,' Hannah says. 'Just you wait. The problem is—'

Lily tunes out again, unwilling to ask what they're talking about, unable to decipher it from the vagary of their contributions.

Uniformed children disembark a bus in front of her and she finds herself once again with a small throng. She turns into Elmwood Avenue and falls into step behind two women, arm in arm. They turn into a restaurant with a fairy-lit awning, and after they disappear into the portico they reappear through the restaurant's glass front. They exchange hugs with an older woman, already at a table. Lily walks on, deciding, without deciding, not to go home. Eventually she sees a sign that says 'Walk-ins Welcome' and it's sufficient to lure her inside.

She likes the cape – its forgiving expanses. Underneath she could be anything. She's a severed head placed on top of a rock as a warning to pirates.

'So' – a man with skin like a chopping board eyes her in the mirror – 'what are we doing then?' He weighs up her wet hair in her hands.

'A bit off the length?'

He laughs. 'That's the usual order of business. How much?'

'Two inches?'

'Yeah?'

'Or maybe three?'

'Whatever you're feeling.'

'I guess the thing about hair is, it grows back.'

'That it does.'

'So maybe four?'

'Sure, you don't want me to shave the whole thing?'

'Not after you've gone to the trouble of washing it.'

He laughs again.

He asks if she has any plans for the evening. She doesn't want to debase his question with the inadequacy of her truth. 'Yes,' she says, and he raises his eyes encouragingly. 'I'm having dinner with my mum and my best friend. It'll be their first time meeting.'

'Lovely,' he says. He holds a mirror up to the back of her head. It could be the back of anyone's head.

SIOBHÁN

'All right, mate? Feel like I've barely seen you this week.' Sophie hands her a KitKat, then props herself against the doorframe.

Siobhán locks her phone, then gestures non-committally to the girls sitting behind her. Rebecca had asked if she could get visitation rights, and Siobhán had relented. She's sitting next to Kimberly, although Kimberly seems more focused on defacing Rebecca's pencil case with felt-tip. Ayesha, Amy and Kate have formed a coven, are giggling over a wordsearch. Ayesha's graphite trauma is seemingly forgotten – she gesticulates, enthused. Rebecca says something, which Kimberly ignores. She glances at the triumvirate next to her, who remain giddy and insular. She looks down at her lap, and her face is worried and uncertain. Siobhán makes a mental note to monitor the situation, then turns back to Sophie. 'Been guarding the prisoners, mostly,' she says.

'Learned their lesson?' Sophie says.

'Hard to remember what the lesson was,' Siobhán says. 'Don't smoke? Or don't get caught smoking?'

'Don't pull at that thread,' Sophie says. 'You'll bring the whole disciplinary model down around us.'

'You ever read that Kafka story, "In the Penal Colony"?'

'No? What's it about?'

'Oh,' Siobhán says. 'God knows.'

Sophie laughs. 'Okay,' she says.

'You know,' Siobhán says, 'when I was like, fifteen, I once told a friend of mine, whose sister had diabetes, that it seemed to me like there was no condition worse than diabetes – that I would rather be diagnosed with almost any chronic condition other than diabetes.'

Sophie frowns. 'What does this have to do with Kafka?' she says.

'Oh, sorry, nothing – this is a separate thought.'

'Right.'

'And I said this, to this girl, whose sister had diabetes. I talked about how horrible diabetes seemed, and the mad thing is that at the time I didn't know whether her sister had type 1 or type 2. I didn't even know there *were* two types of diabetes.'

Sophie laughs again. 'Why are you telling me this?' she says.

Siobhán sighs. 'Just,' she says, 'it's something that came into my head today. An example of me running my mouth off about something I had absolutely no clue about. I'm just reflecting on it today as a means of torturing myself, I guess.'

'So, it's one of those days,' Sophie says.

'Something like that,' Siobhán says. Behind her the girls are cackling at something. 'You ever hear that theory,' she says, 'that guilt is in response to a specific stimulus, a wrong you've done, but that shame happens because of some non-specific, pervasive self-disdain and then we build the narrative around it to try and justify our feeling it?'

Sophie raises an eyebrow. 'Can't say I have heard that,' she says.

'Hmm.'

'So,' Sophie says, 'any plans for the weekend? Maybe a trip to the *penal* colony? Wink wink.' She winks.

'Ha ha,' Siobhán says, instead of laughing. 'Nothing much,' she says, and she slumps against the wall. She sighs. Sophie looks at her for a moment.

'Tragic about that fella on the Falls, isn't it?' she says quietly.

Siobhán nods, once again finds herself feeling precipitously congested. She hastily wipes her nose with her finger.

'You seen the "discourse" about it yet?' she says, performing air quotes, and sneering.

Sophie laughs. 'Yeah. Some real hot takes.'

'Sure, when literally all our problems started in 2016.'

They say nothing for a while. Sophie gives her forearms a rub. 'Want to stay late tonight and get some stuff done?' she says. 'We could go for a drink after?'

Siobhán thinks of her phone – of the still-unfulfilled promise of a conversation with Andrew. 'Not today,' she says. 'I just want to go home and sleep.' Sophie looks disappointed in a way that makes Siobhán think she ought to ask how she is. She doesn't, though, and they stand in silence till the bell rings.

He doesn't contact her that night. She paces heavily around her flat, her ululations a distraction from work, then a soundtrack to it.

LILY

She's woken at eight on Saturday by muffled music. She listens to Siobhán stomping across the kitchen. She sits up in bed, monitors the movements. The same song gets played again, and again. Lily gets up, dresses. She leans against the counter, eating biscuits, waiting. At eight fifty, Siobhán leaves. Lily waits five minutes, then leaves too.

She isn't someone on whom rushing looks natural – her legs are too short, and the little heels on her boots, along with her small, harried steps, make her look like a Shetland pony. At the bus station, Siobhán goes to the shop, and Lily plants herself on a bench. Siobhán emerges, goes to stand eleven, boards the bus. She goes upstairs, so Lily stays down. The bus pulls away from the kerb.

They arrive in Derry, two hours later. They cross the blue bridge, looping around the roundabout with the two out-stretched figures whose hands never touch. They sweep along the river – the wintry sun on its surface is aurous. Lily wants to point things out to Siobhán: the footbridge she and her mother would walk across to get to the hotel by the river where they'd drink cider on Saturday afternoons; the theatre where they once went to see the pantomime at Christmas. Afterwards, they met Yvette in the foyer, who, when asked how she was, shouted, 'I'm a poster girl for leaving your husband!'

The bus rolls into the station forecourt. Lily waits until Siobhán has disembarked, then follows. She almost loses the glossy head among taller people but then retrieves it. Siobhán gets into a taxi. It drives off.

In films people can get into a taxi and say, 'Follow that car!' Lily watches the car reach the end of the road, turn right, then vanish. She starts pursuing on foot, realizes she doesn't know where to follow it to. The world ceases with the limit of her eyeline. She stops, pivots, walks, stops.

Her mother preferred the train. She couldn't wait to turn sixty, to get her travel pass and navigate the country for free. One day, they went to Whitehead. The sky was pale blue with mottled white in one direction, platinum in another. They got chips from a white-walled chippy in town, then walked to the water, past the terraced buildings, painted yellow and green and orange and blue and mint. Her mother had her swimsuit on under her trousers, so she stripped off and went for a swim. Lily sat on a wall eating their chips. There were children learning how to sail, and the shallow water was a consommé of small bodies. Her mother finally emerged, slick like an otter, and Lily handed her the towel.

'Did you know,' her mother said, conjuring a shell from somewhere, 'that it's not the sea you can hear inside a shell? It's just the sound of air in a cavity, which happens to sound a lot like what we understand to be the noise of the sea.'

'I did know that,' Lily said.

'Really?'

'No.'

They meandered back through town, and behind a café a gazebo had been erected, and people were reading poems inside. They went in and sat for a while, listening. The rain started, and more spectators bled in. 'Poets must like the rain even more than ducks do,' her mother whispered.

'Why would ducks like the rain?' Lily whispered back.

'Shh. You're embarrassing me in front of the poets.'

A man stood up to read, and the rain inveigled its way in through a narrow fissure in the tent's roof. Droplets landed on the sound equipment and the microphone began to crackle and sputter. When he said, 'Let me see if I can just fix this here—' and reached for a wire, several people in the audience shouted, 'No!' in unison. He jumped back, shaking his hand. 'Ooh,' Lily's mother said. 'Now it's a pantomime as well.'

She tries to sleep on the bus back, but she can't. She watches the white-hatted hills in the distance; reads the pro-life signage strung around lamp posts in Dungiven; crosses her fingers as they glide over Toome Bridge. As the bus soars over the M22, Divis Tower comes into view. The middle-aged woman across from her takes a can of pre-mixed gin and tonic from her bag, taps the tab twice with an acrylic thumbnail, then clamps it to her open mouth when an arc of white foam spits sideways. The bus pulls into the station, and the twenty-minute walk home takes her an hour.

The first thing she smells, on entering Siobhán's flat, is vanilla. Siobhán has left two candles lit, in the living room-cum-kitchen. They're melted to their last millimetres. Lily looks around, nervous, but there's nobody there. She blows the candles out, and the vanilla is accompanied, then, by the sonorous odour of smoke. She turns on the light and glances at her surroundings, feels a prickle of anxiety at how much more into disrepair the flat has fallen. The candles sit in their pots on old, ossified stains. She remembers how she pictured it, before she was ever here: the fleshy plants, stretching. Now, there are bed sheets draped over chairs and a broken airer leaning against the wall. The cream, elasticated sheet has a permanent, yellowing stain at its centre. There are piles of exercise books and printouts on every surface, and when she peeks into the bedroom the curtains are closed and the bed is unmade: the duvet is bunched to one side in peaks, like a mountain range. The books on the shelf have listed to one side: *NW*; *Tristram Shandy*; John Ashbery's *Collected Poems 1956–1987*; *The Secret*. In the days since she was last here, the place has deteriorated. What had seemed the slightly dishevelled, chaotic arrangement of someone busy and fulfilled has become a place of abandonment and decline. There are empty wine bottles by the bed and a half-empty packet of ham slices on the floor. Clothes lie crumpled across surfaces. She returns to the kitchen, looks at the spilt cereal on the counter. She stands among the detritus of an unhappy person.

'So what was the plan here, exactly?' she imagines her mother saying.

'I would have thought that was obvious.'

'Explain it anyway, for the simpletons.'

'I make her life worse for a while, then, when I think it's had the desired effect, I stop. She's an inconsiderate person, and these vicissitudes—'

'Good word.'

'Shut up. Anyway, she'll be a reformed character.'

'And what was the thing with the mug of fingernails?'

'I don't want to talk about it.'

'Are you accepting feedback at this time?'

'No.'

'Because as rehabilitative strategies go, this is maybe some-what ineffect—'

'No.'

'And I'm just wondering if there might be some avoidance strategies happening, and maybe—'

'I said no.'

The smell of something else makes itself known, competing with the moribund candles, and she realizes the oven is on. She opens it, and smoke bursts from three forgotten charred saus-ages in a glass oven dish. She turns the oven off, puts on the oven mitts and takes the dish from the shelf and plants it in the sink. She peels the blackened sausages from the glass gingerly, her fingers burning. She deposits them in the bin, then turns on the tap. Cold water lands in the dish. There's a moment of stillness, and Lily exhales, then: the dish explodes. There's a high-pitched crack, and the dish's form in one instant becomes permeated with fractals. The sink is suddenly full of fingernail-sized slivers of glass, and the brims of the dish tumble over their limits, newly susceptible to gravity. Lily stares at it.

'Shit.'

She plunges her hands into the sink, commences balancing the shards on one palm. The erstwhile dish is still hot from the oven, and she drops the gathered pieces back into the sink. The bits she picked up have already managed to lacerate her fin-gers: small red bubbles appear over her skin. She looks around. A pair of pink rubber gloves sits on the draining board. She pings them on, then opens the cupboard below and finds a plastic bag. Holding the bag with one hand, she places the fragments into it. She's making progress, then: a noise of heavy hail on a ceiling. She looks down – the still-roasted pieces of glass have burned a hole in the bag's base, are now trickling to the floor. She finds another, sturdier bag in the cupboard, swaddles the first, ripped bag inside it, then gets to her knees to retrieve the errant shards. She hears footsteps outside, and she freezes. There's a key in a lock, and the sound of Caz humming atonally as she goes into her flat. Lily resumes the clean-up of the sink, ensconcing the outermost bag in more bags as the hot glass steadily finds its way through each layer. It's a race between them. Eventually she's got it all, and she wraps her jacket around the swaddled parcel of broken glass. She looks at the floor, sees spatters of blood on the cheap linoleum.

'Shit.'

She sets the bundle on the table and wets a cloth, starts wiping. Her hand oozes blood on to the soft fibres.

'Shit.'

She grips the cloth tightly over the cuts. She resumes the clean-up of the floor.

SIOBHÁN

She wakes early, agitated and purposeful, a combination that stunts the completion of any task. She showers, applies too many different products to her skin. She lifts the fitted sheet from the airer, holds it in her hands, then replaces it on the airer. She lights some candles, blows them out, relights them. She pours cereal into a bowl, pours it back into the box and puts some sausages in the oven. An idea forms in her mind, then persists, growing in volume. Eventually, she succumbs to it.

By nine thirty she's on a bus to Derry, mechanically consuming chocolate. She looks up the location of the complex with the bowling alley and the arcade and the cinema and the soft-play area. Eventually, the bus glides past the River Foyle, sidles into the bus station. She checks the route again. She could walk for an hour, or take a taxi. She takes a taxi.

The building is enormous and windowless, making it feel outside of time. She walks in and the sounds of children screaming and pins dropping and arcade games screeching all land at once in a chromatic chord.

'All right, love?' The man guarding the entrance to the soft-play area looks like the sort of man who thinks women are terrible drivers. She wonders where this thought came from, then smiles winningly. 'Hiya!' she says. 'I'm just here to pick up some kids from a birthday.'

He checks a list incarcerated in laminate on a clipboard. He holds the clipboard like it's a watermelon. 'Which name's the party under?' he says.

'The birthday girl's Sorcha. Surname's Darrell.'

'Thanks, love – go on in.'

'Thanks.'

Sorcha is Ellie's cousin. Today is her seventh birthday. Siobhán knows this because Andrew sent her photographs from last year's party at a petting zoo. She knew the location of today's party because Andrew mentioned it a month ago, and last night she scrolled through hundreds of messages to retrieve the relevant ones. She slides on to one of the soft, padded benches that rim the perimeter. She looks around. She finds her.

Andrew's wife is short, slim, blonde. Siobhán's mother has a thing about small blondes – tell her some brief anecdote about a woman and she'll know intuitively that the woman in question is small and blonde. It makes Siobhán laugh, for no reason other than it demonstrates her mother's dogged commitment to correlating negative traits with benign physical attributes.

Siobhán's father cheated on her mother, for six months prior to and two years following Siobhán's birth. The way her mother found out is half funny, half debasing: a friend approached her and said, 'Oh, you've changed your hair back! I really liked the blonde!' The friend had seen Siobhán's father holding hands with a woman in the supermarket, assumed it was Siobhán's mother. Siobhán's primary thought regarding the whole thing is that the canned-goods aisle doesn't seem like the sexiest stomping ground for marital iniquity.

Andrew's wife is fingering her jumper sleeve. Siobhán can see the absence of body fat around her middle. Siobhán wonders if Andrew wanted his mistress to be visually dichot-omous from his wife – soft and padded in the places she's sparse and firm. Perhaps this is the physique achievable when your husband resents your existence, Siobhán thinks. 'I'm unhappy,' she thinks, then, 'I don't have to be kind.' She wonders about texting Andrew to tell him that she is looking at his wife right now. She's always entertaining ways in which she might force him to confront his reality, in case it might spur him to action.

One afternoon, relatively early in their relationship, she went to his office, unannounced. She knew he had office hours and that they largely went unfulfilled, because he would so often spend them messaging her. She was wearing a navy trench coat with only a bra and knickers underneath, the logistics of which she hadn't given enough thought to, as she sat, sweating, on the bus. She trooped over the O'Connell Bridge and on to the unfamiliar campus. The arts building was blocky and brutish and poorly lit, and three times she pursued wrong corridors before finding the right one. When he opened the door his expression was arid, and nonplussed, and she wondered if the trip had been a miscalculation. She wondered if their conviviality was dependent on him controlling when they saw one another.

He offered, stiffly, to take her coat, and when she untied the belt and opened it his face changed. He kissed her, then rotated her a hundred and eighty degrees and fucked her over his desk, and she was so relieved to have elicited a positive reaction she didn't mind that she wasn't quite ready to have him inside her. While he thrust himself against her she tried to imperceptibly wiggle her hips to find a comfortable angle. She inspected the items on his desk and found herself face to face with his wife, beautiful and young in a photo frame. While Andrew moved in and out of her Siobhán memorized the woman's chin-length curls and symmetrical face. The photo must have been taken before they'd exhausted one another.

The woman looks less new, less soft, now. There's grey at her roots and under her eyes. Siobhán watches another mother say something to her, but she doesn't engage. She smiles absently, keeps irritating her sleeve. Siobhán looks into the colour-block maelstrom of the soft playground – there are kids careening down an enormous slide, kids squeezing themselves through padded tubes like peristaltic waste matter, kids disappearing and reappearing in the ball pit. Siobhán can't see Ellie, and not being able to see her induces a kind of proxy maternal worry – a feeling she doesn't know how to metabolize. She turns back and watches the wife instead. She's pacing. Siobhán can sense her anxiety from twenty metres away, and it's inconsistent with the desultory and mercenary egotist that Siobhán has been imagining. Her phone vibrates and she takes her eyes off the woman.

Hey you.

Hi.

I'm sorry I haven't had a chance to message properly till now. Had to catch up on laundry and work.

It's okay.

How are you, sweetheart?

I'm sorry about the other night.

Sweetheart, it's okay. I'm sorry I was angry.

I'm really sorry.

It's okay, really. You just can't really behave like that, you know?

I know.

What are you up to?

His wife is sitting down now. She has removed her phone from her pocket and is tapping at it. The bony promontory of her knee jiggles up and down.

Just catching up on some marking, Siobhán says. *Planning some lessons.*

Your students are so lucky.

Not sure about that – I'm hardly Miss Honey.

Stop it. You're great.

You catch more flies with Miss Honey than Miss Vinegar, although admittedly Miss Vinegar is great for wasp stings.

Hahahahaha!

What are you doing?

I have the new Chuck Palahniuk book to review so trying to get that done while my family's away.

What's the book?

Kind of a memoir – some writing advice etc.

She googles Chuck Palahniuk, then says, *Is it called 'Write Club'?*

He goes offline. Siobhán looks at his wife, who is now talking on the phone – one thin finger pressed to her exposed ear as she tries to listen. Her leg is still jiggling. Her head is bent. Siobhán can't hear what she's saying but she's nodding now, becoming visibly reassured. The call ends and she returns her phone to her pocket. She stands, walks to another mother (who might be her sister; they look similar). She looks up, and she and Siobhán make eye contact, in the way strangers make eye contact – fleetingly, meaninglessly. Siobhán's phone vibrates.

Hahahahaha!

She puts her phone away without replying, and he doesn't

send a second message. His wife is waving in her peripheral vision. Siobhán follows the direction of the wave: Ellie is waist deep in the ball pit, waving back. Something oscillates in Siobhán's stomach, and she stands, then half jogs, hunched, to the toilet. She vomits up various shades of brown, cries quietly into the chemical miasma of the bowl. She books a taxi, and when the driver asks, 'You okay, pet?' she nods silently.

She buys a bottle of Diet Coke in the bus station. Standing on the kerb, she drops the cap, and it rolls into a grate. She chugs the bottle's contents and her abdomen inflates. She remembers the sausages in the oven with a sudden, explosive panic. 'Shit,' she mutters under her breath. She takes out her phone: *Caz, I went out this morning and left sausages in the oven. Can you take them out/turn the oven off please??* When the bus comes she sits in the penultimate row, and after staring at her phone for half an hour, her knee bouncing, she sleeps. She wakes to a hand gently squeezing her shoulder, opens her eyes to the dimming light of Belfast. 'We're here, love,' an elderly woman says.

LILY

She smears the red on the floor into nothing, then balls the bloodied cloth up and puts it in her pocket. She hears footsteps, then a voice: 'Fuck *sake.*'

It's Siobhán, outside the front door. Lily turns, eyes the jacket-wrapped parcel of glass and plastic bag. She hugs it to her chest, takes two steps to the right, one to the left, one back. She glances around, wildly. She darts to the bedroom. Moments later, the key turns in the lock.

SIOBHÁN

Even if all means of measuring time ceased, the sky would always betray the idiosyncrasies of a late-February afternoon. Dark and light compete alongside humid and cold. A maroon hatchback sprays puddle water up her legs on the walk home from the bus station. She checks her phone. Nothing, and no good post either – a bank statement and a notice of construction work on the church one street over.

She takes the stairs two at a time. She feels a rip happen somewhere near the crotch of her jeans. At her front door, she sniffs for smoke, then snakes a hand between her legs. She can comfortably insert her two fingers into a split in the denim, finding the sweaty fabric of her knickers. 'Fuck *sake*,' she says. Her breathing is heavy and uncontrolled. Her phone vibrates and she checks it. A message from Mark:

We still hanging out tonight, mucker?

She inhales, exhales, inhales, replies: *Hey, thrill-seeker. Yes. Pub at 7?*

Excellente.

She scrabbles to find her key in her bag, puts it to the lock, drops it. '*Fuck* sake,' she says again. She bends, hears the jeans open their new mouth a little wider, retrieves the key. She opens the door.

LILY

Siobhán walks through the front door and Lily lets breath out through the narrow perforation in her pursed lips. Under the bed is dusty and occasionally fluffy with tumbleweeds of hair. The package of broken glass sits on top of her left hand, and when she tries to extricate her fingers there's a soft rustling, then a soft crunch. She stops moving. She hears Siobhán say, 'Whoopsie,' then she hears the oven door open, then close, then a cupboard, then the fridge. She tries to arrange her hips to make her position less uncomfortable. With her right hand she fondles a small creature of lost hair, tries to stay calm. A laceration on her finger resumes weeping, and she distorts her elbow removing the cloth from her pocket. Pain shoots up towards her shoulder, and she winces. She buries her finger into the cloth's folds. She imagines her mother's laughter, reverberating off the bed slats over her head.

SIOBHÁN

The flat smells smoky – Siobhán suddenly remembers the candles she lit this morning, now extinguished and melted to their last moments. Caz must have taken care of them as well. 'Whooooopsie,' Siobhán mutters. She opens the oven, finds it empty. She pours a glass of wine, despatches it with four deep swallows, then messages Andrew.

Hi Andrew. I just want you to know that if this is getting too much for you – if you're feeling too guilty or stressed about everything, we can stop. I don't want our relationship to make you unhappy.

LILY

The bundle on top of her hand is warming through its jacket outer layer. Her skin itches beneath it. Her attempts to breathe imperceptibly are proving inadequate to actual respiration, and her head is starting to hurt. She hears the repeated *clink* of a bottle neck on a glass, then a demonstrative, cartoonish gulping. Lily takes this as her cue to exhale properly. The throbbing in her brain recedes slightly, and she glances at her surroundings, at the hairballs and the miscellaneous bits of life secreted under the bed, like her. She wonders, idly, what she'll say, when she's caught. Perhaps she'll say nothing, simply hand Siobhán the former oven dish, then leave. Perhaps she'll say, 'I hope you've learned your lesson.' Perhaps Siobhán will murder her in a pique of fright, squashing the neck of the wine bottle into her neck.

Music starts, and Lily listens to Siobhán's tuneless and arrhythmic accompaniment. That something will happen is certain, and Lily's control over what that is seems so negligible, at this point, that worrying about it seems futile. 'This is it,' she thinks. 'This is what will end this.'

SIOBHÁN

She sets her phone on the table, then opens her laptop and puts on 'I Can't Make You Love Me'. She undresses in the kitchen, humming along forcefully to drown out her thoughts, draping her clothes over the sheets that are draped over the chairs. She refills her glass.

LILY

Lily turns her head to the side, resting her cheek to the floor. She watches Siobhán's bare feet and calves dance sluggishly past the open bedroom door. The bathroom door closes, then water starts. Lily waits a few minutes, counting backwards from one hundred. She inchworms her way forward, bumping her head gently along the bed's underside. When she stands her torso is a mottled grey landscape, the fabric of her jumper ashy with dust. She bends over and eases out the great ball of evidence. It feels like a body: warm and malleable and broken-boned. She hugs it to her chest, then creeps out of the flat. She closes the front door so slowly it's like it's resisting, pulling back. In the hallway, she takes three great gulps of air, then descends the stairs. She carries the mound of shrapnel to the recycling bin outside, and as she tips the contents of her jacket into its depths she looks at the smeared streaks of blood across her hands. She almost wishes she'd been caught.

'You can stop this,' she thinks to herself. The thought doesn't stick.

'You can stop this,' she imagines her mother saying, instead. 'Yeah?'

'Yes, enough now.'

SIOBHÁN

Before she can bring the mascara wand to her eye, her phone vibrates.

Sweetheart.

She replies immediately. *I'm serious. You have enough going on, and if I'm just one more source of anxiety then this isn't worth it. I don't want to make your life more difficult.*

You don't make my life more difficult.

Are you sure?

I'm sorry I've been distant recently. It's not about you — I love you.

I love you.

He starts typing, stops typing, starts typing, stops. He goes offline. She tries again.

I want this to be making your life better — not worse. If you're stressed out about making time for me, then what's the point? If we can't see each other, and if you're not happy, then what's the point?

He comes back online. *Sweetheart.*

Siobhán waits. He types.

Sorry — can I just get this review sorted? I'll message you after, and we can talk.

Okay.

Speak soon, sweetheart xx

She returns her phone to the table, resumes applying mascara. She goes to the fridge and rolls a ham slice into a ball and crams it into her mouth. She eats a spoonful of peanut butter and a spoonful of blackberry jam. She holds them in her mouth, lets the different viscosities mingle. She opens the fridge, eats another ham slice, slams the door. She opens the fridge. Another slice. Slams the door. Opens the door, takes the bottle of wine to her bedroom and swigs from it while she plucks her eyebrows. She inspects her legs, which she didn't bother to shave in the shower. She lifts her foot to the sink's rim and shaves her shins with lukewarm water. Pinpricks of blood appear across her skin.

When she was twenty-two and living in Toulouse she dated an American man. He worked as a chef in an anarchist pizzeria, although he could never explain to her in any satisfactory way how a pizzeria could be anarchist when its business model appeared to conform to the business model of all non-anarchist pizzerias. He described himself as a poet, first and foremost. He would send her the poems he'd written about other women. They never seemed very good: tortured end rhymes and mangled similes, various things described as being the sum of their parts. She was always nice about them, though. His mother was dead.

One weekend, they went drinking. An English girl said, 'You two are a gorgeous couple,' and he said, 'We're not a couple.' He never held Siobhán's hand, said instead, 'I have a rep to protect,' in an ironic, facetious tone that meant she couldn't question it. They split the cost of everything, which she didn't mind, but in bars he'd be fastidious in reminding her when it was her round, which she did mind, albeit silently. She would tell him often how handsome he was – he would tell her that her stories ran on for too long and it made him want to strangle her. After two months he commenced the barely perceptible process of emotional retreat.

A fortnight before she was due to leave she tried to message him, realized from the unsuccessful delivery that he'd blocked her number. She went out with the other English-language teachers to a salsa bar, drank an excess of tequila and gin. She kissed a beautiful girl with braids and long legs, said yes when the girl asked if she wanted to go home with her, then absconded from the bar under the guise of using the toilet. She went to an Irish bar, alone, drank vodka, kissed a man who had a tattoo of a playing card on his forearm. She walked in the direction of her temporary home through still-unfamiliar streets at 3 a.m. She met another man in the Place du Capitole. She accepted a cigarette, then let him lead her to a dark corner and insert a finger between her ass cheeks. She doesn't remember what he looked like, now. She woke the next morning in her cubicle of a flat with the lingering stiffness of having been excavated. For the first time since childhood her bedsheets were dewy with urine, and in her mind an idea arrived and installed itself: that it was her inescapable fate to be unwanted.

She takes a long time over her make-up. She replays Bonnie Raitt, and when it ends she plays it again, then again. She persists with the bottle of wine, taking mouthfuls between making sweeping gestures at her forehead and cheeks with a brush dusty with gold powder. Her phone vibrates on the windowsill.

Hi sweetheart.
Hi Andrew.
I've been roped into supervising another PhD.
Oh no.
Need to stop saying yes to things.
Haha – yeah, maybe.

Hahaha! Maybe I'll do a Nietzsche – bring a horse to campus, hug it, get sectioned.

Then the horse can take over the PhD supervisions.

Hahahaha.

She waits for him to bring the conversation round to the obvious threat of their dissolution. He starts typing.

Any plans for tonight, sweetheart?

She pulls the hand towel from the rail. She balls it in her hand and bites into it.

Meeting Mark for a drink, she says.

Oh, fun! Are you getting dressed up?

A little.

You're beautiful.

She starts typing. *Can we talk about our relationshi*—She stops. She deletes. She restarts. She stops. She starts. *Are you sure you love me?* She stops. She deletes. She starts. *No – you're beautiful.*

He starts typing. *Right – I'd better go get the house in some shape before they get home tomorrow.*

Okay.

I hope you have a really good night, sweetheart xxx

Thanks.

She locks her phone. She divests the bottle of its final contents.

At 6.50 p.m., courgette-headed and uncoordinated, she opens the door. She collides with the shoe rack and both pairs of boots and a pair of patent high heels scatter. 'Shite,' she mutters.

She lifts one stiletto by its heel. White flakes snow towards the carpet.

'What the fuck is this?' she says under her breath. She grabs the other heel. More flakes. She lowers herself to the ground, lands heavily on her side. She picks up one of the flakes and holds it close to her face.

'Is that – is that a fucking fingernail?'

She turns to the rack, methodically takes every shoe and tips it in turn: the running shoes, the trainers, the court shoes. White flakes spill from all of them, and soon the carpet is lightly dandruffed.

'Okay, seriously, what the fuck is happening?'

She looks up and down the short hall – the glow from the bulbs muted and sordid, the carpet the shades of an old fruit salad without the redemptive quality of natural light. She has an impulse to knock on Caz's door, share whatever this moment is with her, but then realizes how it will look, combined with the abandoned sausages. The last thing she wants is Caz's concern. She tries to get up, then hears a schism occur in the seam at her thigh – it grows, an inch, two inches. She sighs and abuses the empty hall, defeated.

'Absolute fucking cunt,' she says, to her skirt.

She walks into the foyer.

'Hi, angel.' Caz is on her way in, brandishing shopping bags.

'Not now, not right now,' Siobhán thinks. 'Hi Caz,' she says, artificially brightly. 'Thanks for rescuing those sausages from the oven – I don't know what's wrong with me, I've been such an idiot lately. Anyway, I owe you one.'

'What's that?' Caz frowns.

'The sausages, in the oven? I texted you.'

'Oh God, sorry, angel – I left my phone at Robbie's last night and I've been at work all day. I'm going to get it back tomorrow.'

Siobhán stares at her. 'You're joking, right?'

Caz laughs. 'I assure you, I haven't touched your sausage.' She winks.

'But you took them out of the oven?'

Caz is still laughing. 'This isn't a fucking joke, you idiot,' Siobhán thinks. 'No!' Caz says, holding up her hands. 'Maybe you did, and just forgot? Maybe you're more on top of things than you think!' she says generously.

'I didn't. I'm not.'

'Well, I guess just trust that someone's looking out for you then.' Caz smiles.

Siobhán puts her hands to her cheeks, pushes them upwards to her eyes. She inhales deeply, then holds it. 'You okay, angel?' Caz says.

'What?' Siobhán scrunches her hands into her hair, then exhales. 'Yeah,' she says eventually. She shakes her head, then turns to leave.

'You all right?' Caz says. Siobhán turns back. 'Thought I heard a bit of a commotion in yours earlier,' Caz says. 'You break something?'

'No . . .'

'Oh! Must have imagined it.' Caz looks Siobhán up and down. Her eyebrows, without pencil, are sparse and the colour of cardboard. Siobhán has the sudden impulse to hit her. She realizes that she is furious. She can feel the mould of a fist at the end of her arm, and it feels natural, some kind of reverse phantom-limb syndrome.

'You off out then?' Caz says.

'Yeah.'

'Might there be room for me to gatecrash? I'm feeling fun'n'flirty, and without my phone I have a very boring evening ahead of me.'

'Please, go,' Siobhán thinks. 'Please, please fuck off.' 'Sorry,' she says. 'Not this time.'

Caz's forehead bunches. Siobhán needs her to leave, to stop talking. 'You all right?' Caz asks again. She takes a step forward, Siobhán a step back. Siobhán digs her nails into her palm.

'So, you got on well the other night then?' Siobhán says through gritted teeth.

Caz giggles. 'You're nearly forty,' Siobhán thinks. 'Grow up.' Siobhán can hear the words in her head. She taps her foot, restlessly.

'He's handsome, isn't he – Robbie?' Caz says. 'He's making me dinner tomorrow. I'm completely smitten.'

Siobhán lets the hatch on her callousness open an inch. 'Bit of a gammy eye, though,' she says.

'Has he?' Caz says blithely. 'I haven't noticed.'

'I guess your attention isn't on his eyes.'

Caz takes another small step forward. She looks concerned. 'You sure you're all right?' she says. Siobhán thinks about the oven, about the missing exercise book, about the myriad things going askew. She shakes her head.

'You just left me with those guys, Caz.'

'Oh, Siobhán! God, I'm sorry – I didn't think you'd mind. I figured they'd be lavishing you in adoration.'

'I don't go out *always* with the purpose of getting shagged, Caz. I'm not you.'

Caz looks wounded now, but Siobhán can't stop. She needs control, needs to emerge the more powerful. Everything about this feels choreographed, and Siobhán imagines the studio audience again, aghast beyond the proscenium. With this in mind she amplifies her performance. She cocks her hip.

'You're what, like, thirty-eight, right? Christ, Caz. Might be time to stop measuring your self-worth by whether you can persuade some guy to put his dick in you.'

Caz is flustered, unsure if there's a joke she's not getting.

'That's not – I don't—' she says.

'You know, I spend a lot of time praying, praying to fucking *God*, Caz, that I don't end up like you.' She can't quite bring herself to look at Caz as she says this. 'Wrap it up,' she thinks. 'I have to go now,' she tells the floor. 'But yeah, might be time to try some self-respect, maybe?' She turns and exits, letting the caustic wind stop her thoughts.

Mark arrives back from the toilet.

'Fucking hell, mate – I was only gone a minute! You knocked that back rightly.'

Siobhán pushes his pint closer to his chair. 'Better catch up then,' she says.

'You going hard tonight then, or what?'

'Why not?'

'Aye.' Mark takes a deep drink. 'Why not indeed?'

When she arrived he'd looked her up and down. 'Bloody hell,' he said. She smiled at him, salubrious. She pictured her phone, at home on her bed, her last message either replied to or not replied to: *I love you. I think you should leave her. I promise I'll do whatever I can to make things easier for you. We'll make it work. I can make you happy. I'll do whatever it takes to make you happy.*

'So,' she says now, 'how's the next great work of fiction coming along?'

'Jesus,' Mark says. 'Give me a minute to settle myself before the abuse starts, would you?'

'I'm serious!'

'You've never been serious in your life.'

'I am interested, though, really.'

He talks about his book, and she lets the beer and wine intermingle in her insides, become cooperative with her thoughts. She watches him relax into his subject matter with growing sincerity. She realizes that she doesn't want him to be ridiculous. She wants him to do well, to succeed. She wants him to unconsciously associate his success with her, with her encouragement, with her belief in him. She wants him to understand her as a catalyst to his success, intrinsic to his achieving – that way he'll never want to be without her.

'I'll read it, when it's done, if you want,' she says.

'Really?'

'Of course.'

'Thanks, Shiv.'

She winks. 'You got it, slugger.'

They smile at each other. She feels in control again. Whatever she wants to happen will happen.

The toilet seat is icy. She folds over on herself and holds her temples between her fingers and waits for the walls to cease undulating.

The barman approaches their table.

'Just so you know, guys, that's us at last orders now.'

'Cheers, mate.' Mark glances up, then back to Siobhán.

She takes a drink. '*Mate*,' she says.

'Not this again.'

'Sorry. *Mate*.'

'You're a dick.'

'So are you.'

'Aye, probably.' They eye one another. He smiles. 'So, Shiver Me Timbers' – he punches her gently on the arm – 'why'd nothing ever happen with us, then?'

She laughs. 'You mean, aside from you having a girlfriend?'

'Piss off – I mean before. When we were studying.'

'Because, Markise de Sade, you're a deeply unlikeable person.'

He laughs. 'That right?'

'Completely. I find you utterly reprehensible.'

'But opposites attract, and all that.'

'Oh, we're not opposites – that would imply that you have pronounced and discernible characteristics distinct from mine.'

'And how is it if not that?'

'You don't have discernible anything. You're a quasi-person. You're human—' She glances around, lips pursed in contemplation. 'You're human white wine spritzer.'

He laughs again. 'Fuck off.'

'You're hand soap, dry skin, steamed milk.'

'You're a dickhead.'

'I know, I'm sorry.' She swallows the last of her pint. 'One more?'

'You got the last one.'

'I know, but I'm being very unpleasant, and you're being very indulgent.'

'True.' He scratches at his chin. 'Go on, then.'

'White wine spritzer, is it?'

'Fuck off.' He's smiling. She sets her hand on his shoulder as she walks past.

'You know' – he burps into the back of his hand – 'when I was in Berlin last year I thought, "Shit, I should move here."'

She has her body angled towards him. They're being held in close proximity by the padded grip of his living-room sofa. She's drinking gin and Sprite – 'Sorry, no tonic,' he'd said. Her thoughts feel like pool floats.

'Oh yeah?' she says. The sofa is deep and chubby – it has partially ingested them, making movement tricky. The only light comes from the fairy LEDs strangling the curtain pole. The shadows under Mark's cheekbones are deep, his swarthy upper arm a half-inch from her cleavage.

'Yeah,' he says. 'And then I thought: "Siobhán should come with me."'

'You want to live in Berlin with me?'

'Yeah – we'd have a good time.'

'What would we do?'

'We'd work, we'd drink, we'd—' He puts his hand on her knee.

'Neither of us speaks German.'

'That doesn't matter – everyone there speaks English.'

'That's the kind of expat hubris I bet they really love.'

'Fine – we could learn German.'

'*Wüstenspringmäuse*, et cetera.'

'What's that?'

'Gerbil, I think.'

'See? We're halfway there.'

'*Weltschmerz*.'

'What's that?'

'Can't remember.'

'Practically fluent!'

'Where would we actually work?' she says.

'It wouldn't matter. We'd do whatever to have money. I could work in a bar or a café or a bike-rental shop. You could

258

teach English. In the evenings I could write stuff – *you* could write stuff.'

'I'm not a writer.'

'You should be – fuck's sake, Shiv, you're cleverer than all of us.'

'*You're* clever.'

'Not like you.'

'Stop it.'

He pauses. 'And you're beautiful,' he says.

She pauses too. 'So are you,' she whispers. She leans forward. He moves his hand and finds the pediment of exposed skin between the waistband of her skirt and the hem of her top. He strokes the nodules of her spine, then applies force to pull her closer. They kiss. His tongue slides into her mouth; it finds hers and they curl like otters. She bites his lower lip and he slides his hand up her back and wraps a fistful of her hair around his fingers. She escapes from the rapacious embrace of the cushions and straddles him. He redistributes his centre of gravity to accommodate her weight on his thighs, squeezes her breast hard. The music has run out and the only sound is her soft, animal moaning, his heavy breathing. She puts her hand to his crotch and finds an encouraging solidity. She widens her stance so he can spread his legs beneath her. There is a creak as his foot nudges the table leg, then a *thunk*, then a hiss. They stop, and he looks past her torso.

'Fuck,' he says.

She falls off him and parachute-rolls back into the sofa's maw. He clumsily gets to his feet. His bourbon and Coke extends through the rug's fibres. 'Fuck fuck fuck.' He disappears, reappears with kitchen roll. She stands and watches, impotent, forcing her skirt down over her hips. He dabs at the stain and she wanders to the bookshelf, tries to make herself less of an extra in the film starring him and the carpet. She chooses a book, turns it over in her hands.

'Really, Mark?'

'What?' He looks up at her with incredulity.

'*The Secret*? You a forty-year-old yoga mum now?'

His hostility cracks, and he laughs. 'Fuck off,' he says lazily. 'It's Mar's.' And then her name is there, in the room, like the odour of a blocked drain. They look at one another – Siobhán is finding it difficult not to sway. She puts her hand to the wall behind her as ballast. He abandons the handfuls of brown kitchen roll and half gets to his feet, capsizes, tries again. She wonders what's going to happen. He finds his way to her. He puts his hands to her hips and pinions her to the wall.

'We need to stop,' he says.

'Or,' she says. She leans forward. His hand goes to her throat. He takes it away. She leans forward. They become a poorly made desk toy – clattering back and forth in tandem. Eventually he mutters, 'Fuck sake,' and kisses her. She puts her hands in his hair. He retreats. 'Shit, Siobhán, no. Stop.'

'Why?'

'You know why.'

'Why are you with her?'

'I – we're good. She's good.'

'*We* would be good.'

'Obviously, but like, what am I going to do, break up with her?'

'Why not?'

'We live together, Siobhán.'

'So?'

'Jesus – what do you want me to say? Do you want me to say I love you?'

'Fuck, what?'

'Is that what you want to hear?'

'Do you?'

'I don't know. Maybe.'

'How drunk are you?'

'Not that drunk.'

'Fuck.'

'You?'

'Me neither. I—' she starts, and in this moment, she thinks she does. In this moment she thinks she loves him, just for wanting her. She thinks she could love him for ever, if he'd just choose her. She will love him for ever, if he'll just choose her. 'I love you,' she says.

'Fuck.'

She leans forward, and his hand returns to her neck. He holds her at a distance, like a Geiger counter. They look at one another.

'Christ, Siobhán. You need to go.'

'Or—'

'No. Let me get you a taxi.'

He leaves the room. The atmosphere in his absence plummets in temperature. She hugs herself, and waits.

The clock by her bed reads 04:41. She opens the fridge. Ham. She wriggles into bed, finds her phone. He was last online at eleven fifty-six. He's read her message. No reply. She tries to call him. Voicemail. Sleep.

LILY

She wakes early, removes the tumescent sponge from the shower and puts it in the bin, along with the rhizome of hair she liberates from the drain. She washes her new, shorter hair with raspberry-scented shampoo, makes a cup of tea and a bowl of porridge. She dresses, then reads the Wikipedia entry for Cardisoma armatum, also known as rainbow crabs, moon crabs, patriot crabs. They're called soap-dish crabs within the pet industry, because of their needing to be packed in soap dishes for transport, to stop them maiming each other. She glances upwards, picturing herself and Siobhán and Caz, and whatever other voiceless people live in this building, as tormented and irascible crabs, sequestered in their individual soap dishes, yearning to hurt one another. She wonders if the crabs feel anything when they succeed.

'Did you know that if the young crabs haven't reached land by the time they're fully developed they just drown?' she imagines telling her mother.

'What a wilful commitment to not adapting,' her mother would say. 'When life gives you lemons—'

'Die out of spite?'

'Exactly.'

At 6 p.m., she decides to venture out for dinner. She checks her bank account, feels nothing at the amount on the screen.

★

The semi-detached house was left in the responsibility of an estate agent. A young couple rents it now. They have a baby. She knows she ought to be grateful for the source of income, to be a homeowner in her twenties, with tenants. She also knows that knowing you ought to be grateful is not the same as gratitude. She wonders if the doctor and nurse next door will leave figs for them this summer. She pictures the couple's face ovals, the pale blankness of their baby's, moving through a house that is changing in increments, that was once hers, that is still hers, but in the way a blood sample, extracted, would still be hers. She won't be asking for it back. She puts on her coat and leaves the flat.

She recognizes Siobhán from the back. Her mass of hair is in a great ball at the nape of her neck, and the hair at the roots is in greasy, solidified strata. She's wearing shapeless plaid pyjama bottoms and an enormous black T-shirt. The bottoms don't quite reach her ankles and her bare feet are shoved into her tightly laced running shoes, her heels squashing the padded backs. She stands obstinately at the front door, and a moment later a man appears with a paper bag of food. Lily thinks for a moment about the Baader–Meinhof phenomenon, wonders if Siobhán was always there, this much, or if her obsession has conjured her.

'It's a bit shit you couldn't come upstairs with it,' she hears Siobhán say. 'This door is always unlocked. Normally the drivers just come up with it.'

Lily watches him blush a little. She approaches slowly.

'Sorry, love,' he says. 'I have a couple of stops to make and it takes a while to get the bike all locked up. We only get paid for when we're in transit, you know? Sorry about that.'

'Whatever,' Siobhán says. She turns and strides forward, and she and Lily collide. Siobhán's forearm ram-raids Lily's chest. Siobhán drops the bag, says, 'Fuck.' Lily makes a low *ooft* sound, then takes a step back. Siobhán bends to retrieve the bag, then straightens up. She scowls at Lily, then leaves. Lily looks at the delivery man, who raises his eyebrows in a collusive way. He holds the door open for her, and when she says, 'Thanks,' he says, 'Nice to hear it from someone.' He mounts his bicycle, disappears into the vapour of rain. She watches him go, rubbing the throbbing spot on her chest, feeling the anger slowly reassemble itself on her shoulders and in her jaw.

'Stay calm, Lil.' Her mother's voice arrives in her head, unsolicited. She ignores it. The amnesty is over. She walks outside. The stars are more like perforations in the sky than entities in their own right. They are lightless, soulless. She heads for the alleys of the Holylands, sidestepping throngs of students foxtrotting around puddles on their way to the bars. She forages till she finds something she can use, and when she brings it home it oozes juice on to the carpet.

'What should I do, after you're gone?' she'd asked her mother.

'Brush your teeth,' her mother said.

'I'm serious.'

'So am I. Keep brushing your teeth. Keep eating, keep sleeping. You don't need to do anything remarkable. Brush your teeth until you feel like doing something more fun than brushing your teeth.'

'And then?'

'Go and live, but remember to brush your teeth afterwards.'

After the funeral Lily went home and stood in front of the bathroom mirror. She squeezed paste on to the bristles and commenced brushing. She stared at herself as she did so, and gradually the individual components of her face divorced one another. She stared at the corners of the eyes of the person in the mirror, watched the rim of liquid grow and then spill. Water and white saliva dropped into the sink. She brushed for she doesn't know how long, and when she stopped she curled her lips back. The teeth were white and the eyes were red.

Now, she has a new triangle of exposed enamel above her right incisor, where she has brushed too hard and the gum has started to recede. It was hypersensitive at first, but now it isn't, and the tooth is still white, but it feels feelingless. More feelingless, even, than her other teeth.

The next evening she goes upstairs once more. She can hear Siobhán inside, so she stands for a while, listening. She hears snatches of one half of a conversation.

'No, I know. Sorry . . . I'm going to this week . . . Not really urgent, though, is it?'

Her tone is exasperated and thick, like she might cry. Lily looks at the object in her hands. She sets it outside Siobhan's door.

'I love you,' her mother said. Another ambient evening in the hospice.

'I know,' Lily said. 'You've said it several times today. You're starting to sound slightly desperate.'

'I know,' her mother said. 'But I think I should keep saying it, so my last words to you aren't something stupid, like "My feet are itchy."'

'Not really the time to think about going travelling,' Lily said.

'Ha ha ha,' her mother said, in lieu of laughing. Her capacity to laugh truly had gone – a by-product of her body's failing.

'You forcing yourself to say "I love you" over and over again seems like an undue expenditure of energy,' Lily said.

'I have to spend all my energy, though,' her mother said. 'Otherwise I won't get given as much in the next tax year.'

'Ha ha ha,' Lily said.

She died two days later, after long, indeterminate bouts of supposedly painless unconsciousness. Her last full sentence to Lily was, 'I wonder if the staff here have a tip jar.'

SIOBHÁN

Morning arrives as toothache. She wakes on wet sheets again, but this time she doesn't get up. She locates the dryer parts of the duvet, wraps herself in them, tries to ignore the fetor. She has three missed calls from her mother. She composes a message to Andrew: *Hey, I know that message last night was a lot but I think there was someone in my flat yesterday and maybe even before that and I'm freaking out. They've been doing some really weird—*

She realizes how it sounds: at best, a made-up ploy for attention; at worst, the admission that she's losing her mind. She holds the delete key and watches the words disappear. She messages Mark.

Last night got a bit out of hand, didn't it?

He comes online, reads the message, goes offline. She closes her eyes and mimics sleep.

There is a scenario that arrives, uninvited, when she closes her eyes. It's the image of what she wants so desperately: in it, she is sitting, anxious, on a sofa, in an open-plan kitchen-living room. A man enters. They've had a disagreement, largely her fault – she's been unreasonable or mercurial or erratic. In the scenario, she's thinking that this is it; this is surely the ceiling on his tolerance. This is the point of diminishing returns on her value. She's thinking about how she might broach recovering from this, how she might endure her impending solitude, when he walks in. He sits down next to her, and he says, 'Come here.' She lies on top of him. He strokes her hair and neither of them says anything. She reaches back and places her hand on the side of his face and he places his hand on top of her hand and despite everything that's happened she understands now that some things are strong enough; some things aren't precarious.

Her phone vibrates. Mark.
I won't be carrying on like that again, just so you know.
She replies: *I figured.*
No response. She tries again.
Want to do something this week? I'll behave, I promise.
No response.

Time sifts through the day's net. She drifts into ravines of unconsciousness. She texts Caz: *I'm sorry about what I said.* Caz doesn't reply. She watches Mark and Andrew come online and go offline, and flagellates herself for wanting such uxorious men. She orders doughnuts on Deliveroo, and when the driver is unwilling to deliver them directly to her front door she swears down the phone at him. The laces on her running shoes are in impenetrable knots, and when she can't undo them she crams her bare feet into the holes. At the doorway she's even more unpleasant to him, and she feels remorseful when she's back in her flat, doughnuts in hand. She eats three, puts three in the bin, falls asleep, wakes, fishes the three doughnuts from the bin, eats two. She gets a message from Sophie: *Heard from the head that the kids have been raving about our papier mash men. We're making the other teachers look like slackers. More lesson planning parties this week? xx* She doesn't reply. She cries, but it feels like obligation, rather than alleviation. Her phone rings, and she answers without looking.

'Oh, well,' her mother says. 'It's nice to know you're not dead.' Siobhán puts her fingers in her mouth to stop herself groaning.

'Hey,' she says at last. 'Sorry – been swamped.'

'Not too swamped to message people who aren't your poor mum, I bet.'

'No, seriously, there's a lot happening. But sorry.'

'What's the matter, love?'

'Oh, nothing major. It's grand.'

'Tell me. Tell me what's wrong.'

'Nothing.'

The silence on the line builds. Her mother breaks it, sighing irately. 'You know,' she says, 'I don't think it's unreasonable to expect a little consideration. I don't ask for much.'

'No, I know. Sorry.'

'Have you sorted out driving lessons yet?'

'I'm going to this week.'

'You've been saying that for months.'

'Not really urgent, though, is it?'

'I might like some help occasionally, but maybe that's not urgent to you.'

'Help with what?'

'Evelyn's daughter drives her to and from the airport any time she goes away; she drives her to dental appointments to save her having to find parking; she helps with the shopping.'

'Evelyn and her daughter live together.'

'I see, so once you moved thirty minutes up the road you were absolved of all responsibility, then?'

'No, that's not what I'm saying – it's just a different dynamic.'

'Yes, it certainly is.'

Siobhán sniffs deeply from the pungent duvet, closes her eyes. 'Was there anything else?' she says.

'There's no need for that tone, you know.'

'I wasn't using a tone.'

'Might be time for you to grow up a little, perhaps.'

'Right.'

'After a certain point I really shouldn't be having to remind you to do things.'

'Okay.'

'You know, when I was in my late twenties, I already had—'

Siobhán hangs up. She eats the last doughnut.

He messages at 10 p.m. She's trying to eat soup while lying in bed, cricking her neck and pouring it into her mouth. She thinks of hot oil over battlements. The lingering dampness of her bed makes her feel like she's in a bain-marie.

Hi Siobhán.

She replies, *Hi.*

You know, if I could leave her, I would.

'Just fucking do it then,' she thinks. She doesn't say anything. He messages again.

Is this getting to be too much for you, sweetheart?

She knows the obvious answer. She knows that she's supposed to say, 'No, of course not.' She types it, then pauses. What about any of this has ever been obvious? She knows the correct answer is also 'No, of course not.' She retypes it, pauses again. Why is her happiness incorrect? She types. She stops. She types. She stops. She types. She stares at the question: *Is this getting to be too much for you, sweetheart?*

Maybe, she says finally.

She's never brought about the end of a relationship – even when she's ceased to be happy, she has always waited for the other person to take the initiative. There's never been anything more daunting to her than a self-imposed reset.

She tells him she needs time to think, and his graciousness makes her want to regress, to promise him her entirety, in perpetuity. She wants to say she'll do whatever it takes to make it work: she'll accompany him to dental check-ups, colonoscopies, the post office. If these are his only free moments, their only opportunities to see one another, she'll take them. She'll do anything for him if he'll only keep offering her his perfect, unimpeachable love. She stops herself from saying anything.

She manages an hour of silence, then messages again. They skirt around the subject, talk instead about a family trip to the famine village he took as a child, coriander, *Crash Bandicoot*. When he goes to bed he says, *I really love you, you know*, and she thinks about liquids versus gases, how gases not only take the shape of their container, they fill them completely. She says nothing for a moment, and by the time she says, *I love you*, he's offline. She takes two ibuprofen and attempts sleep, massaging the distension from her abdomen.

LILY

She lies low in the week that follows. She goes to work, to Hope. Marian brings in banana bread, and the smell of it makes her feel faintly nauseous, but she eats it anyway, and tells Marian it tastes great. Hannah tells them that Laura and Chris broke up, and when Lily says, 'This must be a *shit* time for them both,' Hannah laughs mid-bite. Wet banana and bread attach themselves to her computer screen. Hannah says that it's her birthday soon, that they're both invited to go drinking. Marian says, 'I'm a little old for that, love?' and Hannah says, 'Nonsense, Marian! You're a fox! You're only as old as you feel!' Marian laughs, and Hannah doesn't push it. She says, 'What about you, Lily? You can't use age as an excuse.' Lily says, 'I can't,' but then pauses. 'Wait,' she says. 'Actually, maybe.' Hannah cheers, and Marian smiles encouragingly, and Lily blushes. Hannah passes over her phone, says, 'Put your number in.'

She walks with her head down to and from work, doesn't encounter the woman in the rara skirt and fur coat again. In the evenings she watches Djokovic win Wimbledon, then watches Djokovic win Wimbledon again, wondering with each viewing if there might be a different outcome. She stops herself from listening out for Siobhán, in case Siobhán is listening out for her listening. A.M. and P.M. sit next to each other as siblings, made indistinguishable by the season.

SIOBHÁN

Monday brings no abeyance. There's no hot water – she forgot to top up the gas. She tips her head over the shower stall, rinses the shampoo out of her head with cold. A headache swirls in while she's defrosting her scalp with the hairdryer. Her phone vibrates.

I love you. How are you feeling today, sweetheart?

She looks for her keys, fails to find them, swears, smacks her head on the wardrobe door, swears again. The flat is frigid. She pulls another jumper over her partially damp head. Her phone vibrates. She ignores it. She finds her keys.

She's always pictured her deservingness of love in pecuniary terms. Over the course of a day, if she says something to make a man laugh, or sends a particularly flattering nude photo; if they go on a date and her hair is behaving, or she looks well rested; if they go to bed and she makes him come with her mouth, then she's in credit. At night, after the day's final interaction, the account empties, and the following day she has to work just as hard to prove her worth. If something bad has happened the day prior – if they argued, or she took too long to understand a joke, if she looked dehydrated or flabby – then she starts the day in arrears, has to work that much harder to get back into positive figures. She has to earn her place in someone's attentions.

★

She gets into school in time to distribute exercise books and thirty-centimetre rulers on the desks, then swaddles herself in the blanket and picks comprehension passages. She checks her phone. She has five messages from him.

I love you. How are you feeling today, sweetheart?

Have you thought any more about what we talked about last night?

Are you feeling okay about things?

I don't want you to feel obligated to do anything, Siobhán.

I know this is a lot to ask of you.

She curls her knees to her chest on the chair.

Hey, she says. *Sorry — couldn't find my keys/getting stuff sorted for the kids.*

The ticks turn blue instantly. He types.

How are you, sweetheart?

Okay.

I love you.

I love you. She pauses. *I just don't know if I have it in me to do this, any more.*

Siobhán.

I don't know if I can be with someone I never see. It's too hard.

I'm sorry I haven't been available much lately. It'll get better.

But how, though? You're not going to become any less busy.

I'll make time, I promise.

I guess I just wonder if we should stop now, before we end up arguing, or resenting each other.

I could never resent you.

But when I call you — that annoys you.

It's not because it's you calling, but because of how things are. It's not you, it's never you.

But that's not how it feels.

Sweetheart, please.
The kids will be in soon.
Can you call me? On your break?
I'll try.

The kids are in a strange mood – Siobhán hears Luke and Christopher talking cryptically about a birthday party; Kimberly and Rebecca aren't sitting next to one another. Kate has been promoted, Rebecca relegated to the seat at the end of the row. Kimberly eyes her threateningly, then whispers something in Kate's ear. Kate giggles behind her fingers. They look like malevolent corner-figures in a Renaissance painting.

'Girls, c'mon, get on with it,' Siobhán says.

Rebecca looks miserable. When it's time to go through the answers everyone is recalcitrant. Siobhán looks at Kate imploringly, but Kate stares at her desk. At the first break Rebecca doesn't ask to stay with the others – she trudges out, lachrymose. Siobhán watches her go, then beckons to Theresa, who's bustling past with a four-plug extension cord.

'Everything all right, Siobhán?'

'Supervise the girls, will you?'

'Where are you going?'

'I have to make a call.'

'All all right, I hope?' She can't conceal her curiosity. Her wattle bobs excitedly.

'Yeah, fine,' Siobhán says. 'Won't be long.'

'It *is* something important, though, yes?' Theresa is trying to corner her.

Siobhán adopts the tone of explaining the obvious. 'I wouldn't be asking if it wasn't,' she says. 'I'll be five minutes.'

★

She has two missed calls.

'Hi Siobhán.'

'Sorry – had to get someone to supervise the kids.'

'Oh, sweetheart, I'm sorry.' His voice is quivering.

'You okay?'

'No, I just—' and he breaks off. Siobhán presses herself into the corner of the antechamber between the playground and the corridor. He sobs musically down the phone.

'It's okay, Andrew, it's okay—'

'It's not, though. I don't know what I'd do without you.'

'I'm still here, Andrew, I promise.'

'But you're thinking about ending it, aren't you?'

'I don't know, it's just—'

'You are, and I understand that this has put so much strain on you. It's just, I love you, Siobhán.'

She rolls her eyes upwards to dissuade the oncoming tears. She bites the inside of her cheek and watches the kids outside reverberating off one another like dodgems. 'I love you,' she whispers.

'Please don't give up on this. Not yet.'

'I—'

'Please, Siobhán.'

'I have to go, Andrew. The kids – I—'

'I love you.'

'I'll call you again as soon as I can, okay?'

She hangs up, atrophied. She presses her head to the wall, digs her nails into her palms. Her phone vibrates in her hand. She doesn't look at it.

The rest of the morning lollops by, lumpen and nondescript. She watches Rebecca ask Amy something. Amy in turn asks

Ayesha, who in turn asks Kate. Kate's smile is dolomite. She whispers something to Kimberly, who whispers back, magisterial. Kate turns and shakes her head in refusal. Rebecca blushes. When the bell goes for lunch she scurries out, her bent posture like a desk lamp. The inmates are the last to leave.

'Twenty-five minutes, all right, girls?' Siobhán says. 'Then back here for your penance.' Amy has a go at smiling, which Siobhán appreciates. She eats lunch at her desk, cowed and too scared to look at her phone.

Sophie corners her after the kids have been delivered to their parents. Siobhán is watching Rebecca bury herself in the lining of her mother's coat, red-faced.

'Hey,' Sophie says, sidling up. 'So, there's a petition for the needle exchange.'

Rebecca's mother strokes her hair, says something that Siobhán can't hear. Rebecca shakes her head, her face concealed among curly mustard wool. They walk off, hand in hand. Siobhán turns. 'What?' she says.

'The needle exchange closing down – there's a petition you can sign to stop it. Shall I send it to you?'

'Oh, yeah, sure. I'd forgotten.'

Sophie laughs. 'Activist for a day, huh?'

'Christ.' Siobhán presses one eyebrow skywards with her fingertips. 'Give me a fucking break, would you?'

'I'm kidding!' Sophie says. She self-gestures derisively. 'Like I'm one to talk.'

Siobhán appraises her. 'Got your coat back, then?' she says, at last.

Sophie beams. 'Yeah! You'd barely notice.' She points to

where the fabric has been sutured. Siobhán tries to remember what tore it in the first place, fails.

'Looks good,' she says, non-committal. 'Anyway,' she says, 'I'd better get on. See you tomorrow, yeah?' She departs for her classroom. Sophie calls after her: 'You okay?' She pretends she hasn't heard.

That evening he pleads with her, messages arriving in torrents in the intervals between him making dinner and Ellie's bath and bedtime. The more he describes the prospect of being without her as unfeasible, the more she starts to view being without him as the opposite. She finds her resolve in increments, and it occurs to her that all it took was entertaining the possibility of ending it, out loud, for it to seem conceivable. Now that she has, it seems not only like something she will be able to withstand, but something she will be able to recover from. With each conciliatory platitude she convinces herself a little more, and not even his despair can shake her growing conviction.

That is, until he says: *I'll leave her, Siobhán.*

She's at the kitchen table, a stack of annotated maps in front of her. She reads the message once, then locks her phone. She unlocks it, then reads it again. She locks it, and on the third reading the letters become indistinct with the onset of her tears. He messages again, and again.

I'll do it.
I'll leave her.
Just don't end this, Siobhán.

★

278

Who is she to pass up on this? On him? Who will extend to her this magnitude of feeling ever again? The freedom she had just been envisioning curdles, becomes a wilful squandering. She imagines a day, a week spent not talking to him, a life without the anxiety but also without the reassurance, the uninhibited intimacy. A teardrop fuzzes a worksheet and she is ashamed of herself for defacing her students' efforts.

I have work to finish, she says. *I need to think. I'll message you tomorrow.*

She turns off her phone before he can respond. She dabs at the splash with a piece of kitchen roll, absents herself from her mind with marking and laundry. At 10 p.m. she turns her phone on again. Four missed calls and fifteen messages. She scrolls through them, half inured to the sentiments, half grateful for their intensity. She messages Caz, then Mark. Receives responses from neither. She checks what time it is in Bangladesh, phones Tara anyway. It goes to voicemail. Tara calls back an hour later, her voice crackling from poor reception and tiredness.

'Shiv, you okay?'

'Jesus, what time is it there?'

Tara laughs huskily. 'Half three,' she says.

'Go to bed, for fuck's sake.'

'Ah, sure, I'm awake now. What's going on?'

'Nothing worth wasting your time over. How's Bangladesh?'

'Never mind that. Talk to me – is everything all right? You sound miserable. Everything all right with work? Everything okay with Andrew?'

The attempt to formulate an answer makes her tear up. She mumbles.

'Seriously, T, I'm all good. Tell me about you, tell me all about your life. How's well-digging going?'

'I don't dig wells, you idiot.'

'Sorry. Tell me about what you actually do.'

She falls asleep to the sound of Tara talking, then wakes to Tara's chuckling.

'Okay, mate, go to bed. We can talk another time.'

'I'm sorry,' Siobhán mumbles. 'I'm the worst.'

'You are, but I love you. Night night.'

'Love you.'

She rolls from one side to the other. She groans into her pillow. Eventually, she stumbles back into sleep.

LILY

She buys noodles and Tabasco and chocolate. The man on the street outside smiles at her, says, 'Any change, love?' She digs in her pocket, gives him what the shop assistant just gave her. A voice manifests behind her.

'Lily, love. Hi.'

The head of yellow curls with dark roots. Lily had always assumed the dark roots corresponded with lapses in hair appointments, but now she wonders if this is just how she likes it: a spiralized sunflower, its yellow petals spaghettified and coiling from the dark centre.

'Hi, Yvette,' she says.

Yvette wraps her bouclé arms around her. Her hair tickles the skin of Lily's philtrum. She steps back.

'How are you, darling?'

'I'm fine,' Lily says. 'How are you?'

'Oh, you know, keeping going. Just down for the day to do some shopping.' She gestures behind her to the pink man laden with carrier bags staring intently at his shoelaces. 'And you?' she says. 'How are you getting on?'

'I'm fine.'

'Good,' Yvette says, and there's a pause. 'You know,' she says, 'we all really miss her.'

Lily almost laughs. 'Miss who?' she says instead. Yvette looks at her.

Lily's grandmother died when Lily's mother was twenty-two. Lily's great-grandmother died when Lily's grandmother was twenty-six.

'From an ear infection, of all things,' Lily's mother told her.

'That's comforting to know,' Lily said.

'I'm just saying,' her mother said, 'you come from a long line of dead mums.'

'Doesn't everyone?'

'Yes, I suppose, but you come from a long line of young dead mums.'

'What am I supposed to do with that information?'

'Use it to win arguments you think you might be losing.'

'I tried to phone,' Yvette said. 'After the funeral.'

'I know,' Lily says. 'Sorry. I moved.'

'That's okay, love,' Yvette says, and Lily wishes that it would start raining, that Yvette might need to escort her crinkly hair inside. 'You know,' Yvette says, 'a couple of years ago your mum helped me organize a community day at school. It was called "It Takes a Village" day.'

'Okay.'

'I told the pupils this story: would you like to hear it? Do you have time?'

'It's about the village, and the stones, right?'

'Oh! Maybe your mum told you.'

'The villagers donate a stone from each of their houses.'

'Yes, and—'

'And the stranger gets to build a house from their donated stones.'

'Yes, and it's about—'

'But surely no stone in a house is expendable?'

'Well, the point is more that—'

'So, presumably their houses would be irrevocably damaged by this? Left with little to no structural integrity?'

'Yes, but the story is really more of a—'

'So, the moral is that an entire village of people should have to sacrifice their way of life so that one stranger can have a house?'

'Well, no, because you're not meant to interpret it quite so—'

'Have you ever heard of the trolley problem, Yvette?'

'I'm sorry?'

'By the way, the stone you brought her, during chemo. The one that said "Faith". We had "faith".' She does air quotes. 'Whatever that means. She still died.'

'Oh, love, I—'Yvette is wobbling in the wind now, like she's made of gloves.

'I have to go now, Yvette,' Lily says. 'I hope you have a lovely day. It was nice to see you.' She turns and walks away, and all the light in the sky coalesces into the hot nucleus of sun, breaking forth from behind a blanket of cloud. She looks up to it, and laughs.

A new morning. She opens a window and unpacks the boxes, arranges books and ornaments on shelves and surfaces. She gathers together the various cards and places them in a drawer. She peels sheets from the cabbage and googles a recipe, then sautés the leaves in garlic and lemon. She cleans the dark patch on the carpet and goes for a walk, buys a cactus. On her way in she meets Caz, dressed for work.

'Oh! Afternoon, moonbeam,' she says. Lily wonders if, in

Caz's mind, she is a mutable entity, one fungible unit of a community. She brandishes the cactus.

'Hi,' she says.

'Haven't seen much of you recently! How are you?'

'Fine. How are you?' Lily says.

'Oh, not so bad. It's been a bit of a strange week, to be honest, the girl next door and I—'

'Siobhán?'

Caz frowns. 'Yeah,' she says. 'I didn't realize you knew her.'

'I don't, not really.'

'So you didn't hear, then?'

'Hear what?'

'She's gone.'

'Gone where?'

'No idea. We had a fight, so I never got the full story, but she lost her job. A dinner lady at her school, Jean, told me. We do yoga together.'

'Why did she lose her job?'

Caz glances over her shoulder. She leans forward, though there's nobody there but them. Lily matches her rakish posture. When Caz speaks again it's a whisper, and as she speaks the blood thumping in Lily's ears threatens to eclipse the words.

That evening, she goes upstairs. The shoe rack is gone from outside the flat. All that's there is a brownish stain on the carpet, the only evidence of Lily's actions. She holds her ear to the door for a moment, but there's no sound. She knocks, gently. Still nothing. She lets herself in.

The flat is empty but for the furniture that came with it: a cheap artificial teak bedframe, a soiled mattress, a chest of drawers and a bedside table. Every room smells of bleach and the trapped must of a vacuum cleaner.

When her mother first relayed Yvette's story Lily said, 'That's such a stupid story.'

'Be nice.'

'Am I wrong, though? If coming up with parables was something everyone should do, someone other than Jesus would be known for it,' Lily said.

Her mother laughed.

'Also,' Lily said, 'why should a whole community suffer to improve the life of one individual?'

'Have you heard of the trolley problem?' her mother said.

'No.'

'Basically, there's no right solution, but it might seem, superficially, more solvable through the application of arbitrary variants.'

'Which means what?'

'We like to have emotional justifications to hurt people.'

Is knowing someone's circumstances a barrier to objectivity? Or is it only making decisions based on those circumstances that threatens objectivity? She reads the Wikipedia entries for 'ethical subjectivism' and 'ethical objectivism'. 'Maybe you shouldn't try to form an ethical framework from Wikipedia entries,' her mother would probably say.

'It sounds to me,' Lily imagines her saying, 'like what you want is to view the single person in terms of ethical objectivism but yourself in terms of ethical subjectivism, enabling you to do bad things based on the particular circumstances of the situation.'

'I don't know how to make it make sense.'

'I only know as much as you do, I'm afraid.'

'Oh.'

'Yeah.'

During her chemo, they sat in the hospital, flicking through books they weren't reading. 'Do you remember the story about the villagers and the stones?' her mother said suddenly. 'Yes,' Lily said.

'Well, what do you know,' her mother said, 'now I'm like one of the houses.'

'How so?' Lily said.

'Little to no structural integrity.'

Later that afternoon Yvette came to visit. She brought a pebble – it had the word 'Faith' painted on it in sky blue. Her mother started to say 'Thanks', but before the word was over she'd already started laughing. Yvette said, 'What's funny?' and then Lily laughed too. They laughed for longer than the moment deserved.

SIOBHÁN

She wakes, sore-headed and crusty-eyed, to two more messages and five missed calls.

Please give me a call when you get a chance, Siobhán.
I need to speak to you.

The soaking roads have an impossible motility. She goes against their current, fights her way uphill to school. There's a dull pressure in her lower torso – the threat of a UTI. The bray of it conspires with the lowness of the dead firmament. The result is claustrophobic. She wrestles with the oncoming wind.

Although she grew up here, has only ever left for brief periods, Belfast seems a changeable and unknowable place to her. It's inconsistent and paradoxical: too small but too sprawling and wild, safe but only just concealing its unsafeness. She feels both deeply symptomatic of it and estranged from it, and she doesn't know where she could go that would be better. Her phone fizzes recurrently for the duration of the walk.

All morning she projects a mania on to her class, trying to compensate for the fear that she is failing them. She flits from desk to desk like a hummingbird – ignoring her phone. She spends the break with her head pointed in the direction of the detainees, not seeing them but instead trying to remember her own primary-school teachers, if they ever seemed on the cusp of an emotional precipice, if her school experience might have suffered from exposure to such a thing. She wonders if her students can sense her tumult. She adjusts her posture.

'Girls, do me a solid, would you?'

They look up from their diversions – Ayesha, a book; Amy, a wordsearch; Kate, disturbingly, is allowing Kimberly to paint ladybirds on her schoolbag with nail varnish.

'I need to nip out and make a call – if I reduce your sentence by a day, will you sit here and behave and not be jerks?'

They nod with fluctuant sincerity. Siobhán takes her phone from the drawer and shuts herself in the foyer. A text – she hopes it's from Mark, or Caz, but it's her mother. *Driving lessons???* Three more missed calls from Andrew. She inhales, calls him back.

'Hey,' she says. 'How are you doing?'

He sniffs. 'Hi sweetheart.'

'I'm sorry.' She stares at her feet.

'I'm really struggling with the thought of this, Siobhán.'

'I know.'

'I need you.'

She tries out the sentence she's been constructing all morning. 'You know,' she says, 'even if things between us had to change, we could still be in each other's lives. I could still be there for you.'

'Don't say that. I—' He starts crying, this time with enervated gasps of hopelessness. Her eyes get wet at the sound and she thinks about lactation. A boy barrels in from outside. She gives him half a smile.

'I'm sorry,' she says again.

'I don't know if I can live without you.'

'Don't say that.'

'It's true – you're everything to me.'

'Andrew, I—'

'I don't know how to live without you now.'

'Andrew, please—'

'Please, please give it some more thought.'

'But I have, Andrew, and—'

'Please, Siobhán. Just don't decide anything yet.'

'Okay.'

'Please.'

'Okay.'

'I love you.'

'I have to go, Andrew. I'll call later.'

'I love you.'

'I – I love you too.'

In the staff toilet she flaps her hands to gain purchase on the world. She performs an echolalia under her breath, slaps her cheeks, forces her face into a clownish grin. When she thinks about him it threatens her stability, so she doesn't. She thinks about Sophie, a dog rolling in slow motion over a cliff face.

'Where's Kim?'

'Toilet,' Kate replies, inscrutable. There's something off about her, but the fatigue of existing today stops Siobhán from dwelling on it. She starts organizing piles of loose sheets into different piles of loose sheets.

'Guys!' Kimberly parades in, declarative. 'Rebecca's committing suicide in the toilet!' She glances round, notices Siobhán behind the door. Ayesha, Kate and Amy turn to Siobhán. Siobhán looks at Kimberly.

'Sorry, miss,' Kimberly says. 'I was in the toilet.'

'Obviously.' Siobhán sighs. 'Stay here,' she says.

She sticks her head around the door of Sophie's room. Sophie is squeezing Sriracha into a Tupperware box of potatoes.

'Soph, would you do me a favour?'

Sophie glances up, and it occurs to Siobhán that Sophie would probably forgive her any transgression. 'There she is!' Sophie says. Steam plumes from the box.

'Something's up in the toilets,' Siobhán says.

'What do you need?'

'I've got the four horsemen in my room – keep an eye on them, would you?'

Sophie abandons her lunch. 'Right you are,' she says.

Rebecca is in the last cubicle, mewing like a kitten. There's the occasional dull thud, and when she opens the door Siobhán can see an ovoid protuberance growing under her fringe.

'Oh, Rebecca, pet.'

Siobhán lowers herself to the floor. Rebecca's eyes and nose leak on to her chest. Siobhán rubs her child-soft hair with one hand, digs her nails into her thighs with the other to remain stoic.

'Want to tell me what's wrong?'

Rebecca starts a sentence, cries, starts again, cries.

'The other girls aren't being very nice to you, are they?'

A shake.

'You weren't invited to the birthday party at the weekend, were you?'

A nod.

'This has been going on for a little while, hasn't it?'

Another nod. The pooling dampness reaches Siobhán's skin, and she tilts her chin upwards to the speckled ceiling tiles. She gingerly moves Rebecca's fringe to one side and inspects the swelling egg on the small forehead. 'Everyone hates me,' Rebecca lisps, and Siobhán tenses her jaw to stop her on-coming tears.

'Want to go home, Becks?' she says. 'Want us to get your mum to pick you up?'

The forcefulness of her nod bounces Siobhán's cleavage. It would be funny, if there was no context. 'I promise we'll get this sorted out, Becks,' she says, and she wonders how many times she'll use the word 'promise' today, whether she'll fulfil any of them.

'Soph?'

Sophie has her feet up on Siobhán's desk, is singing 'Go Tell It on the Mountain' in a discordant key. Kimberly is grimacing. Siobhán beckons her outside.

'Could you take Rebecca up to the office? See if you can get her mum on the phone.' Siobhán squeezes Rebecca's shoulder. 'That sound good, Becks?' Rebecca rubs her eyes and nods. Under her breath Siobhán says, 'Tell her I'll need to schedule a chat with her about some bullying, and fetch the accident log too, would you?'

Sophie nods, gives Rebecca a smile. 'C'mon, Rebecca,' she says, and extends her hand. Rebecca takes it. Siobhán waits until they've disappeared around the corner, then goes into the classroom. The girls watch her, wary. She checks her phone. Two missed calls. Messages.

Please, Siobhán – I need you.

I love you so much.

I'll do anything. I'll be better.

The thought of losing you makes me feel completely hopeless.
I don't know what I'll do if you leave me.
Please, sweetheart.

Her phone goes again. A text from her mother.
If you don't sort out those lessons soon I'm going to do it for you!!

'Right, girls,' Siobhán says, perching herself on a desk in a way that she hopes might elicit honesty. 'Obviously, I'm not suggesting anything, or accusing anyone, but do any of you know what might have upset Rebecca? She's your friend, right?'

Ayesha and Amy are doe-eyed ingénues. Kate and Kimberly share a glance – Kimberly smirks, then Kate smirks, a palimpsest of Kimberly. God, Siobhán thinks, there's two of them.

'Ayesha, Amy, go get a breath of fresh air, would you?' she says. They comply silently, trot out like lambs. Siobhán attempts a posture of deep thought, even though what she's thinking is that she's not thinking.

'Kate, Kim, come here, would you?'

Even their walks seem tailored with defiance in mind.

'Kim,' Siobhán says. 'Maybe not the most sensitive thing to run around saying Rebecca's committing suicide. But then, you know that, don't you? You know that's not a kind thing to run around shouting about.'

Kimberly can't quite bring herself to look up. Siobhán's sole itches a little – she thinks briefly about the fingernails in her shoes, benches the thought. 'Not now,' she thinks. She sighs.

'Any idea what had Rebecca so upset?'

They shake their heads.

'Did something happen at the weekend? Did someone have a birthday party?'

'I did,' Kate says, and she looks at Kimberly.

'Happy birthday,' Siobhán says.

'Thanks, miss,' Kate says, and she looks at Kimberly. Siobhán looks at Kimberly, who looks at no one.

'Was Rebecca there?' Siobhán says. They shake their heads.

'Right, okay.' Siobhán grips the desk, exhales. 'Why not? She's your friend, right?'

They shrug.

'Since when is she not your friend? She sat next to you up until about a week ago, Kim.'

'We were never really friends, miss,' Kimberly says.

'I feel like that's not true,' Siobhán says. The first bell rings. She has three minutes to try and resolve this, then: more afternoon, more day. Her phone vibrates in her hand. She glances at it.

I don't know if I can live without you, Siobhán. I don't know if I want to.

She puts the phone in her pocket, tries to decommission half of her thoughts. She sighs again. 'Right,' she says. 'You're both clever girls, so I feel like this will have occurred to you, but just in case: if Rebecca is the only one of your friends not to have been invited to your party, Kate, do you not see how that might have been upsetting for her? Kim, you're always making a show of how mature you are. Could you not have predicted that it might be a bit horrible for Rebecca to be left out?'

'God, miss,' Kate says, and her voice is that of someone older. Siobhán stares at her. Kate looks at Kimberly and, this time, Kimberly looks back, and grins. Siobhán's phone vibrates in her pocket. Kate turns back to Siobhán, emboldened, and everything about her is wrong: her posture, her tone. Siobhán's phone vibrates in her pocket. Kate shrugs with indifference, and the cognitive dissonance of child-body with adult-gesture is unsettling. Siobhán realizes she's jealous of these girls, not of their youth so much as of the time they have. Time in which to correct their wrong choices. Every mistake she makes seems perennial and permanent, has lasting ramifications. She's running out of opportunities to start again. The phone vibrates in her pocket. It vibrates. Vibrates again. She realizes she needs to say something.

'Kate—'

Kate interrupts. 'God, miss, it's not our fault Becks wants to off herself.' She shrugs. 'Why not just let her?'

For a second, Siobhán's mind and mouth are in tacit agreement: nothingness. No air, no sound. She thinks of Rebecca: the desolation too pronounced on her small features. Her phone vibrates. It vibrates. Vibrates again. Then, she reaches out.

Everything happens before she can identify, acknowledge, dispel the impulse. She grabs Kate's wrist; plump and soft beyond the scratchy sleeve of her jumper. She raises her other arm. She brings her fingers and palm down on to the back of the small, pale hand, held tightly in position. There's a noise like a cracker, pulled. Then, an open silence. Siobhán lets go. She takes a step away, but doesn't bring her other foot to meet it. She hovers, indeterminate – one foot in the moment that has just happened, one in the moment's after-moment.

She looks at Kate. Kate stares with enormous eyes at the back of her hand, the skin already reddening. She looks up at Siobhán, and Siobhán watches her eyes start to wrinkle at the edges. Siobhán looks at Kimberly. Kimberly looks at her with a new expression, and Siobhán realizes: she's frightened. How did she ever think they were well-matched adversaries?

Siobhán looks at Kate. Kate's hand is balled at her chest, her other hand draped protectively over it. She's crying now, louder, and louder. Sophie appears in the doorway, holding the accident log. The second bell rings. Siobhán looks at Sophie. Sophie looks at Siobhán's hand, still half raised. She looks at Kate, then back to Siobhán. Kate sobs. Now Siobhán's the one who's frightened.

The first time she and Andrew woke up together went like this: she woke first, restless; that initial phase with a new person where you don't quite trust yourself to sleep deeply. Her eyes felt simultaneously dry and gummy with mascara. She inched out of bed like a mealworm, washed her face, contemplated fresh mascara, decided against it, inched back. About an hour later he woke. He slipped one arm around her, his eyes still closed. She was so comfortable she felt bodiless. When he was more awake they talked about their childhoods. She told him about a tracksuit she had as a teenager: maroon and forest green. She wore it on the weekends, when she and Tara would waltz down the Ballymaconaghy Road to loiter around Forestside. She felt cool when she wore it, even when the zip wouldn't close over her expanding breasts. He ran his hands over her body, then, told her how soft her skin was, how beautiful she felt.

He told her about his childhood, playing Rock 'Em Sock 'Em Robots with his older brother, who died later in a car accident, in a collision with a motorcyclist.

'We played it four times a day for two months,' he said. 'It drove Mum insane.'

'Why did you stop?'

'It disappeared! Initially I accused him, because on average I won much more frequently than he did. He was certain our dog had dragged it into the garden and buried it.'

'Did you ever find out what actually happened to it?'

'Oh, it was almost certainly Mum, right? Mum definitely got rid of it. Simplest explanation and all that.'

'Right. Roccam Soccam's Razor.' He laughed, as usual, and she loved him for it. In that moment she loved him more than she'd ever thought herself capable of loving anyone. She thought that, if the situation asked it of her, she would die for him, that she would cease existence if it would somehow ensure his safety, his contentment. She loved him so much.

LILY

She tries to make sense of what Caz told her, fails. The evening slips into inertia. She washes the *Thor* mug and it sits, empty, next to the urn. Siobhán's flat lies empty, and silent, above her.

She undresses, and when she walks from the bathroom to her bedroom she catches sight of herself in the mirror – the tea towel has slipped on to the floor. She looks for a while, taking in the impossible, unfamiliar horrors of herself, then stops looking. She gets into bed and stares at the keloid spine of *Wuthering Heights* until semantic satiation sets in. The window is open behind the curtains, and she can hear a bird making noises, the sound of the rain. She lifts her phone, finds Ellen's Facebook page.

Her hair is shorter, her eyebrows darker. She's smiling in the picture, and the gap between her teeth is still there, a narrow doorway into her mind. She's been promoted, is now head of HR. Lily always suspected, though she never told Ellen this, that HR was so appealing a career to her because it involved trying to pre-empt what people's complaints were, but with the authority to impose your prediction upon them. She wonders how she is, what she does with her Friday evenings, now.

The phone buzzes in her hand, and a message from an unsaved number appears on the screen:

Hey, it's Hannah! I'll be in the pub from about 8. Please come! Feel free to bring whoever xx.

Hannah's birthday. She'd forgotten. She reads and rereads the message, allows those words, too, to soften and decompose into an ancient shapelessness. Eventually, her phone screen turns black through lack of attention, and she doesn't reilluminate it. She thinks about *The Entombment*, about *Three Dancers*, about how there are patterns of behaviour you design and embark upon to justify a feeling that's already there. She thinks about her mother, about how much of her preparation for dying was concerned with preparing Lily for her death. Lily will never be able to thank her for that, will never repay that debt. She thinks about an abortive desire to clink pints of cider in a sunlit garden. She thinks about Ellen.

'Do you think it was my fault?' she imagines asking.

'I suspect there were other things going on,' she hears her mother saying.

'Yeah?'

'Partially culpable, remember?'

She taps her phone and the screen goes bright again. She stretches. She places thoughts of Siobhán into that inaccessible space between mind and consciousness. There's nothing to be done, now. Instead, she does what her mother would tell her to do. She starts typing.

SIOBHÁN

'Any jeans for washing, pet?'

'No, thanks.'

'You sure?'

'Yeah.'

'What about those black ones?'

'I did them recently.'

'What's recently?'

'Like, a few weeks ago.'

'That's not recent – they'll still have that horrible smell of your old flat.'

'They smell fine, and I don't wear them that often.'

'Go upstairs and get them. I'm doing a wash anyway.'

'Fine.'

'Did you bring that oven dish of mine home?'

'What?'

'The one I lent you – I could do with getting it back.'

'I don't know where it is.'

'That was a good dish!'

'It'll probably show up.'

'Any clothes for the charity shop?'

'No.'

'You didn't even think!'

'I know what clothes I have, Mum.'

'I think you must have lots of clothes up there that you'll never wear again.'

'I don't.'

'Have a look at some stage, will you?'

'Fine.'

'If you're going to be here for a while, would you go through some of those boxes? I don't want them cluttering up the landing.'

'I won't be here for long.'

Her mother laughs. 'Okay,' she says.

In her childhood bedroom there's a framed photo from the night of her secondary-school formal. She's wearing a champagne-coloured dress, and her hair is piled on top of her head in a messy cornucopia of curls. She's holding a bouquet in one hand, Tara's hand in the other. Out of shot is Matthew – her first boyfriend. The following morning they woke up together in his house. He said, 'Want some breakfast?' And she said, 'Yes, please.' He got dressed, putting his T-shirt on first. He lurched around, hunting for his boxer shorts. The soft foxglove of his penis bobbed; his scrotum hung like two damp teabags. She started laughing, and he said, 'What – what is it?'

'Who the hell puts their T-shirt on first?'

'What's wrong with that?'

'You look like Winnie-the-Pooh!'

He looked down at himself, started laughing, then looked up at her. They grinned, and when she pulled the duvet up to cover her torso he bent over and kissed the top of her foot. 'Right, dickhead,' he said, straightening up. 'How many sausages do you want?'

They broke up about six months later, when they decided

to go to different universities – she stayed, he left – but she still remembers that morning so clearly. How she thought in that moment that that was how love was, that that was how it was always going to be: an innocuous contentment, perfect for its quietude, its not needing tending.

Outside, there's a crow on the small lawn. The storm has garnished the grass with dead leaves and the crow pecks at a mound of them, as if there might be something precious underneath. Her mother calls from downstairs, 'Are you bringing me those jeans?' Siobhán finds them – there's a hole in the crotch and a brown stain on one knee. Chocolate-coloured. She empties the pockets and finds a bus ticket and a receipt for a bottle of wine. Her phone sits on the bed, and its new stillness is her stillness, its freedom is her freedom. She'll rebuild.

'I've got you a number for that driving instructor as well,' her mother calls from downstairs.

'Okay,' Siobhán calls back. She looks out of the window again. The crow stops its searching. Under leaves there are only more leaves; under bones more bones. She turns away, goes downstairs. The rain stops.

EPILOGUE: CAROLINE

After her mother died she and her father carved out a tradition: they went to the same Chinese restaurant on the last Friday of every month. Her mother's favourite.

The restaurant was right on the Bann, and when they were put at a table by the window she could look out and see the water flowing past. It was like they were on a dinner cruise.

The dim sum always came with a wicker basket of heated hand towels in shiny foil tubes. When she split the packet the smell of lemon bloomed out. She would never use hers – instead, she'd let them air-dry, then flatten them between the pages of a book to preserve them. Her father drove a beaten-up pale blue Saab estate, and the middle seat folded down as an armrest, with a compartment. That's where she kept the cottony shrouds. She had thirty-four at one point, the age she is now, and each held the ghost of a smell, the memory of lemon. On Sundays, she'd volunteer to wash the car, and she'd lower the drawbridge of the armrest and stroke the towels, soft as peaches, and think about the simulation of going down a river.

It was her father who taught her the beauty of the salvaged – he loves antiques, keeps all his old suits in plastic sheeting. Even until recently he dried and pressed flowers between the pages of dictionaries, sprayed pine cones with white-wine vinegar and gold-flecked paint and gave them to her to furnish her living room. 'If something can be preserved, we ought to preserve it, Cazzy. We owe a duty to the ancient. Rapid production, rapid consumption, Cazzy – it just perpetuates our own brevity,' he'd say. As a teenager she didn't understand what this meant.

One day, she came home from school and there was a silver Ford coupé in front of the house. Her father had traded in the estate. 'It was twenty years old, pet,' he said, when she mewed. 'There was no saving her.' The coupé is gone now too – his mobility isn't what it was, not to mention his eyesight. He recently received some encouraging results from a biopsy, so they're going to celebrate this weekend. She'll take him, and the dog, out somewhere. If the weather's good, maybe they'll go to the sea. He loves the sea.

'So,' Robbie says. 'Something I've been wondering.'

'Yes?'

'After we met, how come you didn't text me back for so long?'

He doesn't look like a writer, Caroline thinks – he has forearms like oxygen tanks and a neck as thick as her thigh. He makes her feel delicate, which she loves. She so rarely gets to be delicate.

'I like to ignore the first text,' she says. 'See if they're willing to work for it.'

'I wanted to message again, but I didn't want to seem like a creep,' he says. 'I don't like ignoring signs, you know?'

'Speaking of,' she says. 'Want to know something bizarre that happened to me last weekend?'

'Tell me,' he says, holding her gaze. Her fake eyelashes nuzzle her cheeks with each blink. She can smell the rose of her perfume and the polyester of her top.

'So, Sunday evening, I'm on my way in from work—'

'Where's the hotel, again?' His hand is snuffling at her hip, playing with the grain on her velour skirt.

'Oi,' she says. 'Don't you know it's rude to interrupt?'

'But I interrupted to ask you about yourself,' he says. 'Surely, worst-case scenario, the two things cancel each other out and I stay deliciously neutral.'

'You are deliciously neutral, I'll give you that,' she says, and his hand becomes more assertive.

'Sorry,' he says. 'So, you were saying.'

'The little hotel, just off Malone – you know the one?'

'I do! Nice bar in there.'

'I'll be sure to pass on your esteemed praises,' she says. Their heads nod together then drift apart, as though caught on cross-currents. She loses track of her thoughts.

'So,' he says, 'what happened last weekend?'

'Right, yes! So, I get in from work and head upstairs, and I can smell something strange from the stairwell: a slightly pungent, damp, sewagey odour.'

'Oh wow.'

'And the lights in the hall come on with a sensor, you know? So, it takes a second, and they're flickering, and it's all very slasher film, and then they come on.'

'And? What was it?'

'Well, you know those bins you get in the swimming pool? They're shaped like dolphins, and you put the litter into their mouth?'

'Yeah . . .?'

'It was like . . . the head of one of those?'

'What?'

'Yeah! It was broken off, so it was just this big blue dolphin head with its lower jaw missing and these big, glowing eyes. It was so creepy. Plus, it was filthy – slick with all this greasy, muddy ooze.'

'Fucking hell.' His brow is furrowed with consternation. She's enjoying being a raconteur.

'Yep,' she says. 'And when I lifted it, it had left a horrible brown stain on the carpet.' She shudders. 'Uh, I can still feel how slippery it was.'

'That's so, so weird. What did you do?'

'What could I do? I picked it up and took it to the skip down the road. Got some of its horrible bin juice on my skirt.'

His hand hovers. 'Not this skirt?' he says, reticent.

She laughs. 'No – my uniform skirt. Calm down and put your hand back.' He laughs, embarrassed, and does, this time tugging on it to bring her closer.

'Where do you think it came from?' he says.

'No idea,' she says. 'But it certainly didn't walk itself in, that's for sure.'

'Was it outside your flat?'

'No, thankfully, otherwise I bet my doormat would still reek. No – it was outside my neighbour's place. Who do you have to piss off to get the municipal equivalent of a horse's head outside your door?'

He laughs, shakes his head. She knows everything about her is extreme, but he seems drawn to it. 'Did you tell them?' he says.

'No – we had a bit of a falling-out, and actually, she moved out a few days later, so I didn't bother telling her.'

'Probably for the best she's gone, if people are delivering dolphin heads to her door.'

'Exactly.' She curls her shoulders and claps, trying to squeak like a dolphin. 'Lowers the tone of the neighbourhood,' she says, in what she imagines is a dolphin voice.

He laughs, and she can see the gold crowns at the back of his mouth. She tries to remember what state she left her bedroom in, if it's tidy enough for company. A couple of years ago water started to seep in from the ceiling – a problem with upstairs' shower, apparently. She'd had to throw out her rug, stack her other possessions in one corner to preserve them. She had to keep the window open for a week to stave off mould. Thank God she hadn't met this man then, this beautiful man who's writing a play about two people on a boat, who looks at her in a way that makes her feel vital.

It occurs to her that she might move soon, get somewhere a little bigger, a little nicer. Maybe she'll even look into buying, like her friends keep telling her to. Somewhere off Ormeau or Stranmillis, maybe. A little two-bedroom that's all hers: no inherited mattress with old piss stains, no scored wood in the drawers. She hasn't told anyone, but Dorothy left her some money, not to mention the pay rise she just got. 'Yeah,' she thinks, 'it's time for somewhere new.' She likes the odd girl who lives downstairs, but that's hardly a reason to stay. She can't keep mothering every waif who comes along – the girls who weep through the walls, the girls who need domesticating, the girls who assume they're the only ones thinking thoughts, feeling pain. So often you construct images of people to suit your own purposes, she thinks, to let yourself extract what you need for your sense of self. Caroline relentlessly champions people, coddles them. It's what she's been doing for her father since her mother died and it's what she does for these younger women she finds herself among. It's all she's ever done. The truth is, she doesn't know what anyone needs from her, because you can't know. Maybe it's time she stopped assuming other people are vulnerable just so she can feel useful. Maybe it's time to try existing as if she's a free-standing entity; to offer up love as a gift, rather than a cure.

'I got a promotion today,' she says, and his reaction is exactly what she needs. He beams.

'No way!' he says. 'That's fantastic!'

'He's right,' she thinks. 'It *is* fantastic.' 'Yeah,' she says. 'Assistant manager.'

'Congratulations,' he says, and she gives him what she hopes is a showstopper of a smile. 'He's so gorgeous,' but maybe she is too. Maybe she's the best-looking person in the room. He leans in, and they kiss for just a moment, lightly. 'I'm really glad you decided to text me back,' he whispers into her mouth.

'Me too,' she says.

They part.

'Same again?' he says.

'Yes, please,' she says.

'Gin and slimline, right?'

'Oh – I thought you were talking about the kiss.'

Another laugh. She feels effervescent.

'Yeah,' she says. 'Gin and slimline, please.'

'Won't be long,' he says.

'Here's a question for you to ponder, while you're at the bar. It's something I meant to ask you before, but I forgot.'

'Go on then, Paxman,' he says, and she notices how the angular lines of his jaw thaw when he smiles. She leans in.

'If you were a boat,' she says, 'what kind of boat would you want to be?'

Acknowledgements

As always, massive thanks go to Alice Youell, my editor, and Sophie Scard, my agent and professional hand-holder. I'm very grateful for their inexhaustible commitment to bringing out the best in my work. Thank you also to Tabitha, Beci and everyone at Doubleday, and Kat Aiken at United Agents.

Thank you to Catherine McFadden, for answering my many stupid questions. Thank you, also, to Stephen O'Neill, for reading an early draft. Thank you to Joey Connolly, for lots of things.

Thank you to the CCI in Paris, for a residency which facilitated both the conclusion of this book and the commencement of a new one. Thank you to *The White Review* Short Story Prize, *The Sunday Times* Short Story Award and *The Tangerine*, for variously shortlisting, longlisting and publishing short stories that helped form this novel.

I wrote the first draft of this book while living alone in Belfast, at a time when we were all sequestered in our various homes. I'm so grateful for the friendships that sustained me during that time, as well as the boozy days in Ormeau Park that followed it.

Finally, thank you to my family. I'm a great, squashy dilettante, and I'm very fortunate to have such champions.

About the Author

Susannah Dickey was born in Belfast and grew up in Derry. She is the author of three poetry pamphlets: *I had some very slight concerns* (2017), *genuine human values* (2018) and *bloodthirsty for marriage* (2020). Her poetry and fiction have appeared in *Poetry London*, *The Dublin Review* and *The White Review*, and her fiction has been broadcast on BBC Radio 4. Her critically acclaimed debut novel, *Tennis Lessons*, was published in July 2020. She is currently undertaking a PhD in Creative Writing and lives in London.